Jake and Kate are gettin' hitched!

After a roundup that made even the orneriest stampede seem like a day at the corral, cowboy Jake Griffin finally lassoed the sophisticated Kate Cunningham.

Therefore, the now-happy couple wish to invite the whole town of Brady Corners—jet-setters and closet broncobusters alike—to join them in celebrating their marriage.

Ceremony and reception will be held in the garden behind their house—Spindrift.

Formal dress, with the exception of cowboy hats, is required.

Reluctant Grooms

1. Lazarus Rising
   Anne Stuart
2. A Million Reasons Why
   Ruth Jean Dale
3. Designs on Love
   Gina Wilkins
4. The Nesting Instinct
   Elizabeth August
5. Best Man for the Job
   Dixie Browning
6. Not *His* Wedding!
   Suzanne Simms

Western Weddings

7. The Bridal Price
   Barbara Boswell
8. McCade's Woman
   Rita Rainville
9. Cactus Rose
   Stella Bagwell
10. The Cowboy and the Chauffeur
    Elizabeth August
11. Marriage-Go-Round
    Katherine Ransom
12. September Morning
    Diana Palmer

Instant Families

13. Circumstantial Evidence
    Annette Broadrick
14. Bundle of Joy
    Barbara Bretton
15. McConnell's Bride
    Naomi Horton
16. A Practical Marriage
    Dallas Schulze
17. Love Counts
    Karen Percy
18. Angel and the Saint
    Emilie Richards

Marriage, Inc.

19. Father of the Bride
    Cathy Gillen Thacker
20. Wedding of the Year
    Elda Minger
21. Wedding Eve
    Betsy Johnson
22. Taking a Chance on Love
    Gina Wilkins
23. This Day Forward
    Elizabeth Morris
24. The Perfect Wedding
    Arlene James

Make-Believe Matrimony

25. The Marriage Project
    Lynn Patrick
26. It Happened One Night
    Marie Ferrarella
27. Married?!
    Annette Broadrick
28. In the Line of Duty
    Doreen Roberts
29. Outback Nights
    Emilie Richards
30. Love for Hire
    Jasmine Cresswell

Wanted: Spouse

31. Annie in the Morning
    Curtiss Ann Matlock
32. Mail-Order Mate
    Louella Nelson
33. A Business Arrangement
    Kate Denton
34. Mail Order Man
    Roseanne Williams
35. Silent Sam's Salvation
    Myrna Temte
36. Marry Sunshine
    Anne McAllister

Runaway Brides

37. Runaway Bride
    Karen Leabo
38. Easy Lovin'
    Candace Schuler
39. Madeline's Song
    Stella Bagwell
40. Temporary Temptress
    Christine Rimmer
41. Almost a Bride
    Raye Morgan
42. Strangers No More
    Naomi Horton

Solution: Wedding

43. To Choose a Wife
    Phyllis Halldorson
44. A Most Convenient Marriage
    Suzanne Carey
45. First Comes Marriage
    Debbie Macomber
46. Make-believe Marriage
    Carole Buck
47. Once Upon a Time
    Lucy Gordon
48. Taking Savanah
    Pepper Adams

Western Weddings

KATHERINE RANSOM

MARRIAGE-GO-ROUND

Harlequin Books

TORONTO • NEW YORK • LONDON
AMSTERDAM • PARIS • SYDNEY • HAMBURG
STOCKHOLM • ATHENS • TOKYO • MILAN
MADRID • WARSAW • BUDAPEST • AUCKLAND

HARLEQUIN BOOKS
225 Duncan Mill Road, Don Mills,
Ontario, Canada M3B 3K9

ISBN 0-373-30111-1

MARRIAGE-GO-ROUND

Celebrity Wedding Certificates published by permission of Donald Ray Pounders from *Celebrity Wedding Ceremonies*.

This edition published by arrangement with Harlequin Books S.A.

Printed in U.S.A.

A Letter from the Author

Dear Reader,

I'm delighted that *Marriage-Go-Round* has been selected to be reprinted in Harlequin's HERE COME THE GROOMS program. This book means a great deal to me, since it's the last novel I wrote.

I am deeply touched by Harlequin's recognition of my book, resurrecting it and giving it new life. I laughed a lot while I wrote it; I hope you enjoy reading it.

Happy reading!

Katherine Ransom

Chapter One

"Kate, I've found the perfect man for you!" Laurel Cunningham burst into Daisy Letterer's kitchen, where her daughter Kate was preparing to cater a cocktail party.

Kate Cunningham rolled her eyes. The last thing she needed right now was her interfering mother. The kitchen was aswirl with party preparations, and one of the waitresses had called in sick at the last moment. A few short years ago she would have been a guest at Daisy Letterer's party, she thought wryly—and now she was the hired help. Such were the fortunes of the once rich who put all their financial eggs in a falling Wall Street basket.

"Mother," Kate said, "I'm not interested in any man you've dug up for me. The last one was sixty-five years old and had one foot in the grave."

"This one's different," Laurel said, nibbling on a stalk of broccoli. She arched a plucked brow and smoothed a hand over her flat stomach. "He's rich, good-looking and free as a bird."

"Mother, please," Kate said, waving away Laurel as if she were an annoying gnat. Laurel Cunningham had a way of making Kate wish she lived in California. Maybe with three thousand miles between them, she'd be able to stand her mother's constant advice. "I'm busy."

"That's what's wrong with you, Kate," Laurel said. "You're consumed by this foolish business of yours. If you ever want to get married, you're going to have to stop working so hard and start looking for a suitable man."

"Mo-ther!" Kate said, rolling her eyes. "I don't want to get married! Not now, not ever! Now will you please leave me alone?"

"Kate, darling, you're almost thirty-five years old! You wasted the best ten years of your life waiting for that silly Harry Grenville to marry you, and look where it got you—dumped when your father declared bankruptcy. Harry will be here tonight, by the way," Laurel added, studying Kate's face for any effect her words might have.

"I know that, Mother," Kate said tightly. "But leave it to you to pour salt in an open wound."

"It's been four years since he dumped you. It's time you got over him and found someone new. Like Jake Griffin."

"*Who* is Jake Griffin?" Kate asked, not really paying any attention. Her mother's voice had faded into the background, like the distant hum of the air conditioner in a cool room. Kate was more worried about her first meeting with her former fiancé in over three years. Leave it to her mother to not let her forget that Harry would be here.

"Jake Griffin's the one who bought our house," Laurel said.

At that, Kate looked up. "Oh," she said coldly, "*that* Jake Griffin."

"Now, Katie, you're not giving him a chance. I met him the other day and the man is absolutely gorgeous. If I were ten years younger, I'd go after him myself."

"Then why don't you?" Kate said irritably. With Laurel Cunningham's good looks, she probably could get any man in Litchfield County. In this part of Connecticut, where beautiful women abounded, Laurel Cunningham stood out. Even men twenty years younger than Laurel were enraptured by her charm.

"Darling," Laurel said, smiling archly, "the man is virile. I'm sure he wouldn't be interested in a dried-up old bag like me."

Kate snorted to herself. At fifty-five, Laurel looked no more than forty, with platinum blond hair and a figure that most women would kill for. But then she almost killed herself to maintain it—she exercised the way the Marines held boot camp, as if it were a matter of life and death. Next to her beautiful mother, Kate always felt inadequate—tall, gangly and plain in the extreme. While Kate had inherited her mother's features, she refused to slather on the makeup her mother cherished, choosing instead to wear only a touch of lipstick and mascara.

"Jake Griffin will be here tonight, Kate, and I really think you should make it a point to cultivate him. It's all well and good to slave away in a hot kitchen once in a while, but it's not how you want to spend the rest of your life, is it?"

"Yes," Kate said fervently, hoping to get rid of her mother before she blew her stack. "Now will you please *leave?* I'm busy, Mother. This isn't like throwing a party used to be, you know. This is work now, for money. I don't know why Daisy let you come out to the kitchen anyway. She knows I hate it when you interfere."

"Daisy's my oldest and dearest friend," Laurel said. "She knows it's unnatural for you to spend all your time running a business."

"Then why did she hire me to cater this party?" Kate asked crossly.

"That's neither here nor there," Laurel said airily, waving away Kate's words as if they didn't matter. In fact, to Laurel, they didn't. Laurel Cunningham was one of those women who went through life like a steamroller, smashing everybody's plans underfoot in her effort to do things her way. "Now put a little color in your cheeks and get out there and meet people. You may be the caterer, but that doesn't mean you can't socialize a bit...."

Kate sighed. When you played with Laurel Cunningham you just couldn't win.

"DARLING! You look marvelous!"

"...best sex I ever had was with an overweight secretary from the office after I first married Jill..."

"Simply delicious!"

"...and I told her she'd have to break off with him. I mean, it's simply not *done!*"

"Who knows what will happen when the market opens on Monday? The Dow Jones..."

"...love your hair..."

"It's only a *little* diamond—just three carats..."

Kate nodded left and right, and smiled as she maneuvered through the room balancing a tray of crystal flutes filled with champagne. Her eyes swept the room for overfilled ashtrays, empty glasses, food trays that needed replenishing. For the moment she'd forgotten all about Harry. She was totally absorbed in her work and enjoying every minute of it. Everything was going well. The sounds of laughter and vivacious conversation swelled in the air, punctuated by a combo playing soft jazz.

She passed the tray to one of the waiters and headed toward the kitchen to put out more food. She was almost there when a once-familiar voice carried to her through the crowd.

"Katie? Is that you?"

She turned slowly, and there he was, pushing through the crowd toward her, his lank brown hair swept back from a high forehead, his face as handsome as ever: Harry Grenville, her former fiancé, the man she had once thought she would love forever. He wore a navy blazer, a white oxford shirt and beige twill trousers. She felt a momentary pang as she realized he hadn't changed at all. Not even a bit. But what had she expected? He was Harry, wasn't he? She wasn't sure now if she loved him or hated him. Perhaps she felt a little of both.

He came toward her, both arms outstretched, taking her hands in his and swinging them out wide. "Let me look at you," he said. "You're as beautiful as ever. More beautiful, in fact."

"It's good to see you, Harry." Her heart was beating wildly but she looked as cool as iced tea on a summer afternoon. That was one of the benefits of growing up in society—you learned to appear calm even when you were frantic.

"Is that all?" Harry said. "Only good? Sweetheart, I've missed you terribly."

"Really?" she said dryly. "That's remarkable, considering you had a wife most of the time."

"Please, Kate, don't be sore about the past."

"Sore?" She stared at him. He had broken their engagement and married Jennifer Holliday three months later. She had a right to be a whole lot more than sore. Instead she smiled. "I hear you're in the midst of a divorce."

"Mmm," he said, frowning as he shook his head. "Very nasty business, divorce. I don't recommend it at all."

"Then perhaps you should stay married."

Harry's smile faltered, then he laughed. Typical Harry, Kate thought. He'd never had much of a sense of humor. "I'm rather down on marriage right now, I'm afraid," he said.

"Yes, I imagine you would be."

"What about you, Katie? Are you still available?"

"I'm not married, if that's what you mean."

Before Harry could respond, a ripple of excited conversation moved through the room, then a hush descended. No one spoke for a second or two, then everyone began talking hurriedly as if to cover the surprise that had momentarily made the room as silent as a church. Harry's face turned pale. Puzzled, Kate turned and looked toward the front door.

Outlined in the doorway, Jennifer Holliday Grenville stood in a jeweled white dress whose hem almost scraped the floor. Her black hair tumbled over her bare shoulders, her lips were outlined in bold red, her nails were scarlet talons.

"Oh, Lord," Harry fretted, wiping his brow. "What is *she* doing here?"

"She's your wife, Harry," Kate said mildly. "Maybe she was invited."

"No, Daisy assured me she wasn't. I wouldn't have come otherwise."

"Then maybe that divorce settlement of yours isn't worked out as well as you thought."

Harry suppressed a gulp. Jennifer was heading directly for them.

"Well, if it isn't Katie Cunningham," Jennifer said as she came to a stop in front of them. "It *is* still Cunningham, isn't it? I don't imagine you're married yet."

Kate smiled coolly. "Hello, Jennifer."

Jennifer ignored her, turning to look at her soon-to-be ex-husband. "And look who else is here—my own loving husband!"

Kate arched a wry brow. Oh dear, a scene. Everyone would claim they were mortified, but they'd be talking greedily about it all over Brady Corners tomorrow.

Since losing her money and social standing, Kate had developed an ironic eye that allowed her to see her former friends as she never had when she was one of them. What she had experienced the past four years had at first shocked her, then hurt her, but now she courted a sardonic wit that shielded her from further pain. She accepted her friends with amiable indulgence, seeing them for what they were and refusing to let them bother her.

"Jennifer, for heaven's sake, why are you here?" Harry asked in an undertone.

"Why am I here?" Jennifer hooted with laughter. "Because all my friends are here, darling. Why should I stay in Newport?"

"But Daisy *assured* me," Harry murmured, glancing here and there to see if anyone was watching. Everyone was, but in that genteel way that society has, smiling insincerely, then looking away as if they weren't dying to hear every word that was spoken.

"Take it up with Daisy," Jennifer said. "I called her today and she told me she was dying for me to come."

Of course, Kate thought. Jennifer and Harry Grenville's presence would make Daisy's party the most talked about in town.

Jennifer smiled dazzlingly as she looked around the room. Suddenly she seemed to arch her neck, like a bird preening for its mate. "My Lord," she breathed. "*Who* is *he?*"

Kate followed Jennifer's gaze and felt her heart stop then start up like a horse in full gallop. At the front door, a tall, dark stranger was being welcomed exuberantly by Daisy and Sam Letterer. He wore a black tweed sports coat, immaculately pressed white linen trousers, a white shirt and a black tie with minuscule white dots scattered over it. On his head, he wore a black cowboy hat, which he swept off as Daisy Letterer fluttered around him like a bee around honey. His black hair shimmered with a bluish sheen in the candlelight. With his square jaw, crinkly eyes and broad shoulders, he looked as if he'd just stepped off a Hollywood set. Whoever he was, he exuded sex appeal and power. Every man in the room immediately felt inferior, and every woman quickly patted her hair and sucked in her stomach.

"That's Jake Griffin," someone whispered, and the name rippled through the room like a breeze blowing across a wheat field.

"Jake Griffin, the food-conglomerate guru..."

"Jake Griffin! Didn't he used to date Vanna White?"

"Jake Griffin. He's worth billions..."

"Jake Griffin? Looks more like Adonis to me..."

Kate stiffened. So this was the latest man her mother had picked out for her. Leave it to Laurel Cunningham to go for a certified cowboy. Jake Griffin was the son of a Texas cattle rancher who had parlayed millions into a multibillion-dollar food conglomerate.

Not that that was bad. What bothered her was that six months ago he'd bought her family home, Spindrift, and supposedly had completely gutted it. She'd heard rumors that he'd made it into a regular showplace, but she shuddered to think what a cowboy from Texas had done to it—probably turned it into a gaudy display of nouveau riche excess and ostentation.

But here he was looking like the best-dressed man to step out of the glossy pages of *GQ*. She frowned to herself. She didn't like it when people didn't fit her preconceptions. Jake Griffin was turning out to be decidedly different from what she'd expected. But that didn't matter; if her mother wanted him for her, she didn't want him—no matter how attractive and rich he was.

"Jake Griffin," Jennifer said thoughtfully. "Where have I heard that name?"

"Ordinarily in the pages of *Fortune, Business Week* and *The Wall Street Journal,*" Harry said dryly, "but then you don't read, so I guess that's out."

"Oh, shut up, Harry," Jennifer said. "I know where I heard it. Becky Lord in Newport talked about him. She says he's the richest eligible bachelor in the country. What's he doing here?" She looked straight at Kate when she spoke.

"He moved here recently," Kate said briefly, turning to retreat to the kitchen.

"Where does he live?" Jennifer asked, following Kate like a bird dog on the scent of quail.

"In a house," Kate said dryly. "Like everyone else I know."

Jennifer watched her with knowing eyes. "I'll bet I know where he lives," she said in a sing-song voice.

"My, aren't you clever," Kate said, whisking an empty champagne glass off a table.

"You're still mad at me for taking Harry away from you, aren't you?" Kate turned to go, but Jennifer put a hand on her arm. "And I'll bet you're really ticked that Jake Griffin bought your family's ugly old house."

"If you already knew which house he'd bought, why did you pretend you didn't?" Kate asked, irritation flaring. Jennifer had been a thorn in Kate's side since kindergarten, and it looked like she hadn't changed a bit in the past thirty years.

"She pretended she didn't know because she wanted to rub it in," Harry said, coming up behind them and putting a protective arm around Kate. "Jennifer's like that," he said, sending a chilling look at his wife. "She goes for the jugular the way cats go for tuna. She absolutely delights in stirring things up."

"Oh, hush, Harry," Jennifer said. "You make silly mountains out of anthills."

"And she can't even get her clichés right," Harry said darkly.

Ignoring Harry, Jennifer studied Jake Griffin. "My, my," she mused. "He's better than Tom Cruise and Tom Selleck put together." She threw an amused look at Kate. "What fun it'd be to marry him and live at Kate's old estate. What was it you called that place, Kate? Spendthrift?"

It was a clear and cutting reference to her father's bankruptcy. Kate looked away, unable to believe that Jennifer could be so petty, but she refused to be drawn into a fight. Glancing at Jake Griffin, she said, "Go ahead and go after him, Jennifer. I imagine you'd be perfect for him."

"MARTHA, HE'S HERE," Kate said in a shaky voice when she reached the safety of the kitchen.

Martha Ware, Kate's partner in Lilac Hedges Caterers, was arranging stuffed grape leaves on a sterling silver platter decorated with roses and ivy. "Who's here, sweetie?"

Martha was a plump woman with a round face and bright red cheeks framed by corkscrew blond curls. She was much more than a partner; Martha was friend, confidante and moral support. A former college friend, Martha had been the one to convince Kate to go into business with her three and a half years ago, and now Kate owed her everything.

"Harry's here," Kate said, trying to calm the butterflies in her stomach.

Martha looked up from her work. "So? You knew he'd be here. It's all you talked about for the past week."

"Yes, but Jennifer's here, too."

"Jennifer!"

"Yes, and she's already started in on me. That woman is the bitchiest—"

"It's not polite to call women bitches, darling," Laurel Cunningham's voice reached her from the doorway. "It's just not done."

"But she is one," Kate said. "Jennifer lives simply to bother me."

"Jennifer Holliday lives to bother everyone," Laurel said. "She's the kind of woman who isn't happy unless she brings chaos wherever she goes."

"Well, she's brought it here. Somehow she found out that Jake Griffin bought our place and she's rubbing it in with all ten fingers."

"No toes?" Martha quipped from the sidelines, her eyes sparkling as she watched Kate try to fend off the frustration that always accompanied a visit from her mother.

"Give her time," Kate responded through clenched teeth.

"Don't let her upset you," her mother said, ever practical. "Look at it this way. Jennifer's presence assures that this will be the most talked-about party all week."

"I'd prefer that people remember it for the food, Mother, not the froth."

"Jennifer is hardly froth. She's a powerful woman. You should take lessons from her. It might do you some good."

"Lessons? What kind of lessons could she teach me, other than how to steal someone's fiancé or ruin a marriage?"

"She's a fighter, Kate. She's not afraid to go after what she wants."

"Meaning I am?"

Laurel shrugged. "You did let go of Harry without much of a fuss...."

"What should I have done, Mother?" Kate asked sarcastically. "Chase after him and marry him after the rotten way he treated me?"

"Well, you'd be a guest at this party tonight if you had. Not the caterer."

It was a low blow, but Kate held her tongue. She had learned the hard way that Laurel Cunningham always got the last word.

"Mother, I'm perfectly happy being the caterer. Happier than if I'd married Harry Grenville."

"Really?" Laurel picked up a stuffed mushroom and nibbled on it. "Seems to me the exact opposite. The way I see it, you've never gotten Harry Grenville out of your system."

"You think I'm carrying a torch for Harry?" Kate said unbelievingly.

Laurel shrugged. "Just a little one. Not that it will do you any good to show it. If you want Harry Grenville back, you've got to play hard to get."

"Who said anything about wanting him back?" Kate asked, her temper beginning to get the best of her.

"Well, of course you won't *admit* it," Laurel countered. "But I know you, Katie. And if you take just a little advice from your mother, it'll save you a lot of heartache. Play hard to get. Start flirting with Jake Griffin."

"Mother, he's a cattle rancher from Texas. What in heaven's name would we have in common?"

"Well, how about Elroy Kramer?"

Kate rolled her eyes. "Elroy is old enough to be my father."

"True, but he's single and enormously wealthy. You've got to start being practical, Kate. It will come in handy later on in life."

"If being practical means settling for Elroy Kramer, forget it."

"Darling, all I know is, Elroy looks at you like a beagle looking at a pigeon. If you know what's good for you, cultivate him a little. He might prove useful."

"That's utterly mercenary."

"Women have to be mercenary sometimes. Finding a husband was always difficult at best, and it isn't getting any easier."

"Who wants to find a husband?" Kate asked. She knew she was rapidly losing her composure, but her mother always did this to her. To Laurel Cunningham, nothing mattered but marrying a rich husband. She hadn't even learned her lesson when her rich husband had lost all his money in bad Wall Street investments, then died from a heart attack, leaving her destitute. To Laurel, love was a silly notion found only in foolish romance novels and maudlin movies.

Laurel sighed. "You always say that. I do hope you're just joking."

"Mother, I am happier than I've ever been in my life. I can support myself and meet all my material needs. What would I need a man for?"

"How about warmth on a winter night?"

Kate took the tray of caviar from under her mother's nose. "I'll get a dog," she said, and disappeared into the living room.

Chapter Two

Jake Griffin was surrounded by a dozen people. Mostly women, Kate noticed as she swept by him and headed for the buffet table. Honestly, it was just like her mother to sniff him out and sic him on her. But Kate wasn't interested in any man Laurel Cunningham picked out. Maybe she was just being stubborn, but she wanted to choose her own mate, not have him handpicked for her by her overprotective mother.

Sighing, Kate gave her attention to the buffet, only to be interrupted by a deep male voice from just behind her.

"I saw you come out of the kitchen," the voice said. "Is there any real food in there, or is it all just this fancy stuff?"

Kate turned to find Jake Griffin staring down at the caviar. "That's caviar, Mr. Griffin," she said. "It might be fancy, but I can assure you, it's excellent." Her eyes slid over him. She found herself wanting to put a dent in his male ego. "But perhaps coming from a cattle ranch in Texas you're not aware of that."

He raised dark brows over amused eyes. "You seem to know me, but I'm afraid I haven't had the pleasure."

"Kate Cunningham," she said, not looking up from the stuffed mushrooms. "Partner of Lilac Hedges Caterers."

He looked startled. "I thought you were one of the guests. You look like one and you're sure dressed like one. Is this the kind of food you always prepare for parties?"

"Not always," Kate said tightly. "This happened to be what Daisy Letterer wanted."

"I see." He shook his head. "I'll never understand what people see in fish eggs. It's downright disgusting to me."

Kate smiled coolly. "Perhaps if you stay in Connecticut a while, Mr. Griffin, caviar will grow on you." She turned to go, but his next words stopped her.

"I'm having a big party soon. How'd you like to bid on the job?"

The offer to cater a party at Spindrift hit her like an uppercut from the heavyweight champ. Spindrift had been her home, the place where she would have married Harry Grenville if things had gone the way they should have. Catering someone *else's* party there would be too painful to bear. Slowly she turned to face Jake Griffin. "I'm very busy, Mr. Griffin," she said. "I'm sure there are other caterers available."

His eyes swept over her, taking in the simple but expensive black dress she wore. "What keeps you so busy? Shopping for new dresses?"

Her blue eyes flared but she stayed cool. "No, Mr. Griffin, I have a catering business to run. I'm afraid it doesn't leave much time for shopping."

"You mean to say you do the work yourself? You can actually cook?"

She gave him a level gaze. "I've been known to."

"How are you with scrambled eggs and bacon?"

"Why do you ask?"

"I have a hankering for some bacon and eggs. Maybe you'd come home with me when this thing breaks up and cook me some."

She felt pink color flare in her cheeks. Of all the gall. She was a caterer, not a maid. "I don't think so, Mr. Griffin," she said icily.

"I didn't mean to insult you. It's just that I'd like to see how you cook real food. I'd pay you, of course."

A silky voice oozing with sex appeal spoke up behind them. "Honey, you wouldn't have to pay *me* anything to go home and cook for you."

They turned to find Jennifer smiling wickedly at Jake. "Hello," she said, holding out a hand and looking directly into his eyes. "I'm Jennifer Grenville."

"Jake Griffin."

Jennifer's smile widened. "It's lovely to finally meet you. I've heard so many things about you."

"All good, I hope."

"Good heavens, no!" Jennifer said, her dimples deepening. "All bad. Otherwise I wouldn't have come over and interrupted your conversation with our little Kate."

"I'm not yours, Jennifer," Kate said crisply. "And I'm hardly little."

"Isn't that the truth," Jennifer said, then turned back to Jake. "What brought you to Connecticut, Mr. Griffin?"

"Convenience. My corporate headquarters is in New York. I have an apartment there, but I'm getting tired of the pace. I visited Sam and Daisy about a year ago and liked it here, so I decided to buy a place."

"You're only here on weekends, then?"

"No, with a fax machine, a computer and a bank of phones, I get more work done at home than at the office. I go into the city a couple of days a week now, mainly for meetings."

"Next time you go, give me a call. I'm longing to go shopping. We could ride in together."

Kate kept her head down as she busied herself with the food, but she couldn't help rolling her eyes. Jennifer wasn't about to let the fact that she was still married keep her from looking for Husband Number Two. Disgusted, Kate decided to retreat to the kitchen, but Jake Griffin wouldn't let her. He quickly escaped Jennifer's grasp and caught up with her.

"You two know each other?" he asked.

"Jennifer and I? You could say that."

"But you're not bosom buddies."

"No."

"Short answers," he said. "That's the way I like 'em."

"Good, then you'll like short directions even better. Get lost."

Kate swept through the swinging door that led to the kitchen, but Jake came through right behind her.

"You don't seem to like me, Miss Cunningham."

"Nonsense, Mr. Griffin, I don't even know you."

"Why do I get the feeling you don't want to know me?" he asked, grinning at her as he leaned back against a counter and watched her whisk more shrimp from the refrigerator.

"I'm sorry, Mr. Griffin, but I'm very busy right now. Would you mind leaving?"

"Can I call you about catering my party?"

"As you wish."

"You wouldn't care if I hired someone else?"

"Not in the least."

"No, I guess only a woman who needed the money would care about things like that. You rich society gals obviously don't need it."

Kate groaned inwardly. Somehow he had gotten the idea that she didn't need to work, but she refused to disabuse him. She wasn't about to justify her work by spilling the red ink from her account books. Let him think what he wanted. He was obviously the kind of man who jumped to conclusions. If only he'd jump off the nearest cliff.

"So will you come home with me and cook me some bacon and eggs?" he asked.

"You can't be serious."

"But I am."

"Mr. Griffin, I have dozens of things I'd rather do than go home and cook for you."

"Such as?"

"That's none of your business."

"Do you have a husband waiting up for you?"

"No."

"A hot date?"

She felt like a kettle on simmer. "No."

"Then what else would keep you from coming with me?"

"Bed, Mr. Griffin. I've grown accustomed to sleep. I find I like it."

"So do I, Miss Cunningham," he said gently. "But it's even nicer when there's someone with you."

She went very still. A small shiver of awareness fluttered along her nerve endings, but she decided to ignore his remark.

"Mr. Griffin, I cater parties, not to whims—yours or any other man's."

"This isn't a whim, Miss Cunningham, this is a real need."

This time she couldn't ignore the implication. She lifted her head and looked into Jake Griffin's amused eyes. "Then I suggest you find a woman who can fill it. Good evening, Mr. Griffin. It was interesting speaking with you."

"Sure you won't come home with me tonight?"

"*Mr.* Griffin." She leaned her hands on the counter and considered beaning him with a cast iron skillet. "What does it take to persuade you? Calling the police?"

"Okay," he said. "I just didn't want to give up too easy. Women like you like to be courted."

"Women like me like to be left alone."

"I can't believe that. You seemed pretty interested in one guy out there."

Kate stiffened. So he'd noticed her with Harry, had he? She decided to ignore him. Maybe he'd go away. She gave him a final, dismissing glance, then began shoving stuffed mushrooms onto baking tins for heating in the oven. The door opened and her mother came in, with Harry Grenville trailing behind her.

"Hello, darling, look who's here," Laurel said. "It's Harry. He cornered me and begged me to bring him to you."

"We've already talked, Mother." Kate glared at Harry. "I'm sorry, Harry, but I'm busy in here."

"Not too busy to keep out Griffin," he said.

"He barged in, too."

"How nice." Laurel smiled at Jake. "And you are?"

Kate ground her teeth in an effort to keep from growling. Her mother was playing coy. She knew damned well who Jake Griffin was, probably right down to the exact amount in his checking account.

Laurel offered her hand to Jake and introduced herself. "How nice to meet you, Mr. Griffin."

"You work with your daughter?" he asked.

"Good heavens, no!" Laurel laughed. "This is Kate's little hobby, isn't it, dear?"

Kate went to full rolling boil. Now he'd *really* think she was a rich girl who just worked for the fun of it. "Mother, could you help me with these? They just need to go in the oven and heat for ten minutes."

"Certainly, dear." Laurel stared down at the mushrooms, looking completely helpless. Harry refused to budge. Nor would Jake Griffin. They stood on either side of Kate, who grew more agitated by the moment.

"Harry, if you don't mind..."

"Kate, I just need to talk with you."

"Fine," she said shortly. "Talk."

"In private," Harry said, eyeing Jake.

"Go ahead, dear," her mother said. "Martha and I will hold down the fort here."

Ha! thought Kate. Her mother would have the place in flames in five minutes. "Mr. Griffin," she said, taking her frustration out on him, "would you please leave?"

"Kate!" her mother said, sounding shocked. "There's no need to be rude to Mr. Griffin! Maybe he'd like to hire you someday. He has every right to look around the kitchen." She smiled at him warmly. "Wander around all you like, Mr. Griffin. Don't mind my daughter. She's a bit frazzled tonight."

"Mother!"

Harry took her arm. "Kate, I really need to talk with you."

"Harry!"

"I guess I'm just in the way," Jake Griffin said.

"You bet you are!" Kate snapped.

"Not in the least!" Laurel Cunningham interrupted. "Stay right where you are! Harry, take Kate out on the porch, dear. She needs to cool off."

"I need to do my work!" Kate protested.

Harry took Kate by the arm and marched her out of the kitchen. Once outside, she took a deep breath and slumped back against the porch wall. "Lord," she groaned. "Why does everything go wrong right when I need it to go right?"

"Kate," Harry said. "I hate to see you working like this."

"Well, get used to it, Harry. It's how I make my living."

"I know. My parents tell me you've made an astounding success of yourself. I..." He looked down. "Kate, I feel I owe you an apology."

"That's odd," Kate snapped. "I've felt that way for almost four years now."

"Kate, don't be angry."

"Don't be angry?" she repeated incredulously. "Why not? I have every right to be. You were a complete jerk, Harry. I'm just glad I found out before I married you."

"I guess I deserve that, but from now on I'm going to prove how much I care about you."

"Forget it, Harry. Too much has happened to ever recapture the past."

"That's not true. I realize now I made a terrible mistake. You were always the girl for me. If your father hadn't gone and made such a mess of things..."

"That's right, Harry," she said wearily. "Blame Dad."

"Sweetheart, there was such a scandal. You couldn't pick up the financial pages without reading about the mess. I couldn't be part of *that*."

"Why couldn't you?" she said, bristling. "You were so concerned what others might think that you turned your back on me and my family when times got tough."

"Sweetheart, you have to understand—"

"Oh, I understand, all right. You're shallow, Harry. You'd turn your back on your own mother if she ever did anything that dear old society might frown on."

"I know it looked bad, darling, but I was working in the law firm that handled your dad's bankruptcy. The senior partner called me in. He said it wouldn't look good if I continued seeing you. Conflict of interest. That kind of thing."

"And you bought that?" she asked incredulously. "You let some creepy lawyer tell you to ditch your fiancée because it might affect your *career?*"

"Honey, you make it sound so terrible."

"I don't have to make it sound that way, Harry, it just is."

"Look. I know you're hurt. Let's put the past behind us and start over."

"Harry, there's no way we could ever put the past behind us."

"Sure there is." He took her hand and drew her closer. "Watch."

She let out a tired breath and pushed away from him. "Harry, just leave me alone for a while, will you?"

"Sure, honey, I'll see you at the end of the party."

"Harry, I meant days. Weeks even. I'm very busy, and anyway, you're not even officially divorced."

"It's just a technicality now."

"Marriage vows aren't just a technicality, Harry."

He looked away, clearly chastened. "Of course not," he said, then brightened. "I'll give you a few days, but then I'll be back. I need you, Kate."

"That's funny, you didn't need me four years ago."

"Kate—"

"Harry. Please."

"Okay." He held up a placating hand. "I'll leave. But I'll be back. Trust me."

He left her standing there. She had just let out a long sigh of frustration when a deep masculine voice spoke from the shadows.

"I'd trust him about as much as I'd trust a water moccasin in an aquarium."

Kate whirled around. Jake Griffin was in the shadows, leaning against the porch railing and chewing on a twig he'd pulled from a forsythia bush.

"You lowlife," Kate said. "You were spying on us."

"Actually, I came out for air and realized I'd stumbled into a melodrama, so I just stood here and hoped no one would notice me."

"You could have walked away."

"Not without calling attention to myself and embarrassing both of you."

"So you decided just to embarrass me," she said acidly. "How kind of you."

"I can't seem to do anything right around you, can I?"

"It doesn't appear that way. Why don't you just give up?"

"That's too easy, Miss Cunningham. I'd feel like a quitter if I gave up now."

Kate made a motion to leave. "I'm sorry, Mr. Griffin, but I have work to do."

"I notice you didn't send Harry Grenville packing any too soon."

"As you obviously gathered, I was once engaged to Harry. We had some unfinished business to take care of."

"Maybe you think you finished it off, but it sounded like Harry has other intentions."

"Harry doesn't like to face reality, Mr. Griffin. It's one of his many shortcomings."

"Is Jennifer his wife?"

"Soon-to-be ex-wife," Kate said dryly. "When Harry broke our engagement, he married Jennifer three months later. There's no love lost between Jennifer and me, as I'm sure you gathered earlier."

"Sounds like a soap opera to me." Jake Griffin tilted his head and studied Kate with gleaming eyes. "And I'll bet it isn't lost on you that one way to get back at Jennifer would be to marry good old Harry after the divorce is final."

Kate's face went beet red. She pushed away from the porch railing. "Thanks so much for your opinion, Mr. Griffin," she said icily. "But I assure you you're totally wrong."

Jake smiled to himself, as if knowing he'd touched a nerve. "You don't know much about men, do you?"

"What's that supposed to mean?"

He seemed to consider whether to speak, then evidently decided he should. "Harry Grenville isn't right for you. Don't let getting back at Jennifer get the best of you or you'll make a mistake that will cause you no end of unhappiness."

"Mr. Griffin," she said, her voice trembling with outrage, "your concern is completely unwelcome. From now on, kindly keep your nose out of things that aren't any of your business."

A slight smile lifted the corners of his mouth. "Maybe we'll meet again soon, Miss Cunningham."

"One can only hope you're wrong."

Shaking with anger, Kate whirled on her heel and retreated to the kitchen.

Grinning, Jake Griffin lifted the forsythia twig to his mouth and contemplated the seduction of Kate Cunningham.

Chapter Three

Lilac Hedges Caterers was located in a small cottage on a side street in Brady Corners, just north of Litchfield in Connecticut's Litchfield County. Kate had bought the cottage with a bank loan and set about rejuvenating it. She herself had painted the fading clapboards a bright and jaunty yellow, with white shutters at the windows and flower boxes filled with geraniums and petunias. The top half of the Dutch door was opened to allow the lilac-scented air inside.

"I ordered the flowers and wine for tonight," Kate said to Martha the next morning. "They're being delivered this afternoon. Have you got everything you need? The meat and produce? The fresh fruit? The ingredients for the dessert?"

Martha nodded and gestured at the flour-covered work surface. "They're all set." She closed her eyes and gave herself up to visions of the dessert. "Mmm... *Gâteau St. Honoré.* I lust for it." Martha opened her eyes and glanced at Kate. "Speaking of lust, what was going on between you and Jake Griffin last night? Were you following your mother's advice and trying to make Harry jealous?"

"Jake Griffin is a nuisance." Kate bristled with outrage. "I tried to make it very clear last night that I'm not interested in him in any capacity."

"I don't know why not," Martha said. "He's only the hunkiest man I've ever seen in my life. And he's rich and single and he owns Spindrift. Katie, I'd be after that man if I were you."

"No way," Kate said determinedly, then added offhandedly, "He asked me to submit a bid on catering a party for him, by the way. Not that I really want to. It would be hell to go back to my own home as the hired help."

"I know you loved that place, but are you sure you're not refusing to work for him because you find him a little too attractive?" Martha asked.

Kate threw Martha an exasperated look. "Why would I do that? No, Spindrift was my home. I loved that place, the funny little nooks and crannies, the window seat in my bedroom...." She smiled as she remembered how she used to curl up there, lost in daydreams about the day she'd be grown up with a home of her own.

But enough of memories. Bad things did happen, and there was nothing you could do but get on with life. She dusted off her hands, settling in her chair to begin planning a tea party for Mrs. Jennings.

"Let's see," she said out loud. "Mrs. Jennings's tea party..." She sat back and envisioned the Jennings house, with its high ceilings and tall windows. The living room was surrounded on three sides by French doors opening to a brick terrace, the perfect setting for a fabulous Victorian tea party. "I think we should do it with lots of white linen and lace, a Victorian look, with lilacs and roses and sterling silver and her best bone china. Maude Jennings will love that. She'll be at the antique shops in an instant, scurrying around trying to find a romantic lace blouse."

Kate turned to look wryly at Martha. "You realize, of course, that we're in the business of concocting fantasy."

"How so?" Martha asked, covered with flour up to her elbows as she made the cake dough.

"We weave daydreams and make them come true for people. Maude Jennings is overweight and bored to death in that huge house of hers. Her husband is having an affair with a woman half his age, and her children are smoking pot and ruining their ears on MTV. But Maude can't face all that, so she decides to have a tea party, and for a few hours on that day, she'll escape from everything that gnaws at her and she'll be happy."

"Is that so terrible?" Martha asked.

"No. I didn't mean to imply it was. Perhaps it's the only way most of us get through life, by finding pockets of time where we can escape reality."

"It would seem to me," a deep male voice said from the doorway, "that it would be far better to change reality itself, rather than try to escape from it."

Kate whirled around, her heart suddenly hammering. Even before she saw him, she had recognized Jake Griffin's voice. Sure enough, there he was, leaning one broad shoulder against the doorjamb, one hand hooked over the leather belt that encircled his taut waist.

"I'm sorry," he said, inclining his head. "I'm not in the habit of listening in on private conversations, but the door was open and this is such a cheerful little place...."

"Mr. Griffin," Kate said, straightening her shoulders, "don't tell me you don't listen in on private conversations. This is the second time in as many days you've eavesdropped on me."

He smiled easily, closing the door behind him. "Do you know I haven't smelled bread like that since my mama used to bake it on the ranch when I was a kid?"

"You're evading the issue," Kate said, folding her arms. She hated to admit it, but he looked very appealing in that faded chambray shirt and his grubby jeans. He wasn't wearing a Stetson, but he looked every inch the cowboy. His face was darkly tanned, and little crinkly lines surrounded his eyes. He looked like old leather, she thought to herself—soft and supple. She found herself wondering what he'd be like to touch. She had no sooner thought it than she knew his skin would be warm and smooth. But she was more than a little irritated when her stomach did a funny little wobble in reaction to her thoughts. Okay, so he was attractive. That didn't mean she had to fall all over him.

"What brings you out so early, Mr. Griffin?" she asked, her arms still folded against her chest.

"I needed something at the hardware store. I was driving by when I recognized the name of your catering business. I thought I'd just stop in and see if I could convince you to consider catering that party I was telling you about last night." He looked around and seemed pleased at what he saw. "This can't be all of it," he said. "Isn't there a kitchen somewhere?"

"Through there," Kate said, nodding toward a doorway. "Why? Did you expect to find me slaving over a hot stove?"

"Well, you said last night you can cook."

"I can, but most of my time is spent planning menus and looking for business. Martha here is my partner, as well as the pastry chef. Martha, this is Jake Griffin. Mr. Griffin, Martha Ware."

Martha held up flour-covered hands, laughing ruefully. "I'd love to shake your hand, but you'd end up looking like the Pillsbury Doughboy."

"You were in the kitchen last night," Jake said.

"That's right," Martha said, grinning. "I'm usually in the kitchen, as you can see from my waistline."

Jake smiled easily. "Maybe you can convince Kate to cater my party."

"I'll do my best. Goodness knows, we could use the work."

"Oh? Is business bad?"

"Not at all, Mr. Griffin," Kate said, hastening to respond. "But we've only been in business a little over two years. Start-up expenses are tremendous, so we don't usually turn away clients."

"Then why did you turn me away last night?"

She was stumped. What could she say? That she didn't relish the prospect of returning to her former home as hired help? That would sound foolish. She wished now she had told him about her connection to Spindrift the moment she met him.

"Let's just say last night wasn't my best night," she said. "But after looking over the calendar, I see we can squeeze in another party. Just when did you say you were having it?"

"Not so fast, Ms. Cunningham," Jake Griffin said, his eyes gleaming. "Let's not get ahead of ourselves. First I'd like you to put a few ideas together and price things for me. I'll be speaking with a couple other caterers, also. I'll make my decision based on who comes up with the best menu at the best price."

"Oh." Well, she had walked into that one, hadn't she? Here she thought she had a job with Jake Griffin all sewed up, only to have him turn the tables on her and tell her she was competing with a couple other caterers. "I'll need an idea of the kind of party you're thinking of," she said, pulling a notepad toward her and scribbling his name across the top of the page.

"Why don't you come out sometime next week and we'll talk about all that. I'm in a hurry right now and need to get back. Even though it's Saturday, my secretary is setting up a conference call with some business associates."

Kate glanced at her calendar. "How about Monday morning?" she suggested.

"All right. Monday morning at ten."

She scribbled the appointment on her calendar. "It's a date, Mr. Griffin," she said brightly. "Monday at ten."

"I wouldn't call it a date, Ms. Cunningham," he said gently. "It's more an opportunity to get to know each other a little better."

She looked up, struggling to keep her face from turning pink. His eyes were gleaming with amusement, as if he knew very well the difference between business and pleasure, and he'd make sure she did, too, before he was finished with her.

She arched a brow. "But of course, Mr. Griffin—it'll be an opportunity for a meeting of the minds."

He grinned and let his eyes linger on hers for a few seconds longer than necessary. She felt an explosive reaction in her stomach, as if she were standing on the bow of a sailing skiff in heavy weather and the waves had tossed the boat up and into the sky, leaving her temporarily off balance and shaking. She put an unsteady hand on her desk to regain her equilibrium and smiled uncertainly.

"I'll bring out a few menus for you to look over," she said, straightening stacks of *Gourmet* magazine, lining up notepads, keeping herself busy so she didn't have to look into those surprisingly attractive blue eyes. "You know," she went on, "just a few suggested menus for different kinds of parties. That way you can begin to get an idea about which way you want to go—formal or informal, that kind of thing. Of course, I wouldn't do a really formal dinner for more than twenty-five or thirty people. Much too elaborate and boring, with all those deadly courses. It depends, of course, on the guests. If they're intellectually stimulating, a formal dinner could be wonderful, but for the most part they're deadly stuff. It depends, too, on the host. Can he or she pull it off, keep the conversational ball rolling, so to speak, pair the right couples? It's just all so enormously complicated unless one has a feel for that sort of thing. Personally—"

"Ms. Cunningham," he interrupted gently. "Do you always talk so much?"

Startled into silence, she felt color begin to seep into her cheeks. "Not usually," she admitted, and let herself peek at him.

He was looking at her with the most gentle, amused eyes, as if he found her boundlessly appealing. She felt herself begin to tremble. How long had it been since a man had looked at her like that? Three years? Four? Come to think of it, had any man ever looked at her like that? Certainly Harry Grenville hadn't. He had always been too busy with his own concerns.

"Ten o'clock Monday morning?" Jake asked.

She nodded. "I'll be there."

He inclined his head, his eyes holding hers again for just a moment longer than necessary. Then he turned and walked out of the office. Immediately everything felt less real, less interesting, as if he had drained the world of all color when he turned and left the room.

"I don't know about you," Martha sighed from across the room. "But for my money, that man is unbeatable."

"Ha!" Kate said, straightening her shoulders and pretending to fiddle with the notepad.

"Gorgeous," Martha said, smiling rapturously. "His body, his eyes, everything about him. Simply gorgeous."

Kate gave her assistant a look. "Martha, you hate men. You're always telling me that."

"Not a man who looks like that." Martha grinned. "Anyway, I can dream, can't I?"

Kate glanced past Martha to the window that overlooked the street and caught a glimpse of Jake Griffin getting into some sort of four-wheel-drive vehicle. Unexpectedly she felt again the impact of his eyes on her face.

Filled with warmth, she pushed the memory of Jake Griffin's eyes out of her mind. If she was going to get the offer of catering his splashy party, she'd better come up with a few ideas that would convince him Lilac Hedges Caterers was the one for the job.

IT HAD BEEN almost four years since Kate had driven up the winding, tree-lined drive that led to her family home. She steeled herself for what was to come. Once she rounded the curve up ahead, the trees would fall away and the entire countryside for miles around would be spread out before her.

When her father had declared bankruptcy four years ago, the house had already deteriorated. They hadn't been able to afford the necessary upkeep for years, so the painted trim on the once-gracious brick home had faded and chipped. The shrubs had grown so high they shrouded the windows, making the rooms inside gloomy even on the sunniest of days. Weeds had overtaken the brick walkways and terraces.

Now, approaching the curve, Kate wiped her palm on her skirt. She'd heard that Jake Griffin had gutted the house. He'd spent almost as much on renovation as he'd paid for the entire estate. She dreaded to see it. The house she had once called home had been wrecked, she was sure, by a former Texas cowboy from a broken-down cattle ranch. There were probably bearskin rugs on the floors, gun racks on the wall and a deer carcass over the mantel....

She wanted to close her eyes and keep them closed. Instead she punched the accelerator on her ancient BMW, gritting her teeth and telling herself that no matter what Jake Griffin had done to her home, it didn't matter. The past was gone. The future was all that mattered now. She rounded the curve and gasped, then coasted to a stop.

It was magnificent. Every detail was perfect. This was the way the house was supposed to look, yet she couldn't remember it ever being so lovely. Perhaps in her grandparents' time, but certainly not since she'd been born. The windows sparkled in the sun. The shutters gleamed with a new coat of black enamel. Even the pinkish red bricks of the three-story Georgian seemed new.

The overgrown evergreens around the house had been replaced with magnificent plantings of rhododendron and azalea. The brick walkway was free of weeds. The lawn was groomed as if it were the eighteenth green at a prestigious golf club.

Tears welled up in her eyes as she gazed at the house she loved so much. But she told herself to be grateful that Jake Griffin had hired a professional to redo the place. He hadn't wrecked it after all.

Kate dashed the tears from her eyes. This was no time to get sentimental, especially over a house that was no longer hers. She parked her car at the front door and got out. It felt strange ringing the bell. She had always used the back door. She used to run pell-mell into the house, calling out for her beloved father, laughing and giggling with friends, her cheeks pink from riding her favorite mare, her blond hair tumbling in disarray around her shoulders....

The door opened and brought her back to the present. Jake Griffin stood before her. "Hello, Mr. Griffin," she said brightly.

"Ms. Cunningham," he said. "Please come in." She didn't even look at him; she was too absorbed in being back in her home. Memories assailed her. She looked at everything, peering down the wide hallway, into the open doors that led to what had been the drawing room in her parents' time.

Her eyes fell on a sideboard against the wall. A huge arrangement of spring flowers was reflected in the Chippendale mirror above it. Silver candlesticks gleamed on either side of the arrangement. A blue-and-white Chinese bowl held potpourri.

"That sideboard is magnificent there," she said before she realized that Jake probably didn't know a thing about furniture. He'd probably paid an expensive decorator to come in and redo the place completely. "Why don't I just look around?" she suggested. "I'll have to look over the place anyway if you choose me to cater the party." She knew she should wait for an invitation, but she couldn't. This was her home, and a mixture of joy at being here, and sorrow that it wasn't hers, welled up inside her, blurring her usual good manners.

She turned and gazed at the magnificent circular staircase, carpeted now in Williamsburg blue. Once, she had dreamed of sweeping down that staircase in a glorious wedding gown of white satin and lace, her face radiant as she walked toward Harry Grenville, who would be waiting for her in the drawing room.

She turned away abruptly and crossed the wide hall to what had been the drawing room. It had been redone, as had the rest of the house, and it was more beautiful than it had ever been when she lived here. The furniture was new, upholstered in a bright yellow chintz print, and the faded paint and wallpaper had been replaced. Now everything sparkled and gleamed, from the mahogany tables to the gilt-framed mirror over the marble mantel of the fireplace.

She sighed wistfully, completely forgetting Jake Griffin. It would be an even more beautiful place for a wedding now, she thought. And once again the thought of Harry Grenville threatened to intrude. As usual, she pushed it away. It didn't do any good to think about things that could never happen.

Kate turned and forced a smile at Jake. It was too painful to be here. She wished she could leave. She didn't want to come here ever again. Yet she knew she couldn't afford that luxury. As always, making a living was a pressing matter.

"I've seen enough," she said, swinging around on her heel and striding toward the back of the house. "Is the garden room still off the kitchen?"

"You've been here before?" he asked, sounding surprised.

She paused, missing only a single beat. "Yes," she said, and let the matter drop.

"I call it the sun porch," Jake said.

She stood in the doorway to the sun porch and gazed at the room that had always been her favorite. In her parents' time, the wicker furniture had been old, its white paint faded to a pale blush of color, the flowered cushions matted down from years of use. Now it was new, with plump forest green cushions. Lush plants hung from the overhead beams, and the white-painted French doors that surrounded the room on three sides were all open, allowing the sweetness of the early-summer air to enter.

"Oh," she said, her voice quivering slightly as tears threatened to blur her vision. "It's so lovely...."

"I'm glad you like it."

Something in his voice made her pull herself together. She decided to get down to business and leave as quickly as possible.

"Well, Mr. Griffin, let's talk about your party."

He held out a hand, indicating a chair. She took a small leather notebook from her bag but remained standing. "First of all, let me thank you for considering Lilac Hedges to cater your first party."

"You have a good reputation. I checked you out. I'm told you do excellent work."

"We do our best."

"Evidently."

Kate looked up and found him watching her. His face was unreadable. It was a perfect poker face, revealing nothing of what he thought. She busied herself with her pen, fumbling with it to hide the unaccustomed confusion that gripped her. She was used to men who were tall, handsome, short, fat and everything in between. They spoke glibly and charmingly, at great length. Jake Griffin, she realized, hardly spoke at all.

"Well!" she said brightly. "About this party of yours. Perhaps we could have a Texas-style barbecue—steaks on the grill and good old-fashioned vegetables like green beans and corn on the cob. Home cooking is coming back in fashion, you know," she said. "We could do the whole thing with red-checked tablecloths and pitchers of iced tea and tin buckets filled with bottled beer."

Jake took out a slender cheroot and a box of matches. Using his thumbnail, he lighted the match and puffed on the cigar, then leaned back comfortably. Watching him, Kate remembered her father. Her mother hadn't allowed him to smoke in the house, so he'd been reduced to sneaking out to the garage and smoking with George, the chauffeur. But she couldn't imagine Jake Griffin letting any woman tell him what to do.

"Is that what you think I'd like? Simple, unsophisticated food served unpretentiously?"

She swallowed thickly. Oh boy, now she was in for it. No matter which way she answered, she had probably cooked her goose. Rather than suggesting a menu, she should have waited for Jake Griffin to give her a few cues. That was the first rule in business—give the customer what he wanted, and never try to guess what his tastes were.

"Well," she said, her mind racing, "from your reactions at the party, I gather you didn't approve of the food, especially the caviar. I figured you wouldn't want an elaborate French buffet."

"Do you like your work, Miss Cunningham?"

His question surprised her. No one had ever asked her that before. Her friends had been supportive when she opened her own business, but many had seemed embarrassed for her. It wasn't easy for them to see her carrying trays of food at the very homes where they were guests. But by now they were used to her working while they partied, and most of them admired the way she made the best of things.

"As a matter of fact, I love my job. I'd do it for free if I had to. I love planning parties and preparing menus."

"Perhaps you could come up with some ideas for menus," Jake said and stood up. Suddenly the interview seemed to be over.

He escorted her down the hall. She looked around, remembering the days she had helped her mother put on small parties. They had never had much money, but what they lacked in funds, they made up for in imagination and hospitality. Genteel poverty, it seemed, had its uses after all.

At the front door, she turned and held out her hand. "I'm sorry for the way I treated you Friday night at the Letterers'."

"Oh? How did you treat me, Ms. Cunningham?"

She looked away, embarrassed. "I'm afraid I was rather rude."

He shrugged as if it didn't matter. He opened the door and looked out at the BMW, raising an appreciative brow. "Nice car."

"It's an oldie but goodie," she said, smiling. She'd owned the car since she was sixteen. She kept it in perfect running order with the help of a teenager who worked on it lovingly every Saturday afternoon. To Kate it was as comfortable as an old shoe, and every bit as familiar. She would have loved a new car, but she couldn't afford one, so she lavished care on the only one she had.

Jake's eyes swept from the car to her, taking in her deceptively simple yellow linen skirt and white blouse. In the Talbot's catalog six years ago, this outfit had cost a small fortune, but she had cared for them with all the solicitude she lavished on her car, so it was almost impossible for all but the most discerning eye to see how old they were.

"Perhaps I shouldn't even be talking to you about working for me," he said thoughtfully.

"Why not?" she asked. "We may not have as big a name as some of the other caterers, but we're just as good as our competitors, if not better."

"But there's the matter of need, Ms. Cunningham. I always feel better knowing I'm giving my business to someone who truly needs it."

Hot color swept into her face. "Are you in the habit of always making sweeping assumptions, Mr. Griffin?"

He frowned thoughtfully. "Surely you can understand my feelings, Ms. Cunningham. I grew up relatively poor. I find it more rewarding to help out people with real need."

"Well, guess what?" she said acidly. "Just because I drive an antique car and wear nice clothes, doesn't mean I'm rich. I have to work, too, Mr. Griffin, just like all the other peons. So bundle up your damned scruples and shove them up your chimney. If you want the best caterer, give me a call. If not, drop dead."

Whirling on her heel, she left him staring after her, his mouth curved into an amused smile, his eyes filled with admiring laughter.

She rushed down the steps and hurried toward her car, her cheeks blazing with heat, her skirt flashing around her legs as she raced to put as much distance between them as possible. She yanked open the door to her car and got in, finding the ignition despite the way her hands were shaking. She threw the car into reverse, spinning around in a huge semicircle and careering down the driveway.

Damn Jake Griffin anyway. Blast him and his stupid assumptions. There were plenty of other clients in Litchfield County. She didn't need that bullheaded Texan.

Chapter Four

"So you just stomped off?" Martha asked incredulously. "You numbskull!"

"It's not just any job, Martha, it's Jake Griffin's job. Put yourself in my place—I'd be going back there putting on a party, yes, but not the way I used to dream about. It wouldn't be *my* party, Martha. It'd be Jake Griffin's. I'd be the hired help, in the place that was once my own home."

"There's nothing to be ashamed of about putting in a good day's work and earning your keep. I can tell you most of your so-called friends would give their eyeteeth to have what you have right now."

"Yeah, right," Kate said sarcastically.

"I mean it. Do you think there's much self-esteem in whiling away your day sitting at the country-club pool? Uh-uh. Self-esteem comes from working at something you're good at, and being able to take care of yourself, and you do that every day, Kate. Those so-called friends of yours envy you like hell, and they put you down in subtle ways because they really can't stand themselves and their empty lives."

"And I'd give anything to have their so-called empty lives," Kate admitted ruefully.

"No, you wouldn't," Martha said, grinning. "You'd like a little less financial pressure maybe, but you've grown so much in the past three years, I almost don't recognize you at times. You're a career woman at heart, though that's the last thing you ever expected of yourself. You're making it on your own, Kate, and sometimes that's rough, but you're doing it. You have an awful lot to be proud of."

"So what should I do?" Kate asked resignedly. "Beg Jake Griffin for the job?"

"Why not just get three different menus ready and drop them by his place? Tell him you're in the running and you expect to win."

"Good grief, Martha, you make everything sound so simple."

"Hey, I grew up knowing I'd have to work my way through life. I wasn't born into money the way you were."

"Well," said Kate, "looks like I'll have to do it, and to hell with my silly pride."

"Thataway, Katie. You can do it."

"Yeah." A rueful smile broke across Kate's face. "It's just that I wish I didn't have to do it for Jake Griffin."

"Hey, who knows?" Martha said, grinning. "Maybe something will happen between you two."

"We'll probably come to fisticuffs."

"Kate, the man is gorgeous, and as far as we know, he's available. Stop forecasting doom and go after him."

"There's no man on earth I'd like to go after less."

"I hope you're not talking about me, Katie."

Kate turned to find Harry Grenville standing in the doorway smiling at her. For a minute she was eighteen years old again, seeing him as she'd first seen him, with windblown brown hair, wearing a tennis sweater and white tennis shorts, carrying a racket and grinning at her as he walked by her at the golf club.

But this wasn't the twenty-two-year-old she'd first seen. This was Harry eighteen years later, wearing an Irish knit sweater and tweed slacks. He still looked every inch the well-to-do and up-and-coming male most likely to succeed, but there were lines in his face, and his hair was rapidly thinning. He was still as slender as he had been though, and she felt that familiar pang she'd always experienced upon seeing him.

How many times in the past three years had she imagined this moment—Harry showing up at her shop and looking around, impressed by all she'd accomplished? She swept a trembling hand across her lemon yellow skirt and smiled nervously.

"Hello, Harry," she said, deciding to ignore his comment. "What brings you to Lilac Hedges?"

"I wanted to see you and this business everyone's telling me about. It's incredible, Katie. I wouldn't have ever thought you could do it."

Her smile faded. "Actually, I've done very well, Harry," she said coolly. "There are a lot of things I'm capable of you probably wouldn't have guessed I could do."

"Well," he said, briskly rubbing his hands together, "this is all quite charming. It's hard to believe you actually make money at it."

If Harry had stopped by to renew their courtship, he was sure botching it, Kate thought darkly. A few more condescending words from him and she'd throw a bottle of her famous vinaigrette at him.

"Harry, it's been nice seeing you, but I'm afraid I have work to do."

"Come now, Kate. At noon? Surely even you take lunch."

"Yes, I eat a salad at my desk. It does wonders for the figure."

"I won't have it," Harry said. "You're coming out with me. We'll go to The Lily Pond. I've already made reservations."

"Harry," she said, shaking her head at him, "didn't you hear what I said? I'm working."

"Just this once. I wanted a chance to talk with you. Please, Kate, as a favor to someone you once cared for."

"Harry, that was a long time ago. I'm busy now."

Harry turned to Martha, who was pretending to be absorbed in making apple pies. "Martha, can't you convince her to come to lunch with me?"

"Hello, Harry," Martha answered ironically. "Nice to see you again, too."

His smile faltered then resumed its one-hundred-fifty-watt charm. "Still as droll as ever. How are you, Martha? How're Tom and the kids?"

"They're doing fine." Martha seemed surprised Harry had even remembered her ex-husband and children.

"Martha, come on, be a sport," Harry said. "Tell Kate to take an hour off and have lunch with me."

Martha turned to Kate. "If you don't, he'll probably stand around and pester us all day."

"She's right," Harry said.

"All right," Kate said, taking a deep breath. "But just this once, Harry. I have a business to run. I can't be taking time off whenever anyone has a whim to eat lunch with me."

"I promise. From now on I'll call and make a date with you instead of stopping by unannounced."

Kate crossed her arms. "Harry," she warned, "you're not taking me seriously."

"But I am!" he said, grinning as he took her by the arm and escorted her past Martha. "From now on, I'm going to take you very seriously." He threw a wink at Martha and slammed the door shut after them.

Kate shrugged her arm out of Harry's grasp. "Mother tells me you're here for a couple weeks to visit your folks. How are they, Harry?"

She had always liked Harry's parents. They were pleasant and had always welcomed her into their lovely home. Even after Harry had broken their engagement, they had been gracious to her, extending sincere invitations to dinner every time they saw her. Somehow Kate had always found a reason to decline. It seemed less messy that way.

"They're just fine," Harry said, opening the door to his silver Lexus LS400 and helping Kate in.

"We could have walked, Harry," Kate pointed out when he was behind the wheel and headed for The Lily Pond. "It's only a mile away."

"Why walk when we can ride in luxury?"

She arched a brow. How typical of Harry. She recalled how Harry had always liked her to gush over his cars and high-tech toys, but if he was angling for a compliment today, she wasn't about to comply. She had spent entirely too much of her life oohing and aahing over Harry. It would be nice if he'd ooh and aah over her for a change, but she supposed the chances of that happening were akin to landing on Mars in a rowboat.

"That's right, darling," Harry said. "Put your head back and relax. I hate to think of you slaving away at a dull job, Kate. Let me pamper you while I'm here."

The unexpected words were like flowers to a bee. She closed her eyes and felt herself begin to unwind. How lovely to be pampered! She smiled lazily. "Harry, it's not a dull job."

"No? Well, that's wonderful, Kate. I'm so pleased for you."

She opened her eyes. Could it be true? Had Harry changed? He certainly seemed to be giving her all his attention and solicitude. She glanced at him and found him looking at her with warm eyes.

"You're terribly beautiful, Kate, darling," he said quietly. "More beautiful than I even remembered."

"Perhaps it comes from working."

"Don't joke, Kate. I'm very serious about getting back together with you again and taking care of you properly."

They pulled up in front of the restaurant where a liveried valet stepped forward and opened Kate's door. "Harry," she said, stepping out, "please."

"All right, darling," he called, handing the boy the car keys and a very large tip. "But I won't be put off too much longer."

"Don't I have any say in all this?" Kate asked wryly as he opened the door and escorted her into the soaring cathedral-ceilinged lobby with its small pool lined in turquoise tiles. A large stone fish sculpture spouted water from its mouth, and goldfish darted among the underwater plants. Dozens of coins lined the brilliant floor of the pool, and a large lily pad floated on the water, a small gold frog seated on its surface.

"Reservations for two for Grenville," Harry said, and the hostess smiled brightly.

"Oh, yes, Mr. Grenville, right this way, please."

She led them past a gigantic aquarium that took up an entire wall, then into a dining room furnished in bleached woods with pink-and-green geranium-print upholstered chairs. Kelly green carpets covered the floor. The entire outside wall was glass, with French doors leading to a brick patio. In warm weather diners ate outside, but today most of the diners were content to look out at the lavish display of late-blooming tulips, geraniums, petunias and flowering shrubs that surrounded an even larger pool outside, stocked every summer with goldfish and frogs.

Their table was in front of a bay window, tucked away behind a huge ficus tree, out of the way of traffic and most other diners. Only one other table shared this tucked-away space, and when Harry held out Kate's chair, she saw his face drain of color. About the same time, she heard Jennifer's lilting voice.

"Hello, Harry," his wife called. "Having lunch with little Kate, I see."

"Oh, good grief," Harry said under his breath, then pasted on a smile. "Afternoon, Jennifer." He inclined his head stiffly to her companion. "Griffin."

At that, Kate froze, lifting wary eyes. She was seated directly across a small space from Jake Griffin, whose blue eyes gleamed at her over a glass of wine.

Jennifer and Jake Griffin. Terrific. Just terrific.

"Did you plan this, Harry?" Kate asked pleasantly under her breath when he'd taken his seat. "Or is it just our extraordinary luck?"

"Kate, I assure you, I had no idea they'd be here. Do you want to leave?"

"Of course not," Kate said, studying the luncheon menu. "Why let your wife chase you away from having lunch with your former girlfriend?"

"I'm sorry, Kate, this must be terribly embarrassing for you."

"Not in the least," Kate said dryly. "I love having Jennifer looking daggers at me over lunch."

"Well, she has no right to. It was she who filed for the divorce."

Kate glanced up at Harry. "I'm sorry," she said softly. "Has it been difficult for you?"

He stared down at the sparkling-white linen tablecloth, his forehead knitted into frown lines. "It's been a complete circus. Just a mess. First she says she wants the divorce, then she says she doesn't. Honestly, Kate, I don't know what would make Jennifer happy."

"Do you mean you're still interested in trying to find out so you could try to make her happy?"

"Absolutely not. It never really worked for us, Kate. Oh, the first year or so was wonderful but that was just—you know..."

"Beginner's luck?" Kate asked, an eyebrow lifted over ironic eyes.

Harry shrugged. "Who knows? I can't understand women. I've never been able to comprehend what you women want from a man."

It was Kate's turn to shrug. "Love? Companionship? Caring? A little attention once in a while? Isn't that what you men want from women?"

"Yes, but—" he lowered his voice and leaned toward Kate "—Jennifer wanted all my time! It was impossible! I have a successful career that requires a lot of time and energy, and she was always badgering me to come home from work early or take her on a trip to Europe. Honestly, I sometimes wish she had a career to keep her busy. She's like a child sometimes, always needing to be pacified."

"Then you can see why it might be beneficial for a woman to work?"

"Can you imagine Jennifer trying to hold down a job? One little setback and she'd be gone, up in arms about the impossible demands placed on her."

"Why did you marry her, Harry?"

"I don't know. She was around, I suppose. After I broke up with you she just started showing up wherever I was, and pretty soon we began to meet for cocktails. One thing led to another and before you know it, we were engaged."

"Short engagement, Harry," Kate said dryly. "What was it? All of two weeks?"

"Jennifer wanted it that way, and whatever Jennifer wants, Jennifer gets."

Kate slid her gaze toward Jennifer, who at this moment was gazing flirtatiously into Jake Griffin's eyes. "It looks like Jennifer wants Jake Griffin now."

"Imbecile," Harry spit out. "If she got lonely being married to me, can you imagine what it would be like being married to a workaholic like Jake Griffin?"

"Is he a workaholic?" Kate asked. "If so, he sure finds time for lunch."

Harry glanced at the other table and harrumphed. "Jennifer's after him. The poor guy hasn't got a chance."

Kate sat back and studied her former fiancé. "You look unhappy, Harry," she said at last. "Are you sure you want this divorce?"

"Of course I want it! That way I'll be free to marry you."

"Whoa, Harry," Kate said, holding up her palm as if to ward him off. "Let's settle back to a leisurely trot."

"Okay, I guess I am coming on too fast," Harry admitted.

"Like a freight train," Kate sighed, and then realized that Jake Griffin was watching her. She looked away quickly, feeling confused as pink color filled her cheeks. What was it about Jake Griffin that set her on edge? She wondered how she'd ever submit three menus to him now. Why hadn't she said something when she first saw him? Now it was going to be even more awkward than it would have been.

"Kate?"

She looked up to find Harry studying her. "The waitress is here."

"Oh!" She ordered a Cobb salad and white wine and smiled at the waitress, then found her eyes drifting toward Jake Griffin again. He was really quite extraordinarily attractive, she thought, studying him covertly as she sipped from her water glass. Her gaze went to his hands. She remembered how she had felt on Saturday when he had dropped into her office and took her hand in his. She felt a sudden glow of warmth and looked up. Startled, she found herself once more staring into Jake Griffin's amused blue eyes.

Hurriedly she looked away, but not before Jennifer had seen the exchange.

"Perhaps we should put our tables together," Jennifer suggested. "It's really quite foolish to be seated so close together and not talk."

"I don't think it's foolish in the least," Harry snapped.

Jake raised an eyebrow and grinned, his eyes pinned on Kate.

"I wasn't asking you, Harry," Jennifer said coldly. She gave Kate an artificial smile. "Actually, I was thinking that Kate might like to join us. We haven't had a chance to talk in years."

Astonished, Kate cleared her throat. "Perhaps we'll get a chance to talk some other time," she said tactfully.

"Oh, come on," Jennifer said. "Let's put our tables together."

"Jennifer." Harry's voice took on a tone of warning.

Jake Griffin stood and said, "Yes, why don't we?"

"Oh, Lord," Kate said under her breath. She raised her gaze and stared at Harry imploringly. "Do something," she hissed under her breath.

"What can I do?" he whispered back, then stood and pulled out a chair so the other couple could join them.

"Well!" Jennifer said when she and Jake had seated themselves. "Isn't this cozy?" Her eyes flickered over Kate's outfit dismissively as she fingered an elaborate emerald peacock pin on her white silk suit.

"Cozy as a bug in a rug," Kate said dryly, refusing to look at Jake.

"I hope you don't think we're interfering," Jake said.

"Of course they don't!" Jennifer said. "My goodness, Kate and I have known each other since grade school."

"Kindergarten, actually," Kate said. "You colored my new red shoes with purple crayons the first day of school."

"And you've never forgiven me." Jennifer smiled slyly.

Kate let that slide by, but wished she had a bludgeon. If she hit Jennifer with one good shot, she'd be out of it for a couple hours at least and they could eat in peace.

"Jennifer," Harry said, "are you visiting your parents?"

"Yes. They're heartbroken about our divorce, but I've told them it can't be helped. Irreconcilable differences and all that."

"Yes," Harry said darkly, "I have brains and you don't."

Kate choked on her white wine, and Jake's lips twitched in a grin.

"Harry," Kate suggested hurriedly, "tell us about your trip to Switzerland last year. I heard you had a lovely week of skiing in Gstaad."

"It was terrible," Jennifer said. "Harry was angry at me the entire time."

"You were flirting with every man in sight, Jennifer. It was hardly a relaxing vacation."

"I get bored skiing, Harry," Jennifer said with a pout. "I need to have a little fun!" She rolled her eyes. "But there was good old Harry, out on the slopes at 8:00 a.m. and not back till dinner. Ugh. It was incredibly boring."

"If you had skied, it would have been fun."

Jake looked across the arena toward Kate. "Are you still angry with me?" he asked quietly.

She looked down, hiding her eyes behind her lashes. While Harry and Jennifer went at each other, she and Jake seemed suspended in a pool of quiet. She raised her eyes and shook her head. "In fact, I've decided to submit three menus to you, if you'll accept them."

"Of course I will. I really don't know what I said that upset you so much, but I'm sorry I did."

Suddenly Jennifer stopped her tirade and glared at Jake. "When did you upset Kate?" she demanded, then realized how she sounded and softened her words with a smile.

"It really doesn't matter, Jennifer," Kate said.

"But it does!" Jennifer trilled, batting her lashes at Jake. She tapped his hand playfully and said, "You bad boy. You mustn't upset our little Kate any more."

Kate rolled her eyes and wondered if ladies were ever sick to their stomachs in public. Right about now she felt she might be. It was almost too much to believe that Jake couldn't see through Jennifer, but she supposed men were blind when it came to attractive women—they saw what they wanted to see and ignored the facts.

But Harry was studying Kate's expression. "When did you see Griffin?" he asked her in a low undertone.

"It doesn't matter, Harry," Kate said quietly.

"But it does! I want to know when you saw him!"

Looking up, Kate saw that Jake was aware of what was going on between her and Harry even while Jennifer continued focusing her attention on him. She raised her eyes heavenward and let out an exasperated sigh. "Harry," she said baldly, "mind your own business."

Jennifer's head came up like a beagle sighting geese. "Harry, stop bothering Kate."

"Jennifer," Kate said through her teeth, "I can take care of myself, thank you."

"Can you?" Jennifer asked, oozing warmth and concern. "But your father couldn't take care of himself. I'm worried maybe you've inherited his . . . er . . . weakness. . . ."

Kate felt as if she'd been slapped. Two red spots burned in her cheeks as she stared at the woman who batted such innocent lashes. Picking up her pocketbook, she slid back her chair. "Don't ever say anything about my father again," she said in a low voice that trembled with anger. "Now if you'll excuse me, I have to get back to work."

"But, Kate!" Harry catapulted from his chair.

"Katie, you mustn't go!" wailed Jennifer.

Jake Griffin said nothing, but watched the unfolding scene with more than polite interest.

"Harry," Kate said threateningly, "be quiet. Jennifer—" She paused. She was a lady and ladies didn't get involved in public scenes, but sometimes it was important to say what you felt and the niceties be damned. "Jennifer," she said at last, "drop dead."

Turning on her heel, she strode from the dining room, leaving a waitress staring after her, a Cobb salad still in her hand.

Kate was outside when Harry caught up with her. "Kate!" he called. "Let me drive you back to your place. I'm so sorry, Kate. Jennifer's being a bitch."

"I want to walk, Harry," she said coolly, striding along without looking at him. "It will help me work off my anger."

"You've got to forgive her, Kate," Harry said, walking next to her. "She doesn't know what she says sometimes."

"No, Harry, I don't have to forgive her, just as I don't have to forgive you for what you did to me. Sometimes I think you two deserve each other."

"Kate! Why are you angry with *me* now?"

"Harry, I've *been* angry with you, but I've acted polite and kept my temper because that's what ladies *do.*" Her eyes flashed as she strode along angrily. "Well, I'm sick of being a lady. I'm sick of acting as if everything's just peachy when in fact I'm mad as hell. Harry," she said, coming to a stop and turning to face him, "go to hell, right along with Jennifer."

She left him standing openmouthed in astonishment and walked away, exhilaration churning in her bloodstream, making her feel as if she could take right off and fly. Lord, she was pumped right now! She could take on an army, melt steel, chew nails into mush. She'd just taken on thirty-four years of training and had finally done something she wanted to do rather than what she'd been taught she *should* do! No more nice girl. Kate Cunningham had finally broken loose.

Chapter Five

"Way to go!"

Martha's eyes glowed with exuberance as Kate regaled her with the story of her lunchtime escapade. "You should've told him to take a hike when you saw him at the Letterers' the other night. But at least you did it today. Oh, Katie, I'm so proud of you!"

Kate had kicked off her shoes and was sipping a cup of tea and sharing a blueberry muffin with Martha. She was amazed, but she felt like a million bucks. She'd had not one moment's doubt about how she'd acted—until her mother intruded on her thoughts.

"My mother will croak if she ever finds out," she said. "And she will find out. She has an underground circuit that leads directly to anything that smacks of a scene or scandal."

"She may give you a hard time, but she'll get over it," Martha said.

"Ha. She'll be on me like fleas on a dog. There'll be no letup. She'll scold and berate and tell me how ashamed she is at how I acted." Kate rested her chin in her hand. "She'll tell me she can't hold her head up in the community, that she raised me to be a lady and I acted like a common something or other." Kate glanced at Martha and shook her head. "It won't be pretty."

"You can handle it," Martha said.

Sighing, Kate hoped she could.

"I'M SO ASHAMED!" Laurel Cunningham stormed that evening. "I can't hold my head up in the community! I raised you to be a lady, Kate, not some common harridan! How could you do this to me? And in *public?* My Lord, Kate, at The Lily Pond!" Laurel closed her eyes and shook her head, looking as if she'd just swallowed a sour grape. "What am I going to do about you, Kate? What am I going to *do?*"

Kate studied the *New York Times* Sunday crossword puzzle, trying to figure out what a five-letter word for a seabird was.

"Kate, you're not listening to me!"

"Yes, I am, Mother," Kate said, yawning. She hoped her act was working. Inside, her stomach may be mush, but she was unflinchingly sticking to her game plan: Don't let her know she's reached you. Act like you know what you're doing. Act as if you believe in yourself. And by all means, don't let her see you sweat.

"Oh, Kate," Laurel said sorrowfully, trying a new approach, "what am I going to do with you?"

The shrillness was gone. The modulated voice was back, this time with a resigned tone and sorrowful shake of her head. In times gone by, these exact tactics had caused Kate massive amounts of guilt and had resulted in pounds of apologies and resolves to change and be more like her mother wanted her to be. Today Kate filled in the six-letter word for courage: spunky.

She'd probably find out later on it didn't fit, but she liked the sound of it right now.

"Spunky," she said out loud. "A six-letter word for courage."

"Nonsense," Laurel Cunningham spit out. "It's mettle. *M-e-t-t-l-e,*" she said, spelling it out.

Kate sighed. "You're probably right."

"I'm *always* right!"

"No, Mother, you aren't," Kate said, surprising her mother so much that her mouth fell open.

"I beg your pardon?" Laurel said.

"You're not always right, Mother," Kate repeated. "Sometimes you're dead wrong, particularly when it comes to me and my life and what I should be doing."

Tears sprang into Laurel's blue eyes. "How can you say that?" she gasped, dashing a tear away. "I'm your mother, Kate! I love you!"

"That I won't dispute," Kate said more quietly. "I know you love me, and I know you want what's best for me, but taken over a lifetime, your advice is worth diddly squat."

Laurel stared. "Diddly *what?*"

"Squat, Mother," Kate said tiredly. "Now, if you'll excuse me, I've had a hard day and I'd like to go to bed."

"Bed? It's only eight o'clock! You should be going out, trying to meet a nice man! There's a bridge tournament at the club tonight, darling. I'm sure you'd meet someone charming if you'd go."

"At a bridge tournament?" Kate said. "You've got to be kidding."

"Kate, as you should know very well by now, I never kid."

It was true. Laurel Cunningham had absolutely no sense of humor. Jokes left her cold. She found comedies and comic strips and stand-up comedians boring. She was the only person Kate knew who didn't laugh when someone slipped on a banana peel.

"Mother, it was nice of you to stop by and tell me how everyone in Litchfield County is abuzz over my abrupt exit from The Lily Pond. I am sorry if I've caused you grief, but you'll just have to get over it." Kate stood and threw the puzzle down on the coffee table. "Now, good night, Mother. See you in my dreams."

"Kate," Laurel said, "I think this catering business of yours is having a very bad effect on you."

Kate had to smile. She couldn't help it. The funny thing was, her mother was right, though in a roundabout and totally wrong way.

"What do you think I should do, Mom? Close up shop? Go to work for Martha Stewart? All the family money is gone, lost in a bunch of wrongheaded investments and a couple racetracks along the way. So what should I do, Mom? You tell me."

"Kate, I think you may be coming down with something. Run yourself a nice hot bath and get in bed like you want, darling. We'll talk when you're feeling better."

How like her mother. Running when things got tough. Smooth over the ugly and gloss over the bad. Pretend that all was well when the damn roof caved in and act as if everything were terrific when all hell had broken loose. But never, *ever* admit that something might be wrong.

"Thanks, Mom," Kate said, deciding it wasn't worth arguing about. "A nice hot bath sounds great."

"Goodbye, dear," her mother said, air-kissing her cheek. "Take it easy, darling."

Kate walked her mother to the door, then closed it with a tiny slam and tapped her fingers on it. "Okay, Mom, I'll take it easy. I'll run my bath and the world will get all pink and fuzzy and all problems will disappear and everyone will find money growing on trees in the morning."

When a knock sounded on the door a few minutes later, Kate shouted, "Go away, Mother! I've had enough for one night."

"It isn't Mother," an irate male voice called back.

Kate froze, then peeked behind the lace curtain that shielded the sidelights. Oh, good grief. Jake Griffin. What would happen next? Would the sky fall? The earth buckle? Damn it all to hell, had the greenhouse effect already taken place?

She opened the door and found Jake Griffin standing there, his face a mask of anger. "Why didn't you tell me?" he snarled.

She stared at him blankly. What was she supposed to have told him? From the looks of it, it was mighty important. "I beg your pardon?"

"How was I supposed to know it was your parents' home? My lawyers handled the paperwork. I never even knew the former owners' names."

Stunned, Kate stared at him, then gestured for him to come in. "Let's go sit down and have a brandy," she suggested. "It looks like this is going to be a long night."

Jake followed her into the living room. It was furnished with things taken from her parents' home and was charming, with one wall lined in floor-to-ceiling bookcases, a fireplace, French doors opening onto a brick terrace and a window seat tucked into a bay window. Two camelback sofas upholstered in forest green damask sat facing each other in front of the fireplace, with a Chippendale table between them on a navy-and-emerald oriental rug. The wide-board floors shone, and Waterford crystal glittered in the light from china lamps. A large navy wing chair sat angled in a corner.

"How did you find out?" Kate asked as she handed Jake a glass of brandy.

"Jennifer, initially."

"Oh, Lord, I'll bet you got an earful."

"I talked with the Letterers later."

Kate sipped the brandy and sat on the edge of one of the sofas. "It was awkward for me, Mr. Griffin. I didn't even want to go out there when you first suggested it."

"For God's sake, call me Jake!"

She raised her eyebrows at his vehemence, and he sat opposite her. "I'm sorry," he said more quietly.

She shrugged. "It doesn't matter."

"But it does. I feel like a fool. I'm just so damned sorry. I made so many assumptions about you, and then to find out what had happened..."

Kate smiled at him. "Thanks for apologizing. It helps."

"I am sorry, Kate," Jake said. "Especially about your father. It must have been very rough on you."

She looked at the logs laid in the fireplace and wished they were lighted. She'd like to feel the warmth from a good roaring fire right now. She supposed she'd have to settle for the warmth from alcohol instead.

Kate glanced at Jake. With a start, she saw compassion glowing in his eyes as he watched her. Immediately she felt warmer, and it wasn't from the brandy.

"Losing the family home was terrible," she said quietly. "And finding out Dad had declared bankruptcy was painful, but losing my father was..." She stared down at the amber liquid in her glass. "You knew he had a heart attack right after declaring bankruptcy?"

"The Letterers told me," he said.

She looked away. "Would you mind lighting the fire?"

Jake got the fire going, then came back and sat down.

"Thank you," she said. "It feels good sitting here with you."

"I'm glad."

She smiled and nodded at his drink. "You're not drinking."

"I'll finish it in good time."

She smiled and looked at the fire, which was beginning to eat up the kindling. "I used to be terribly angry at him for leaving Mother and me to cope with the mess he left behind."

Jake didn't say anything; he sat and looked at her with those marvelous warm eyes that were filled with equal parts of understanding and compassion. "It must have been rough," he said at last.

She nodded. "But I'm doing okay. The catering business is going pretty well, so that helps. I keep busy."

"Will you go to dinner with me tomorrow evening?" he said unexpectedly.

She couldn't help it. She laughed. "That's a quick change of subject."

"I'm sorry," he said. "I didn't mean I wasn't listening to you. I've been listening, but it's so nice being with you, I thought of asking you to dinner. Would you?"

"Well..." She felt suddenly flustered. Did she want to go to dinner with Jake Griffin? What if he hired her to cater his party? It wasn't the best idea to get personally involved with a client. "This is awkward," she finally said. "I mean, I'd like to cater that party for you, but..."

"But?"

She shrugged. "I don't like to get involved with clients."

"We won't be getting involved," he said easily. "It's just a dinner."

She smiled. "Just shoveling food in our mouths, eh?"

He laughed. "Perhaps a little fancier than that. There's a very nice inn not far from here. I thought we could go there."

"The Inn at Fielding Point?"

"Yes, that's it."

"It is nice," she said and nodded. "Okay. I don't suppose one dinner with a possible client would hurt."

"You can bring the menus with you, if that makes you feel better," Jake said. "I'll go over them with you over drinks."

"All right. That sounds fine."

"Good. I'll pick you up at seven-thirty?"

She nodded and rose to walk him to the door. "That'll be fine."

"Till tomorrow then," he said, and unexpectedly leaned forward and kissed her gently on the forehead. "Good night, Kate," he whispered softly.

She felt chills go up and down her arms. She lifted her head and looked into his eyes and felt herself falling into a long and lovely field filled with sunlight and golden grass. "Good night, Jake," she whispered back.

She felt a sudden shock of recognition. She wanted him to kiss her again, really kiss her. She wanted him to take her in his arms and hold her and kiss her the right way, the way a man kisses a woman he adores. Instead he reached out and pushed a stray strand of golden hair behind her ear.

"You're very lovely," he said.

She wanted to curl her fingers into his lapels and draw him to her. She wanted to melt into his arms and feel his warm lips on hers. Kiss me, she wanted to plead. Kiss me.

"Good night, Kate."

"Good night."

He closed the door softly behind him.

She stood in the hall with her forehead pressed into the door, her eyes closed, seeing his warm eyes again, feeling the incredible warmth fill her as it had when he'd actually been looking at her. She felt his hand on her hair, his breath on her face, heard his voice again: Good night, Kate.

"Good grief," she said out loud. "This I don't need."

She'd gone too long without a man's companionship, and this was the result—falling for the first man her mother shoved her way. And a cowboy at that!

She pushed away from the door and told herself to get real. Hammering hearts and pounding pulses were for teenagers. Right now she needed a contract to cater Jake Griffin's party. If she wasn't careful, all she'd get was a night in his bed....

"A DATE?" Martha said the next morning. "Oh my God, Kate! That's wonderful!"

"It's not a date," Kate said. "It's a business dinner. We're going to discuss a few options for his party."

"Kate, the smart woman always pretends it's just business at first."

Kate gave Martha a dark look. "Will you stop it? It's just a friendly meeting."

"Sure. And I'm just a polar bear."

"Jake Griffin is merely a potential client. Nothing more."

"Sure," Martha said dryly. "Like if Paul Newman walked in you wouldn't faint right on the spot. Honestly, Kate, loosen up. It's time you got involved with someone. You could use a hot love affair right about now. Or does it bother you that your mother's the one who suggested you go out with Jake Griffin?"

"Speaking of whom," Kate said, ignoring a subject too close to the truth, "Mother appeared last night just as I knew she would, woebegone and distraught, claiming she didn't know how she could live in Brady Corners after what I'd done yesterday." She sighed. "I've got to do something about her, but I don't know what. She is just so concerned about me all the time."

"Maybe it's time she found a new man," Martha ventured.

"A new man." Kate turned the idea over and felt a burgeoning sense of hope. Maybe there was a way out of this mess after all! "You're right, that's just what she needs. Someone to fuss over the way she used to fuss over Dad and the way she's fussing over me now."

Kate frowned as she went through the catalog of available men in the area. Half the men in Litchfield County were after her mother, but she'd have none of them. Laurel Cunningham was completely unrealistic about men; she wanted someone as handsome as Adonis, as rich as Croesus and better in the sack than Kevin Costner. Kate smiled to herself. What her mother really needed was someone like—

"Elroy Kramer!" she cried. "Mother and Elroy. Can you see it? Just the other night at the Letterers' she was trying to foist him off on *me*."

Martha and Kate broke into peals of laughter.

"I've got an idea," Martha said, her laughter evaporating as she began to plan an attack.

"Well, don't keep it a secret."

"What if your mother found out Elroy was lonely, or needed someone to talk to, something like that? Your mother is the perfect codependent. She'd fly to his rescue the moment she thought he needed someone. Meanwhile I could talk to Elroy and tell him your mother has a crush on him but she won't admit it. So when your mother approaches him asking how things are with him, he'll think she's just using that as an excuse to talk to him...."

"I don't know, Martha," Kate said, gnawing on the idea. "What if Elroy isn't interested in my mother?"

"Be real, Kate," Martha said deadpan. "What man wouldn't be interested in your mother?"

"That's true. I suppose it could work."

"Of course it will work. Trust me."

Kate felt vaguely uneasy, but decided to go along with it. After all, anything was better than having her mother constantly on her back.

"LAUREL CUNNINGHAM is interested in me?" Elroy Kramer said. "Really?"

"Yes, but she won't admit it, of course," Martha said. They were in line at the checkout counter of The Gourmet Grocery. Martha had been there for half an hour, waiting for Elroy to show up at his usual time to buy a quarter pound of fresh-roasted coffee beans, a chocolate croissant and the morning paper.

Elroy adjusted his red bow tie and smoothed his rumpled brown cardigan sweater. Beaming at Martha, he brushed his few strands of hair across his bald spot. "She's such a lovely woman. I'd never have believed it."

"Well, it's true, Mr. Kramer," Martha said, smiling to herself as he took off his horn-rimmed glasses and began to polish them. "I imagine she'd use any excuse to approach you.'

"She wouldn't need an excuse!" Elroy exclaimed. "I'd be honored to go out with her."

"Yes, but she doesn't know that. After all, Mr. Kramer, you're a very wealthy man. You could have any woman you wanted."

He put his glasses back on and stared at Martha, dumbfounded. "I could?"

"Sure you could!" Martha said, laying it on. "Any woman would give her eyeteeth to land you."

Elroy lifted his chin and straightened his shoulders. "Well, that's kind of you to say, Martha. Very kind, indeed."

"I just thought you should know," Martha said, then waved and disappeared from the store, leaving Elroy standing bemused at the back of the line, his corduroy trousers bagging around his knees.

"ELROY'S DEPRESSED?" Laurel Cunningham said, staring at Martha. "Why, the poor man! How did you ever find out?"

Martha had stopped by to drop off a dozen blueberry muffins from Kate. Laurel was visiting a woman whose husband was ill in the hospital, and she had called Kate for some ideas about what to bring when she visited.

"Well, I don't know for sure he's depressed," Martha said. "It's only a hunch. I just saw him in the store and he looked . . . I don't know, kind of lonely, forlorn. I think it's a real shame. He's the nicest man, but he's never married."

"I'll have to think of a way to cheer him up," Laurel said, already casting about for ideas.

Martha let out a relieved breath. "That would be so nice of you, Mrs. Cunningham."

But Laurel didn't even hear Martha. She already had an idea. She'd been after Kate for years to cultivate Elroy. What if she told Elroy that Kate was secretly crazy about him? Nothing would turn the old coot on faster, or she'd miss her guess. And that way Kate would have a level-headed older man to take care of her, and *she* wouldn't have to worry herself sick about Kate anymore.

Satisfied she'd come up with the perfect plan, Laurel saw Martha to the door and immediately went to the phone.

"Elroy?" she said when the phone was answered on the fourth ring. "This is Laurel Cunningham."

"Laurel! How nice to hear from you." Elroy leaned over and peered in the mirror. Maybe that little Martha who worked with Kate was right. Maybe Laurel Cunningham did have a crush on him.

"Elroy, I need your advice. I was wondering if you could meet me for dinner tonight?"

"I'd be delighted, Laurel." How like a woman to pretend she needed advice when in reality she just wanted to be with him! "Why don't we go to The Inn at Fielding Point?" he suggested. "It's quiet there. We can talk without being bothered."

"That's wonderful, Elroy," Laurel said. "I'll see you about eight o'clock."

"Eight tonight," he said, smoothing his hairs over his bald spot. "Terrific. See you then."

Elroy hung up and rubbed his hands together briskly, beaming at himself in the mirror. Finally, at age sixty-five, he was going to have a little fun!

HARRY GRENVILLE stared disconsolately at the phone. He wasn't used to sitting around all day. He wished he could just call Kate and ask her out for dinner. Kate was a good sport. She'd always known how to cheer him up. Not like Jennifer.

Harry groaned and got up and began to pace his room at The Inn at Fielding Point. Dammit all. Why couldn't he get Jennifer out of his mind? She was a total scatterbrain, without scruples and utterly shallow, yet she intrigued him still. But he'd been a fool to marry her. Women like Jennifer were made for secret assignations and romantic affairs, not for the long haul. No, for settling down, for steadiness and security, he needed a woman like Kate. He should have married her in the first place and to hell with what his boss had said.

True, Jennifer was exciting. She was magnificently beautiful. She was intriguing and exhilarating and baffling. She made his blood boil, his temper soar and his pulses pound, but she wasn't the kind of woman you married. Went to bed with, yes. Even now he felt desire leap within him just thinking about her.

Swearing to himself, Harry picked up the phone and dialed the dining room. He made a reservation for dinner for himself at eight. Dammit, why had Kate been so stubborn about him not calling her? She was exactly what he needed—sweet, intelligent, kind, sensible. And the other day, she'd shown a side of herself he hadn't known existed. It appeared she had more gumption than he'd given her credit for. Yes, Kate was the answer to all his problems. The only problem was, she didn't want to speak to him as long as she lived.

JENNIFER GRENVILLE stared at the decorating magazine, not seeing the glossy pages. Her thoughts were focused on Kate Cunningham. She hated it that she thought about Kate so much. Sometimes it seemed as if her entire life had been spent trying to get what Kate had. She'd thought her most fulfilling moment had come when she'd stolen away Harry Grenville, but now she wasn't so sure. If she could marry

Jake Griffin and come back to live at Spindrift, maybe she'd finally best Kate for all time.

But something niggled at Jennifer. She didn't want to think about it, of course. She never liked thinking about unpleasant things, and thinking about Harry was particularly unpleasant lately. She just wished the divorce was over. Maybe then she could get him out of her mind. He had the most amazing way of popping into her head just when she least expected him.

Frowning, she decided to make reservations to go out to dinner. She'd heard that Harry was staying at The Inn at Fielding Point. Maybe she'd go there. After all, it wouldn't hurt to run into him again. For some reason, she liked the idea of making life miserable for him. Smiling to herself, she picked up the phone and dialed the inn.

Chapter Six

The goal was to look businesslike, efficient and not at all attractive. A long-sleeved navy dress with prim white collar and cuffs was perfect for dinner with Jake Griffin. For the finishing touch she swept her hair back in a loose French twist with a tortoiseshell comb.

Into a trim leather folder she tucked the three menus she'd come up with that afternoon and then sat to await Jake Griffin's arrival, her feet primly crossed at the ankle.

But as soon as she heard the doorbell ring, warm color swept into her face and her heart started beating much too quickly. She forced herself to walk sedately to the door, but when she opened it she had a swift desire to close it again real quick and run and hide in her closet.

Jake Griffin obviously hadn't tried to make himself look businesslike and unattractive. He wore a buttery-soft tan suede sports coat, faded but immaculately pressed blue jeans and a white silk shirt open at the collar.

Then she caught sight of a hint of crisp black hair beneath the vee of his shirt. Get a grip, girl, she told herself. But her eyes remained fastened on the sun-browned warmth of his neck. Her stomach felt like a Ferris wheel.

"Hello," she said, her voice much too breathless for her liking.

The corner of Jake's sculpted mouth lifted appreciatively. "Hello to you, too."

"Well, I'm all set."

Jake grinned at her, his eyes crinkling in amusement. "You look good enough to eat."

She stared at him, astonished. "What?"

His grin widened. "There's something about a woman in a high collar and long sleeves that drives me crazy. I always want to slowly undo all those delicious little buttons that keep her body hidden from sight and nuzzle the soft skin of her neck."

"Oh," she said weakly, and considered dashing upstairs to change into a bikini if long sleeves made him feel that way. She forced a tepid laugh. "Well, Mr. Griffin, this is a business meeting after all."

"Business doesn't have to mean no pleasure, Kate," Jake said, taking her arm and guiding her toward a long silver limousine.

"A limo," she said, coming to a stop. "How...how nice." Now she was getting scared. Men used limos as a means of seduction, or at least that was what she'd always found. They inevitably pulled out a bottle of champagne, put on a seductive disk and closed off the driver's compartment from the back, and there the woman would be—a sitting target for his advances. At least that was what had happened in her experience. Maybe Jake Griffin would prove her wrong.

She wasn't wrong. They had no sooner settled in their plush seats than Jake slid a black-mirrored window into place between them and the driver. He touched a button and the low, sultry sound of a saxophone filled the air. A bottle of champagne chilled in a silver ice bucket; two crystal glasses were waiting on a mahogany tray.

"Well," Kate said, "let's get down to business."

"Later, Kate. Let's just sit back and get to know each other a little better."

She arched a wry brow and inched toward the corner of the seat. "Mr. Griffin, I don't have any desire to get to know you better."

"Not even a little bit?" he asked, grinning as he poured a glass of champagne and held it out to her.

She pushed the glass away. "Not even a smidgen." She pulled out the three menus and handed the first to him.

"Tex-Mex," she said. "I thought it would be a fun idea, what with you coming from Texas originally."

"I haven't lived in Texas since I was a kid," he said, tossing the menu onto the seat between them.

She shrugged and handed him the second. "Roast suckling pig."

It went the way of the first. "Can't stand the looks of a trussed-up pig on a spit."

She gave him a glance and wondered how *he*'d look all trussed up on a spit. She handed him the third. "Elegant nouvelle cuisine."

He shook his head and deposited it with the others. "I really think you need to get to know me a little better before you can cater a party for me."

"I agree completely, Mr. Griffin—"

"Jake."

"Jake. But you insisted that I present you with three possible menus. I just did and you refuse to even consider them."

"I'll consider them after we've had a chance to talk awhile," he said, and handed her the glass of champagne.

She stared at him then took the glass. The client was always right—at least they had to feel they were, she thought disgustedly. "How many people do you plan to invite?" she asked, hoping to get him back to business.

"Kate, why don't you relax and let me get to know you?"

"I told you last night, Jake—I don't want to get involved with a client."

"That's not it and you know it isn't. You know what's really going on?"

"Why don't you fill me in."

"You've still got a crush on Harry Grenville."

"What?"

"It's very clear. You're the only one who doesn't know how you feel about Harry."

She almost sputtered she was so angry. "You've met me three times, Jake Griffin. You've seen me at the most a total of a half an hour with Harry. Just where do you get off diagnosing me?"

"Because that's the only possible explanation. I'm a reasonably presentable man, Kate. I've yet to meet a woman who didn't respond favorably to a request to have dinner, yet you are doing your damnedest to keep me at arm's length."

"Your ego is immense!" she said. "How do you live with yourself?"

He laughed easily and poured her more champagne. "I just think you need to recognize what's going on and come to terms with it. Put Harry behind you, Kate. He's no good for you."

"And you are?"

He smiled lazily. "I might be."

"Spare me," she said, rolling her eyes. "About the only thing worse than Harry Grenville is a man with an overstuffed ego."

"Meaning me?"

"Bingo."

He laughed and reached out to take her hand. "Kate, relax. Stop putting up your defenses against me."

"Stop trying to scale them." She pulled her hand from his.

He sighed and took his hand away. "All right, let's talk about business."

"Well, we're here now," she said, and opened the limo door without waiting for the driver to do it for her. "Let's talk about it over dinner."

Jake got out of the limo and put a hand on the small of her back to escort her toward the inn. She gave him a look and stepped away from his hand. "Let's get something straight, shall we? This is business and nothing but business. No holding my hand or putting a protective arm around me or looking deeply into my eyes. Treat me like I'm sixty-five years old and overweight with a hair growing out of my chin."

He laughed out loud. "Never in my wildest imaginings could you be overweight with a hair growing out of your chin."

"Well, then, at least make me sixty-five."

"When you're sixty-five, Kate Cunningham," he said gently, "you'll be as lovely as you are right now."

She looked at him and felt her resolve melting. How could you fight a man who made you feel special, adored, desired? She looked at him, a plea shimmering in her eyes. "Please," she said softly, "don't try to seduce me. I'm feeling very weak right now and I don't need to be seduced."

"On the contrary, Kate," he said. "Seduction is exactly what you need."

They were in the shadows and there was no one around. It was the simplest thing in the world to step into his arms and let him kiss her, and so she did. It was a dizzying kiss, filled with magic, carrying her out of herself, past the *shoulds* and the *ought tos*, bringing her directly into confrontation with her very womanly desires.

His lips were the sweetest she had ever known, his arms the strongest. She felt dizzy and overwhelmed and filled with yearning. She didn't want the kiss to end, didn't want to ever step out of his embrace, but it did end and she had to step away. It was the hardest thing she'd ever done.

"Now," he said softly, smiling at her, "that wasn't very bad, was it?"

She looked into his eyes, feeling as if she were falling into a deep and magical spell. "It was lovely," she whispered.

"Kate." He took her in his arms again and kissed her again until she could only cling to him, lost in his arms, turning round and round as if on a marvelous golden carousel—dizzy, aroused, trembling with awareness of him.

"Ohhh," she breathed, and her voice shook and her fingers curled into his lapels and she buried her forehead against his strong chest.

He held her against him. "I think I should call the limo back and whisk you off to my place and keep you captive until you fall in love with me."

She had to smile at that. He was utterly absurd. "I thought you were a confirmed bachelor."

He shrugged. "Even confirmed bachelors get lonely."

She smiled and looked up at him, her eyes shining. "How many women have you seduced with that line?"

He shook his head, his blue eyes strangely serious. "None, I'm afraid. I've never said that to a woman before."

She searched his eyes and felt suddenly confused. She looked away and stepped back. "We'll be late for our reservations."

"Mustn't do that, must we?" he asked gently.

She met his eyes again and saw that they were wonderfully warm and filled with promise. "I suppose we mustn't," she whispered softly.

He put his arm around her and escorted her toward the inn. "No protective arm around you," he said mildly. "No looking into your eyes." He pulled her gently toward him, his hand on her waist. "No more kisses, either, I suppose."

"Not one," she said, laughing.

He stopped at the front door and turned her to face him, lowering his head and kissing her softly but firmly. "When you tell me no, Kate, I seem to only want to do it even more."

"No," she whispered.

He kissed her soundly then, strongly, the way she'd wanted him to kiss her last night when he'd left her home, leaving no doubt that he found her desirable.

"Let's go in, Kate," he said when the kiss ended. "Otherwise I won't be responsible for what happens between us."

She put a trembling hand on her stomach and willed it to stop dancing, took a deep breath and followed him into the lobby.

They were seated at a small table for two in a shadowy corner. Candles were lighted at the table, casting a golden glow around them. Kate felt as if she were shining, as if a hundred candles burned inside her right now, illuminating her from within. Jake ordered more champagne. It was going to be a perfect evening, Kate decided. Absolutely perfect. Nothing would be able to spoil it.

"Katie!" a too-familiar voice trilled from nearby. "What are you doing here?"

"Mother?" She felt her perfect evening begin to evaporate like snow melting on a warm day.

"I had no idea you'd be here tonight!" Laurel Cunningham gushed as she approached the table.

Kate met Jake's amused eyes. "Mother, you remember Jake Griffin."

"Of course, how could I forget? Mr. Griffin," Laurel said, holding out her hand. "So nice to see you again."

"It's a pleasure to see you, Mrs. Cunningham."

"Darling, you know Elroy Kramer."

Flabbergasted, Kate looked up to find Elroy standing behind her mother, his eyes sheepish behind his horn-rimmed glasses, his little red bow tie bobbing up and down in nervousness. Her heart went out to him. Being with Laurel Cunningham must be a little like fishing for trout and landing a barracuda. Yet she was happy that Martha's plan had already begun to bear fruit.

"Hello, Elroy, it's so nice to see you. This is Jake Griffin. Jake, Elroy Kramer."

The men fell into conversation and Laurel bent to whisper in Kate's ear. "Why didn't you *tell* me you were going after Jake Griffin?"

Kate rolled her eyes. "Because I'm not," she said in a low voice. "Honestly, Mother—"

"That's quite all right, dear. I'll just mind my own business."

That'll be the first time, Kate thought dryly, but smiled and watched as Elroy escorted her mother to a nearby table. Kate looked across the table at Jake. "I see Mother hasn't wasted any time," she said. "Only this morning Martha put a bug in her ear about Elroy Kramer. I'm hoping she'll turn her full attention on him and leave me alone for a while."

"I see. Too attentive for your liking, is she?"

"Mother is. . ." Kate paused to contemplate her mother. "Mother is a typical concerned mother. She pays entirely too much attention to my business and not nearly enough to her own."

"Exasperating."

"Exactly."

Jake looked past Kate, his eyes twinkling. "Well, if you find your mother's presence unnerving, how will you react to Jennifer Grenville's?"

"Oh, Lord. Not Jennifer."

"I'm afraid so, and they're bringing her this way."

"Oh, God." Kate wished she could bury her head. "This is turning into a date from hell."

Jake grinned and nodded at Jennifer. "Good evening, Jennifer. Nice to see you."

Jennifer's eyes lighted up when she saw Jake, but she stopped when she saw who was with him. "Kate Cunningham?" she said. "My goodness, you're like a bad penny. You show up everywhere."

"Hello, Jennifer," Kate said dryly. "Nice to see you, too."

"I'm eating alone, I'm afraid," Jennifer said. "Mind if I join you?"

Appalled, Kate could only stare up at her. How could she be this bold to invite herself to join them? It was incomprehensible to Kate, totally unbelievable.

"I'm sorry," a familiar voice said from behind Jennifer. "You'll have to excuse Jennifer. She's being outrageous again."

They turned to find Harry Grenville standing there, eyeing his wife sardonically. "You're here alone?" he asked Jennifer.

"Yes," she said, defiantly flouncing her hair at him.

"Then join me." He took her by the elbow, and with an apologetic look over his shoulder at Kate, marched Jennifer away to his table.

Kate looked back at Jake. "My mother and Elroy and Jennifer and Harry."

Jake sighed. "A bad dream."

"Worse than that," Kate said. "A nightmare."

His lips quirked with humor. "Shall we leave and find another place to eat?"

She laughed. "No, I think we should stay and watch the show."

"You think there'll be one?"

"With Harry and Jennifer and my mother around? Indubitably."

"Then my chances of having a romantic tête-à-tête with you are shot."

"I'm afraid so," Kate said, smiling.

"Drat."

Her eyes twinkled. "You'll get over it."

"Not if you spend the evening looking at Harry Grenville."

"Who's looking at Harry?"

"You are. Your eyes just naturally seem to drift toward him."

"Rubbish."

He sighed, looking at her consideringly. "Were you very hurt when he broke up with you?"

She looked down. "At the time, I thought I'd die."

"And now?"

She lifted laughing eyes to his. "I'm glad I didn't."

"I think we should leave them to their various devices," he said softly, a smile breaking across his face. "And concentrate totally on each other."

"Sounds lovely."

Jake took her hand and brought it to his lips. "*You're* lovely."

Kate felt as if she were floating. Even at the height of loving Harry Grenville, had she ever felt like this?

Chapter Seven

"He's kissing her hand!" Harry Grenville muttered. "Dammit to hell, what's gotten into Kate to let him carry on like that?"

"What's it to you?" Jennifer snapped. "*I'm* your wife, Harry, not little Kate."

"Not for long, thank goodness. Anyway, I never stopped caring for Kate."

Jennifer flounced her hair. She hated it when Harry talked about Kate. Why wasn't he paying attention to *her?* It seemed as if she'd spent a lifetime living in the shadow of Kate Cunningham. She just wished Kate would drop off the face of the earth.

Sulkily Jennifer ordered a double martini. "You know, Harry," she said with a pout, "if you hadn't continually thrown Kate up to me, we might have had a chance with our marriage."

Harry turned his attention to his wife. "What do you mean? I never threw Kate up to you."

Jennifer rolled her eyes. "Of course you did, constantly. It was 'Kate always did this' and 'Kate always did that.'" Jennifer grabbed a bread stick and tore off the wrapper. "If you loved her so darned much, why didn't you marry her when you had the chance?"

"You know why I didn't marry her."

"Harry, you've never faced the truth once in your life, have you?"

"What are you talking about?"

"If you truly loved Kate Cunningham, nothing on earth would have stopped you from marrying her—not scandal, pestilence or flood."

"Then why are you throwing it up to me now that I still love her and she ruined our marriage?"

"Because—" She broke off and let out a frustrated breath. "Oh, never mind, Harry. Just sit there and look at her with those doglike eyes of yours."

"I'm not looking at her, Jennifer!"

"Harry, sometimes I wish I had a camera so I could take a picture and show you what you're doing. You say one thing and do the exact opposite."

"Jennifer, you are describing yourself! That's *exactly* what you do! It's so exasperating! I've never been able to stand that in you. Never."

Jennifer blinked back a tear. "Well, then," she said quietly, "it's just as well we're getting a divorce, isn't it?"

Astonished, Harry stared at her. "Jennifer, if I didn't know you, I'd think you didn't want this divorce."

She lifted her chin and gave him a severe look. "Of course I want this divorce. Don't be stupid, Harry."

"You aren't mature enough to be married, Jennifer. You're still a child."

"You didn't think that when we were in bed."

Stricken, he looked at her and felt a surge of desire almost overcome him. Dammit, she was a witch. He could hardly wait to get the divorce and be rid of her. He needed someone like Kate. She was such a lady, so cool and calm under fire.

"Good Lord!" he said in shock as he stared at Jake and Kate. "She's letting him rub her foot under the table!"

Jennifer began to do a slow boil. "Will you stop *looking* at her if she upsets you so much?"

"But this isn't like Kate." Harry shook his head worriedly. "I must have hurt her terribly when I broke up with her. She lost her father and then me and all the family money...." He stared at Kate, whose face mirrored erotic contentment as Jake Griffin massaged her foot under the table. "This is disgusting!" he said under his breath. "A lady would never do that in public."

Without preamble Jennifer stood and poured a pitcher of water over his head. "Harry, you are an ass."

Turning, she stalked out of the dining room.

For a moment, pandemonium reigned. Harry jumped up and bellowed in rage. Jennifer crashed through the door into the lobby. Waiters came running, dabbing at Harry, whose face was beet red. A vein throbbed in his forehead as he batted away their hands.

"Oh, we're so sorry, Mr. Grenville."

"So sorry."

"Yes, so very sorry, Mr. Grenville."

"Good grief," he shouted. "Leave me alone! I didn't drown! It's only a little *pitcher* of water, not a damned *pool!*"

Kate put a hand to her mouth as peal after peal of laughter rippled through her. "Oh, Lord," she gasped as tears began to stream down her face. "Oh, that was so funny!"

Jake tried to hide his laughter behind his large hand but it was no use. He didn't know which was funnier—Jennifer, Harry, the waiters or Kate's reaction. He laughed until his sides hurt, then saw Laurel Cunningham's face and broke into even louder laughter.

"What?" Kate gasped. "What is it?"

"Your mother."

She turned to look at Laurel and was struck by another spasm of laughter. Her mother sat rigidly, staring at the tablecloth, her face a mask of disapproval. Across from her, Elroy was laughing uproariously, but Laurel Cunningham sat like a rock, perhaps afraid to budge in case her entire world collapsed.

But watching her, Kate sobered. Slowly she saw something she had never seen in her mother: anguish and pain and terrible confusion, all valiantly held at bay by Laurel's rigid control. Suddenly Kate was overcome with empathy for her mother. Without even thinking, she went to her and put her arms around her.

"Mother," she whispered. "It's all right."

Something in Laurel seemed to give way. She lifted frightened eyes to Kate. "It's all too much for me. It's just all too much."

"What is, Mother?"

"Oh, Kate, everything. Trying to hold it all together." Her mother dabbed at the tablecloth with a linen napkin clutched in her hand. Tears welled up in her eyes. "Darling, I'm so scared."

Elroy realized what was happening and sobered rapidly. "Laurel, it's all right," he said, reaching out and taking her hand. His voice was low and kind and his eyes were filled with compassion. "It's all right, dear. Let me take you home."

Kate looked up at Elroy with appreciation. "I can take her home, Elroy, but thank you so much for your kindness."

"No," he said, standing up and putting a solicitous arm around Laurel. "I'll take you home, dear. You've just had too much these past few years. It catches up to all of us, you know."

"You'll be fine, Mother," Kate said gently. "Jake will bring me to your place to stay with you tonight."

"Oh, Kate," she said, beginning to weep softly, "I'm making a scene and I've never made a scene in my life. I can't forgive myself."

"Yes, you can, darling," Kate said. "And scenes can be marvelously restorative, you'll see."

She watched Elroy protectively lead her mother away and felt a deep sense of gratitude for his kindness and understanding. Turning, she found Jake at her elbow, his face grave.

"I'm so sorry, Kate. I had no idea there was a problem."

"It's all right, Jake. I didn't, either, until..." She looked at him. "It was like a flash, and suddenly I saw her and I understood what she was going through. I've never understood her before, never realized what she was feeling."

Jake led her back to the table and poured some champagne. "Tell me," he said, and Kate knew she could.

"All of a sudden I understood her attempts to hold it all together, to get through each day, to stay in control. I think just now if I hadn't gone up to her and given her that hug, she'd have just pulled herself together like she's always done, good old invincible Laurel Cunningham, steady at the helm."

"But you did hug her," Jake said softly.

Kate frowned thoughtfully, sipping the champagne, grateful for its pungent bubbles. "Yes, and when I did, something gave way inside her and her world started to collapse. I think she must be feeling terribly afraid right now, but I think it's the best thing that could happen to her."

"Why's that?" Jake asked gently.

Kate sighed and lifted her shoulders and gazed around at the dining room. The other diners had gone back to their meals. The storm created by Jennifer and Harry had passed. Both were gone, as were Laurel and Elroy. "She needs to let go," Kate said at last. "We all do. But she was raised to be rigid and in control and always spit-polish perfect." Kate gazed down at the table, then lifted sad eyes to Jake. "I was, too, but thankfully I began to find out a few years ago that people aren't machines. We break if we can't bend. I hope Mother will find that out, too."

Jake reached out and took Kate's hand. "I like you very much, Kate Cunningham," he said, smiling at her. "Very much indeed."

She smiled and felt radiance burst inside her. Her eyes took on a sparkle. "It was terribly funny what Jennifer did, wasn't it?"

Jake's mouth began to quirk. "Terrific."

Kate's smile grew until she was beaming at Jake. "I wonder what he did to send her over the edge?"

"Who knows? I think she should have done it sooner, though. He's a prig."

Kate's eyes danced. "You don't like Harry much, do you?"

"I can't understand what you ever saw in him."

"He was my first love," Kate said. "And though you may find this amazing, there's a part of me that loves him still."

Jake's smile evaporated. "You can't be serious."

"Well, I am," Kate said, slightly affronted by his attitude.

"Kate, it's obvious that even Jennifer sees through him to what he is."

"And you think I should be able to also?" she said sharply.

"Well, shouldn't you? You're an intelligent woman, Kate. Good Lord, it's about time you came to your senses about him."

Kate lifted her chin defiantly. "I'm so sorry that you disapprove of my feelings for Harry, but the fact remains that I once loved him and part of me still does."

Jake snorted and socked back a dose of champagne. "Women."

"You can take me home, then, Mr. Griffin," Kate said coolly.

"Don't be ridiculous. We haven't even ordered yet."

"Well, let's not order!"

They eyed each other angrily across the candlelit table. "Kate, don't be ridiculous."

"Odd," she said shortly. "It was I who thought you were being ridiculous."

"Stop talking like a rich girl."

"I once *was* a rich girl," Kate said. "Pardon me if I still sound like one."

The waiter appeared and looked indecisively from Jake to Kate and back to Jake. "Um... would you like to order?"

"Yes," said Jake.

"No," said Kate.

Jake glared at Kate, who glared back. Then she lifted a cordial face to the confused waiter. "Check, please," she said graciously.

The waiter looked at Jake, who sat like a rock, staring at Kate with stormy eyes. "Er... okay," the waiter said and scurried away.

"I begin to see now why Harry Grenville didn't marry you," said Jake. "You're much too willful."

Kate felt as if she'd been struck, but she refused to show it. "It's always so wonderful when a man shows empathy and understanding," she said snidely.

"You are a witch when you want to be."

"And you, sir, are a fool."

When the check was paid, Kate raced from the inn toward the silver limousine, Jake right behind her.

"You don't have to run," Jake said testily. "I'm not going to attack you."

Kate gave him a chilly glance and opened the car door. The driver came awake and sat up. "All right, Mr. Griffin," he said happily. "Back to your place as planned?"

Kate turned her head and stared at Jake with menacing eyes.

"Er, no, Waldo," Jake said. "I'm afraid there's been a change in plans."

"You lowlife," she said in an undertone, giving Jake a withering look. Leaning forward, she said to the driver, "Please take me to 1250 Edwards Crossing."

"Yes, ma'am," Waldo said, tipping his hat and starting up the car immediately.

Kate slid the window closed with a thump. "So," she said coolly. "You *were* planning a seduction scene."

Jake shrugged negligently. "One can always hope."

"And you have the nerve to talk about Harry." She settled back into the corner of the seat, as far away from Jake as she could get.

"He probably wouldn't know how to seduce a woman."

"Harry is a gentleman," Kate said. "He wouldn't want to seduce me."

"If he wouldn't want to seduce you, he isn't even a man."

Kate rolled her eyes as if to say one had to make excuses for boors, but she didn't say another word.

They rode in uneasy silence until Jake finally said, "Look. I still want to consider you for catering my party."

"Do you?" Kate said frostily. "How eminently sensible. I'm only the best there is in Litchfield County."

"Modesty is always so becoming in a woman."

"And manners in a man."

He growled and pulled the champagne bottle toward him, pouring some into a glass. "Flat," he said disgustedly.

"Just like the evening."

"Oh, be quiet, Kate."

"Not on your life. You almost convinced me, but luckily all your precious plans fell apart at the seams."

"Convinced you of what?"

"That you were serious!" she hooted. "That you really wanted to get to know me." She gave him a knowing look. "Oh, you wanted to get to know me all right, but in the purely biblical sense!"

"Good heavens, you'd think it was a capital offense for a man to want to take a woman to bed!"

"So you admit it!"

"Yes, I admit it! Good Lord, you're a very attractive woman! I'd be a damn fool not to want to make love to you."

"Ohhhh," she said, shaking she was so angry. "Just stop talking. I can't stand to hear it."

"What is so damned awful about wanting a physical relationship with a beautiful woman?"

"First of all," she said, bristling, "I'm not some little tramp you can wine and dine and then take home for dessert. I should have known when you propositioned me at the Letterers' that you wanted just one thing."

"Well, what do you expect from a man, then, Princess Katherine? Should I take you to the opera and then merely kiss your hand? Should I admire you from afar and write love letters to you for weeks on end? What is so horrible about two red-blooded people who are attracted to each other just...just..." He let out an explosive sigh. "Just doing it?"

For some reason she didn't quite understand, her lips were trembling in an effort to smile, but she resisted it. She didn't want him to know she had already accepted the absurdity of their quarrel. Perhaps she was foolish, but she *did* like a man to court her. All women did, didn't they? Who wanted to be looked upon as a piece of meat in the market, picked up because one looked succulent? One wanted to be wanted for one's mind and soul as well as one's body. At least she did.

By the time she'd thought it all out, she was back to being hurt. Men were impossible, she thought dismally. They didn't understand women's needs. They thought women were foolish or even hypocritical. Cut to the chase—that's how men thought of things. Can the stupidity and get to the meat and potatoes. Well, dammit, she didn't want to be anyone's meat and potatoes!

"Well," Jake said, "aren't you going to answer me?"

"A woman wants flowers," she said shortly.

"Oh."

"And to be courted."

"Courted."

"Yes. And she wants to be valued for herself, not for her body parts."

"Good heavens, Kate, I value you for yourself."

"Ha!"

He rubbed his chin and stared at her thoughtfully. "So I should bring you flowers next time?"

"What next time?"

The corner of his mouth turned up. "You're very angry with me, aren't you?"

"Very."

"Quite miffed, in fact."

Oh, she did wish he wouldn't use that gentle tone of voice! It really got to her. She had to fight to keep from turning toward him and melting into his arms.

"Miffed," she said coolly, "is a rather trivial word to describe what I'm feeling."

"Perhaps you could come up with something more—" he reached out and trailed a finger over her hand "—descriptive."

She shivered at his touch but steeled herself to fight him off. She couldn't give in now, not after standing on her high horse and telling him off the way she had.

She turned her head and said to him, "I'm feeling very angry."

That sat him back. "I see."

She smiled in the darkness. "So don't even think about calling me for another date."

"Another date?" he said. "But this wasn't a date, my dear. It was a business meeting, remember?"

"Semantics."

"Mmm," he said darkly. "How you women love to twist words."

"Ha."

He sighed. "All right. I'll behave myself. Why don't you come out to my place for lunch and we'll discuss the party I want to give." He looked at her. "Would that be all right?"

"I suppose so."

He smiled. "Don't do me any favors."

She found herself smiling also. "All right."

The car slowed and turned into Edwards Crossing, a luxury condominium where her mother rented an apartment.

"Well," she said, regretting now that the evening had turned out so badly, "we're here, I'm afraid."

"I'm sorry about tonight," Jake said. "The next time I'll bring flowers."

"Let's not plan any next time," she said. "I'll just come out to your place for lunch and we'll discuss the party and..."

"And?"

She shrugged lightly. "We'll get to know each other. You'll see me at the market. I'll see you at the post office. You'll drive by and wave. I'll see you at a party."

"Sounds like it could take forever."

"Women usually like to take it slow," she said in a low, throaty voice.

"Egad," he said. "My pulse is skyrocketing."

"Just as long as nothing else is," she said, putting a seductive hand on his thigh. She leaned over and kissed him long and slowly, then got out of the car.

He slid the window down and said, "You are a cruel wench with ice in her heart."

"Good night, Mr. Griffin," she said, smiling down at him. "Thanks for an... interesting evening."

"It's nothing. I could do it again," he assured her. "Maybe Jennifer could push Harry in the pool the next time."

"And risk my mother having a nervous breakdown?" She smiled. "I think not."

"Tomorrow for lunch?" he asked.

"I'm busy tomorrow," she said over her shoulder. "I'll call you later in the week."

"Don't keep me cooling my heels too long," he called to her. "I'm not a patient man."

She refused to look back at him. Men needed to be kept off balance. It was a fine art, but she thought she had the knack of it.

But she hadn't figured on Jake Griffin. He came bounding from the car, racing up the sidewalk to her. He grabbed her and spun her around to face him and took her in his arms.

"Don't leave me like this," he said in a low growl. "I want to kiss you one more time."

"Good grief, Jake," she said, laughing as she pushed at his shoulder. "Good night!"

"Kiss me," he said. "Kiss me like you mean it."

She went up on tiptoe and kissed him on the end of his nose. "Good night, dear sir."

"You are a tease."

She smiled and nodded. "Yes, I am."

He walked with her to the door, his arm around her. "All right," he said. "I guess I'll have to court you."

"Well, don't make it sound like a chore!"

"It will be, I'm sure," he said. "All that scurrying around trying to impress you when we could already be in bed lustily enjoying each other."

"Even as we speak, I suppose," she said dryly.

"Most definitely," he said in an almost hoarse voice. "You have no idea how disappointing this evening has been for me."

"And for me, also," she pointed out coolly. "Take me seriously, Mr. Griffin, or don't take me at all."

He slid his hands into his trouser pockets and rocked back on his heels. "All right. Roses in the morning."

"Don't *tell* me," she said exasperatedly. "Surprise me!"

"She wants to be surprised, too. All right," he said, and turned on his heel and walked away into the night. "See you around, Princess Kate."

Smiling, she watched until the long silver limousine completely disappeared, then she turned and rang the bell at her mother's door.

Chapter Eight

Laurel Cunningham was sitting in front of the fireplace in the living room, a glass of brandy in her hand when Kate walked in. She was all smiles. It was as if nothing had happened in the restaurant. The old Laurel was back in charge and nothing was going to upset her applecart.

Sighing, Kate wondered how much of that had to do with Elroy Kramer. Maybe Martha was right about her mother and Elroy. Was her plan working already?

Elroy came to the door. He stared at Kate with dazed eyes. The first warning bells went off. Obviously, from the look on Elroy's face, things hadn't gone very well.

"You look confused, Elroy," she said.

Elroy swallowed nervously, making his bow tie jump against his throat. "I guess I am." He glanced into the living room.

"Kate, darling," Laurel called. "Is that you?"

"Yes, Mother."

"Well, do come in. I've been telling Elroy all about you."

"About *me?*" Kate looked at Elroy.

He shrugged. "She's been babbling ever since we left the restaurant about . . . about . . ." He swallowed, looking utterly miserable.

"About what, Elroy?" Kate asked, beginning to worry now herself.

He lifted his hands helplessly. "About how you and I would be perfect for each other. She says you've had a . . ."

He shook his head and looked as if he wanted to drop off the earth.

"She said I've had a what, Elroy?" Kate asked darkly. She might have known it. Her mother was ruining everything.

He shrugged helplessly. "She said you've had a crush on me for years. I tried to tell her that was preposterous, but she won't listen. She just keeps going on and on that you need an older man to take care of you."

Kate could only stare at Elroy. Mother was at it again! "Have you ever heard of denial, Elroy?" she asked at last.

"Denial?"

"Yes, it's a defense mechanism. Mother depends on it the way addicts depend on drugs. It gets her through."

"I don't understand."

"That's all right. Neither do I."

"Kate!" her mother said. "Do come in and sit with Elroy and me and have some brandy. I'd like you two to get to know each other."

Elroy and Kate looked at each other and sighed. It was a losing battle—a little like trying to get the wind to stop blowing.

She sat on the couch and said, "Mother, I've just been talking to Elroy."

"Wonderful!" Laurel enthused, winking at Elroy delightedly. "I've been telling Elroy all about you, dear."

"So I hear."

"Now I don't want you two to be bashful around each other. Elroy, sit on the couch next to Kate."

So much for Martha's plan, Kate thought.

"Now I know there's quite an age difference between you two," Laurel was babbling gaily, "but you mustn't let that deter you. Oh, yes, people may talk at first but it'll die down. You'll see." She smiled flirtatiously at Elroy. "You naughty man! You're still sitting a mile away from Katie. Now get on over there and sit next to her, Elroy! Right this instant."

Kate couldn't stand it a minute more, but there was nothing she could do about it. Her mother was like a locomotive—she just kept going until she derailed. Kate sat back and watched her, thinking that if the Defense Department knew about her, they'd have the most potent secret weapon in the history of the world.

To Kate's surprise, it was Elroy who rallied. He seemed to straighten his frail shoulders, then said, "Laurel, you've been talking like an idiot ever since we left the restaurant."

Stunned, Laurel sat and stared at him. "I...I don't know what you mean," she uttered when she caught her breath.

"Yes, you do, you just don't want to admit it," Elroy said, warming to the subject. "Kate isn't any more interested in me than I am in her. It's you who needs someone to take care of you, Laurel. Stop nagging Kate all the time. She's doing just fine by herself. You're the one I'm worried about."

Laurel sat back, ashen. She put a thin hand to her wan face and stared at him with huge eyes. "I...I don't know what you're talking about."

Elroy nodded knowingly. "Oh, yes you do. You think it's disgraceful to be weak. Tonight in the restaurant, your world spun out of control and now you're desperate to keep it from happening again. But it won't work, Laurel. You can't make life be the way you want it to be."

Kate watched Elroy with awe. Elroy Kramer had always been around, ever since Kate could remember, but she didn't know him all that well. He was a quiet, bookish little man with an astonishing facility for investing wisely. He wore rumpled tweeds and baggy cardigan sweaters and usually looked down shyly when people spoke to him. She'd had no idea he was so kind, and she found her heart warming to him. And he wasn't just kind—he understood.

"Tonight," Elroy continued in a more gentle tone, "you've spent a great deal of time trying to convince me that I'd be perfect for Kate, that she needs an older and wiser man to take care of her. In fact, I think that's what you really want for yourself. So, if you don't mind...I'd...er..." He faltered, the enormity of what he'd just been saying finally hitting him. He stared at Laurel with frightened eyes, then went on, mentally giving himself a boot. "I'd really like to see you again. That is, if you think it's all right. I mean, I wouldn't want to interfere where I'm not wanted. . . ."

Laurel Cunningham sat and stared at Elroy, all defensiveness gone. She looked utterly wiped out, as if the emotional toll from tonight had been too high. All fight seemed to have left her. She sighed and looked at him and said, "I think that would be very nice, Elroy."

"You do?" Elroy's face was transformed. He went from being shy and uncertain to looking as if he'd just been given a reason for living. "You mean that?"

"Of course she means it," Kate said before her mother could change her mind.

"Stop talking for me as if I'm dead," her mother snapped. She looked back at Elroy and smiled tentatively. "It's been a very long time since I've had a man I could lean on, Elroy."

"I'd like you to lean on me," he said shyly.

Kate stared at them, but they didn't even see her. They sat looking into each other's eyes dazedly. Kate got up quietly to leave, then realized she didn't have a car. She stood irresolutely, not wanting to interrupt her mother and Elroy. They were like kids just discovering each other.

"Mother?" she finally said.

"Oh. Are you still here, Kate?"

Kate shrugged. "I don't have a way to get home. I expected to stay here tonight."

"Nonsense!" Laurel said. "There's absolutely no reason for you to stay here. Elroy will drive you home, won't you, Elroy?"

"Of course. I'd be delighted to."

"Then it's all set," Laurel said, getting up. She put a hand to her head and said, "Oh, my. I'm utterly exhausted. All this emotional turmoil is tiring." Then she flashed a bashful smile at Elroy. "I'll look forward to your calling, Elroy."

Suddenly Kate felt more like the mother than the daughter, chaperoning two would-be lovers. Maybe there was hope for Martha's scheme, after all. She bid her mother goodnight.

"Kate?"

She turned around to find Elroy and Laurel standing there hand in hand. "I'm ready to take you home now," Elroy said.

"If it's too much trouble, Elroy..."

"It isn't any trouble at all," he assured her, then turned to her mother. "You're sure you'll be all right?"

"I'm fine," Laurel said, looking into his eyes. "Now."

He beamed and Laurel giggled and Kate rolled her eyes. But she was happy for them all the same.

"Good night, Mother," she said, leaning over to gently kiss her mother's cheek.

"And, dear," Laurel said, "I do hope I didn't spoil your date with that nice Jake Griffin."

"No, Mother," she said. "And it wasn't a date."

"Well, my going out to dinner with Elroy wasn't a date, either," she whispered. "But look what happened!"

"Yeah," Kate said with a smile. "A miracle."

IF ELROY SMILED any brighter, Kate thought wryly, they wouldn't need the headlights.

When he pulled into her driveway, he said, "I'll walk you to the door."

"Oh, no need, Elroy. I'll be fine."

"It's no trouble, Kate. I wouldn't want anything to happen to you. Your mother would never forgive me for not protecting you."

Smiling, she walked to the door with him, where he leaned over to kiss her gently on the cheek. "Good night, Kate."

Suddenly a dark figure came barreling out of the shadows, hurling itself at Elroy with a loud curse. "Okay, Griffin!" he shouted, landing a punch squarely on Elroy's nose. "Keep your hands off Kate!"

"Harry?" she screamed.

"Elroy?" he said, staring down at the older man who lay on the ground holding his nose. Harry Grenville looked up at Kate. "Elroy Kramer?"

"Harry," she said, going down on her knees to help Elroy sit up, "you are a certified jerk."

"But, Kate, how was I to know you were with Elroy? You were with Jake when I saw you at the inn."

"Yes, and that was none of your business, just as my being with Elroy right now isn't any of your business. How dare you hit this poor man!"

"But I—I thought you were with Jake Griffin."

"And you thought you were hitting Jake, I suppose!" snapped Kate as she held a handkerchief to Elroy's bloody nose. She picked up Elroy's glasses and tried to fit them over his nose but he shouted with pain. "Ohh," she said, "I'm so sorry!"

"Let me help," Harry said, holding out his hand to help Elroy up.

"Get away from us," Kate ordered. "Just get away, Harry. You've already done enough harm."

"Good Lord, Elroy," Harry said when the older man was once again standing, "I'm so sorry. I had no idea it was you."

"Get away, Harry," Kate threatened. "Or I'll deck you myself."

"Now, Kate, let's not be upset."

"Let's not be upset? You might have killed him!"

"Oh, Kate," Harry said, putting an arm around Elroy's frail shoulders and leading him toward the house. "Just open the door."

"It's all right," Elroy wheezed, the handkerchief held to his nose. "I'm fine. You can let me go."

Kate turned on a light and led Elroy to the couch. "Harry, do something useful for once in your life and get some ice."

"I don't need any ice," Elroy said.

"Get some ice, Harry," Kate threatened.

"Honest, I don't need any ice." Elroy looked back and forth from Kate to Harry.

Harry rushed toward the kitchen. "Ice!" he shouted. "I'll get some ice!"

"And wrap it in a dishcloth," Kate yelled after him.

"Well," Elroy said, "it appears Harry doesn't like it when you go out with anyone else."

"Harry is a moron," Kate snapped, then rushed to apologize. "Oh, Elroy, I'm so sorry. Are you all right? Can I get something for you? An aspirin? How about a brandy?"

She poured the drink and handed it to him. "Here. This will make you feel better. Is your nose broken?"

"No, it's fine, just a little sore is all."

Harry rushed in with the ice. "Here, Elroy, put this on your nose."

Kate stared at Harry with murder in her eyes. "Do you mind explaining what you were doing here, Harry?"

"Oh, Kate, don't ask."

"Why?" she said. "Because it would only show you up for the fool you already are?"

Harry turned to face her. "I suppose I deserve that," he said, sighing. "I'm sorry, Kate. I guess I had no right coming here."

"You guess exactly right. The problem is, why didn't you realize that before you even came?"

Harry lifted his hands and let them fall again helplessly. "Oh, Lord," he said, dropping into a chair and putting his head in his hands. "What a nightmare tonight has been."

"Don't be too rough on him, Kate," Elroy said, peering at her from over the huge mound of ice on his nose. "It looks like Harry's had a rough night."

"Does that mean he had to take it out on *you?*"

"Oh, for crying out loud, Kate," Harry said. "I thought I was hitting Griffin."

"We've already established that, Harry. Can you elucidate, or is any coherent statement beyond you?"

"It's Jennifer," he said mournfully, staring at the rug as if his life were over.

"Harry," Kate warned, "start making sense."

"She's after him. And all because you want him."

Kate sat down. It looked like it was going to be a long night. "Say it again, Harry," she said. "And this time put a little thought behind the words."

"Oh, for crying out loud," Harry said. "Don't you realize what's happening right under your nose?"

"No," Kate said curtly, "but I'll bet Elroy does."

"Leave Elroy out of this a minute," Harry said. "Good grief, Kate, I'm glad I didn't marry you. You're turning into a regular she-devil."

"Harry, you came to my house with the intentions of hitting the man I was with. And you think *I'm* turning into a she-devil?"

"Oh, just forget it," Harry said. "The point is, Jennifer wants Jake Griffin because you've caught his eye."

Kate held her head. Headaches like this one didn't even begin to subside with a couple of aspirin. She'd need codeine before she was through. "So that explains why you came here to hit him."

"No, dammit," Harry said. "If you'd just let me explain. I came here tonight to talk to you, but I fell asleep out on the porch in that old swing. When I woke up, all I could see was someone kissing you, and naturally I thought it was Griffin, and I'm so damned frustrated I did the first thing that came to mind. I hit him."

"Except it was Elroy," Kate pointed out, grabbing a piece of ice from Elroy's nose bag. She held it to her head and counted to ten. Something had to cool her temper down or she'd give Harry a bloody nose.

"Yes," Harry said, glancing at Elroy. "Sorry about that."

Elroy shrugged it off and smiled shyly. "I'm just fine," he said. "You two go on talking."

"You see, Kate," Harry said, not even bothering to listen to Elroy, "I figured everything out tonight."

"After Jennifer poured water on you or before?" Kate asked acidly.

Harry gave her a beseeching look. "Please," he said. "Just listen, okay?"

She let out a long breath. "Fine. I'm listening."

"It was after Jennifer dumped the pitcher of water on me," he said, "that I realized I love her."

Startled, Kate raised her head and stared at Harry. "Well, you have a funny way of showing it, running around after me and trying to get a divorce."

"I know," he admitted. "I've been blind. But Jennifer has a way of driving me crazy. I thought we just weren't compatible, but tonight she made me see that if I'd really loved you, Kate, I would have married you no matter what had happened to your family. But I didn't marry you, I married her."

"And now, from all accounts, you're divorcing her."

Harry sighed. "I know. I'm a fool. But Jennifer is just as much at fault as I am. She won't admit she cares about me. She's too damned busy trying to get what you have."

"What's that supposed to mean?"

"I'm not sure, but it hit me tonight that Jennifer has spent her entire life wanting what you've got. She took me away from you and she was happy for a while, but now she's got her eye on Griffin, and I swear it's because he's interested in you."

"Harry, that doesn't explain why you hit Elroy just because you thought he was Jake."

"It's hard to explain. I was frustrated, and it just seemed like everything was Griffin's fault. If he wasn't around, maybe Jennifer would come to her senses and realize she really loves me."

Kate stared at Harry, anger percolating in her like coffee in a pot. She didn't like to admit it, but it hurt to find out that Harry really wanted Jennifer. Even though she'd said she didn't want him, it had been gratifying to find out he wanted her.

She wished she could hit him, just once, the way he'd hit Elroy. She realized now why Jake Griffin had told her she still had a thing for Harry. She did. It was foolish, beyond all comprehension and undoubtedly ridiculous, but she still wanted Harry Grenville. And she had called *him* a fool!

"What's the matter, Kate?" Harry asked. "You look put out."

"I have a headache," she grumbled.

"I bet it's not as bad as mine," Elroy said sheepishly.

"Elroy, I'm sorry," Kate said, getting up and going to him. "What can I get you? An aspirin? Another brandy? More ice?"

"It's not from the nosebleed," Elroy said, looking from Kate to Harry. "It's from listening to Harry. What's wrong with young people today? Don't you know how to communicate openly and truthfully?"

Harry stared at him. "What do you mean?"

"What do I *mean?* If you love Jennifer, why not just tell her?"

Harry shook his head. "Oh, no, you can't do that with Jennifer. You have to play these little games."

"Game playing is what makes all these problems," Elroy said.

"You don't understand, Elroy," Harry said. "You see, I know what I want now, but Jennifer doesn't know what she wants. She really loves me, I swear she does, but she's so busy trying to get what Kate has that she doesn't realize what she's doing."

"Why does she want what Kate has?" Elroy asked.

Harry shrugged. "I think she's been this way since childhood. It's jealousy or something. She hates Kate. She's spent her entire life trying to better Kate, and now she's at it again, this time with Jake Griffin."

"Well, that's simple then," Elroy said. "Make her think Kate wants you and she'll go after you again."

Harry looked at him consideringly. Kate stared, then said, "I thought you said all these little games were the root of the problem."

"Yes, but if what Harry says is true..."

"Would you, Kate?" Harry asked eagerly.

"No!"

"Why not? It wouldn't be for real. And you could still see Jake on the sly."

"Harry, it wouldn't work. Anyway, why should I help *you?*"

He reached for her hand. "For old times' sake?"

"Harry, right now all I want to do is slug you," she said, pulling away from his grasp. "How do you expect me to pretend I'm crazy about you?"

"Oh, Kate, it wouldn't be for very long. I'm sure Jennifer would come to her senses in a week or so."

"Jennifer doesn't have any senses to come to."

"Come on, Kate. Please. Just this one favor."

"No," she said, standing up and pointing toward the door. "Now get out, both of you. I've had it with you, Harry. And take Elroy with you."

"I'll talk to you tomorrow, Kate," Harry said as he walked away with Elroy. "Maybe tomorrow you'll be in a better mood."

"Don't depend on it," she said, and slammed the door and burst out crying. Men. She hated the entire lot of them.

Chapter Nine

"Your life is so much more exciting than mine," Martha grumbled the next morning at work. "Here you've got one man trying to seduce you and another begging you to help him save his marriage. Honestly, Kate, you have all the fun."

"Ha," Kate said flatly. "If this is fun, I'm a Mutant Ninja Turtle."

She was still mad, but she didn't know who she was madder at—herself for still wanting Harry, or Harry for wanting Jennifer. It was painful to admit it, but her pride was hurt.

Dammit, Harry had left her once and married Jennifer, and now he was doing it again. It would have soothed her wounded ego considerably if he'd had the good sense to come home, see her again, and realize how much he'd always loved her. As it was, he had come home, seen her again, and realized he'd always loved Jennifer. Great. She was the dumpee in the only relationship that had ever mattered to her. She felt like a clown. Just put an oversize pair of shoes on her and paint a big flower on her head and be done with it.

She opened her checkbook and began paying off the stack of bills in front of her. No time like the present to tackle unpleasant tasks.

"It seems to me that everything is working out great," Martha said. "Your mother's seeing Elroy, Harry's trying to get Jennifer back and Jake Griffin is after you. What more do you want?"

"Jake Griffin is trying to seduce me," Kate said, eyeing Martha pointedly. "That's hardly cause for celebration."

"In my book it would be. I'd give anything for a man like that to try to seduce me."

"Harrumph," Kate said sourly. "What greater ego gratification than to know a man wants you for one night then would dump you."

"Who says he'd dump you? Kate, one thing you seem to have forgotten: men love the chase. So you never let them know you want them. You string them along, tease them, make them want you so bad they think they can't live without you."

"Is that how you got Tom?" Kate asked, referring to Martha's ex-husband.

"No," Martha admitted. "I asked him to marry me and he just kind of agreed."

"So much for the chase theory."

"Look, we can't talk about Tom and Jake Griffin in the same breath, okay? They're in different leagues. Jake is a chase kind of guy. He's the kind you have to drive crazy before you give in."

"I'm not planning on giving in. I'm sick and tired of men. They're totally ridiculous, and I don't want to have anything more to do with them."

"Then let's see how you're going to deal with this," Martha said.

"What?" Looking up, Kate realized a delivery boy had entered the shop. He was holding a long flower box, looking from Martha to Kate.

"Ms. Cunningham?" he asked. "Kate Cunningham?"

"That's her," Martha said, grinning as she pointed out Kate.

The boy grinned back and handed Kate the box. "Have a nice day, miss."

"Mmm," Kate said, staring down at the box.

"Well, open it!" Martha urged.

Sighing, Kate undid the ribbon and lifted the cover from the box. There they were, a dozen perfect red roses lying on a bed of fern—just as Jake Griffin had promised. "Roses in the morning," he'd said, and sure enough, here they were.

"Ooooh." Martha hung over Kate's shoulder to stare at the flowers. "They're beautiful."

"Mmm." Kate shoved them to one side as she began to write out another check.

"Aren't you even going to open the card?"

"Why should I? They're from Jake Griffin. Big deal."

"Well, if you're not opening it, I am." Martha took out the card. "Aha," she said, arching a brow at Kate. "Aren't you the prissy one? Thinking you know everything. They're not from Jake Griffin after all."

Startled, Kate looked up. "They're not?"

"Nope," Martha said, handing her the card. "See for yourself."

"Please, Kate," the card read. It was signed Harry.

Kate tossed the card on the roses and shoved them aside. That odious man was still trying to convince her to help him get Jennifer back. Tough luck. She wouldn't do it for all the money in the world.

And what was the matter with Jake Griffin? Hadn't he promised to send her flowers in the morning? She glanced at her watch. It was almost noon. It looked as if he were going to disappoint her yet again. Damn him anyway. All men were louses.

When the door opened from outside, Kate froze at the female voice that spoke. "Well, what have we here?" Jennifer Grenville asked from the doorway. "Is it really true that you actually *work,* Kate? Jake tells me you do, don't you, Jake?"

Kate steeled herself. It was bad enough that Jennifer was here, but she'd brought along Jake Griffin. The rat. Hadn't he said he was going to court her last night? Strange way of courting her, she thought sourly, and swiveled around.

"Hello, Jennifer, Mr. Griffin." She nodded her head formally.

The corner of his mouth lifted in amusement. His blue eyes danced. "Good morning, Ms. Cunningham. Jennifer here wanted to see where you work."

"How sweet of you to help her find me," Kate said.

"Flowers?" Jennifer asked, spying the roses. "Do you send them to yourself, Kate?"

An urge to slug Jennifer passed. She shrugged negligently and tossed Jennifer the card. "No, darling, your husband sent them to me."

Jennifer stared down at the card. Her face grew red. "How sweet," she said coldly. "What's he asking you to do, Kate? Marry him at long last?"

"As a matter fact," Kate said nonchalantly, deciding that a little white lie would put Jennifer in her place at least for a while, "he is. Of course I've refused him." She looked disdainfully at Jennifer. "I've never liked used cars, so I'm not too fond of the idea of used men."

"Harry's better than you deserve," Jennifer said hotly. "He's just too foolish to realize it."

"Ladies," Jake said, taking Jennifer by the arm, "things are heating up in here. Why don't we leave, Jennifer, and have lunch like we planned."

"Why don't you buzz off?" Jennifer said, and turned and stalked out of the room.

She couldn't help it. It was so funny Kate had to laugh. She felt her lips tremble as she looked at Jake from under her lashes. "Oh dear," she said soothingly. "I'm sure she didn't mean to be so rude."

"You little devil," he said. "You goaded her into that."

Kate shrugged. "It's nothing she doesn't deserve."

Jake leaned against her desk. "Did Harry really ask you to marry him?"

"Of course," she said airily. "Why wouldn't he? It's me he really loves."

"I doubt it," Jake said. "It's Jennifer he really wants, or I'll miss my guess."

Startled by his perception, Kate stared up at him. "What makes you say that?"

"Human nature," he said. "It happens all the time. People often pretend they want what they don't want, and want what they pretend they can't stand."

"Oh? Where did you get this insight, Mr. Griffin?"

"Watching people. Take you, Ms. Cunningham. You think you want Harry, but you really don't. Of course, you'd never admit you wanted Harry, so you spend all your time playing foolish little games while the man you really want has to cool his heels."

"And I suppose you think you're the man I really want?"

"Uh-huh."

"Rubbish."

He grinned. "It would be so much nicer, Kate, if we let Jennifer and Harry battle it out and went off by ourselves and just enjoyed each other's company."

"In bed, I presume."

"There and other places. I'm told you like horses. We could go horseback riding. And the theater and art museums and antique shops. Do you like that sort of thing?"

She did, but she'd never tell him that. "Mr. Griffin, I have work to do."

"And so, it seems, do I," he said, and reached down and took her by the arm. "And plenty of it, by the looks of it. Come on, we're going."

"Where?" Kate gasped as she trotted along behind him, her arm firmly in his grasp.

"Lunch first, since Jennifer left me in the lurch. Then we'll see. We'll find something to keep us busy, I'm sure."

"But I really do have work to do!"

"It can wait. That's one thing I've learned in the last twenty-five years in business—work can always wait. It'll still be there when you come back."

"Martha, call the Drapers for me. Tell them I have their menu ready. Tell them they can stop by and pick it up or I'll deliver it later in the week. And check with Edie to see if she can waitress for me Saturday night."

"That's right," Jake said, ushering her out the door. "Delegate."

"And Martha?"

"Go," Martha said, her eyes gleaming as she stood in the doorway watching Jake Griffin kidnap her boss. "Don't worry about a thing. I'll handle everything. Just enjoy yourself."

"Fat chance," Kate mumbled, but Jake only laughed and helped her into the passenger side of his car.

"Settle back," he said when he got in and started the car. "Enjoy yourself, like Martha said."

"Where are we going?"

"To lunch. Then we'll play it by ear. Spontaneity is the spice of life, don't you think?"

"Not in the catering business."

"Speaking of which, I'm sending the invitations out at the end of the week. The party will be in two weeks. Can you cater it for me?"

"Just like that? No other interviews?"

"That's right. I've decided to hire you. I spoke to the other caterers but they didn't seem...er...they didn't seem to be as much fun as you."

"Fun," Kate said flatly. "That's how you decide who will cater your parties? If they're fun?"

He shrugged. "I want you to cater my party, Kate. Don't make me give you reasons. I don't have good reasons. I want you and that's that, as far as I'm concerned."

"Whatever Jakey wants, Jakey gets, eh?"

He threw her an amused look. "Something like that."

"Okay, so tell me about this party of yours. What are we doing? A Tex-Mex buffet or an elaborate sit-down dinner?"

"Neither. I want to have an old-fashioned picnic, out in the yard. You know, hot dogs and beans and hamburgers and corn on the cob and a dozen different salads and iced tea by the gallon and beer. Think you can handle that?"

"I don't see why not." If she was surprised, she didn't show it. Already her brain was calculating how to make an old-fashioned picnic into something different and unique. She wanted to retain the mood of a picnic while presenting it in an entirely new way.

"That's why I want you, Kate," Jake said. "You're confident."

She shrugged. "You put on one party, you can do any other. It's all the same after a while. The menus might vary and the kind of decorations you use, but in the end feeding two hundred people is the same as feeding two."

"Okay, so that's settled. Let's not talk about business any more, all right? Let's just try to get better acquainted."

Kate smiled to herself. "Okay, so tell me about yourself—everything, from your first tooth to your last girlfriend." She knew what Jake Griffin wanted, and she was going to put up a battle. She wouldn't give herself away. Jake Griffin would have to work to get her.

"I'd rather just tell you about my dreams," Jake said.

"Dreams," Kate said wistfully. "I don't know that I have any. They all seemed to die a few years ago."

"That's the problem with dreams," Jake said. "When they come true, you have to replace them with new ones. Take me, for instance. I had a dream to leave Texas when I was just a kid. I don't know why, but I'd look at that flat landscape and try to see beyond it, try to see all the cities I'd read about, Chicago and Detroit and New York. So I studied hard, and when I was ready for high school, my father sent me to a prep school up north. I never went back. I went to Yale and then set up an office in New York and set about making a business for myself."

"It appears you were very successful."

"Yes, but those dreams are fulfilled. For the past year or so, I've been planning new dreams to replace the old ones."

"And what are they, Mr. Griffin? A bigger business? More money? A house in the Caribbean?"

He smiled. "What I want more than anything on earth is a real home," he said. "Someplace where I can leave the world behind and have a family waiting for me."

Startled, Kate glanced at him. "A family?"

"Kids," he said, smiling. "Babies. Do you know I've never changed a baby's diaper?"

Kate snorted. "Neither have I, but it's not the first thing on my wish list."

"Don't you want kids, Kate?"

She rested her head against the back of the seat. "I don't think about it. I can't or I'd go batty. I have a business to run and it hasn't been easy. You spirited me away today, but normally I'm there from eight in the morning to eight at night. I don't have a social life or a personal life. Everything's work, trying to make a go of it."

"Don't you want a family someday?"

"I wanted one, but now..."

"Did you give up that dream when Harry broke your engagement?"

"I guess I did. Everything fell apart, and I had to work like hell to make a go of the business. And there hasn't been any time to date, and the men who used to ask me out have either found someone else or stopped asking."

"So you're a career woman."

"I guess I am."

"With no plans to settle down and have kids."

"I suppose if someone came along and we fell in love I'd want that, but I just don't feel as if it's going to happen."

"You have to want something, Kate, before you get it."

She turned her head and studied Jake Griffin. Was this just another line designed to make her fall for him? "How many women have fallen in love with you because you told them you wanted kids?" she asked quietly.

He glanced at her, his eyes gleaming. "You don't think much of me, do you? Do you honestly think I'd use that as an excuse to get a woman to fall for me?"

Kate shrugged. "Wouldn't you?"

"Kate, you don't know me at all."

"I suppose I don't. We've barely talked. Generally it seems we spar when we see each other."

"And whose fault is that?"

"Where are we going?" Kate asked, ignoring his question. She knew whose fault it was—Jake's—only he'd think it was hers.

"You'll see." He grinned at her. "And all your pretty little misconceptions about me will fall apart."

"We'll see," she said dryly. "You'd have to go a long way to convince me you're just an affable guy looking for a sweetheart to settle down with and marry."

"Oh ye of little faith."

"Mmm," she said. "Seeing is believing."

He pulled off the road suddenly and cut the engine. "Open your eyes, Kate," he said. "Stop looking at me with preconceptions and see the real man beneath your image of him."

"The real man," she said, turning in her seat to rest her back against the door so she could face him. "Sometimes I think it's impossible to get to know someone, really know them. Sex interferes, or business matters pop up, and there's no time to really just talk with a person. People don't take walks anymore, have you noticed that? We're all too busy. So how do we expect to get to know someone if we haven't even the time to do the simplest things together?"

"Do you have any idea what I want to do to you?" he asked softly, his eyes smoldering with heat and sensual promise.

She lifted her shoulders and let them fall. "I can't imagine."

"I want to take you in my arms and carry you into that meadow over there, past that rock wall and through the trees and lie down with you under the sun and kiss you and never stop kissing you. I want to unfasten all your buttons and undo all your bows. I want to touch your skin, Kate, and make you mine."

She was out of breath just listening to him. No man had ever talked to her like this. She didn't know they could talk like this, except maybe in a movie script. "Well," she said, ever practical, "it'd be hell on my bottom without a blanket."

He sat back and laughed out loud, his teeth shining and his eyes dancing. Lifting her hand to his lips, he kissed it lingeringly. "Someday, Kate, I'll do it. I'll drive you here and take a blanket and carry you into that meadow and make love with you in the sunshine."

"Well, I hope a police cruiser doesn't come by."

"You can't take me seriously, can you?" he asked. "You have to always make jokes."

She withdrew her hand from his. "It's safer that way," she said.

He put a hand out and played with the hair that danced at her temple in the breeze. "I want you to trust me. I won't try to seduce you until you tell me you want me to."

"Oh, heck, Jake, don't take the fun out of things. Don't get serious on me!"

"Then you like games, like the ones you play with Harry?"

She shrugged. "Life's serious enough as it is. No sense in taking the fun out of flirting."

"So you just want a mild flirtation with me, is that it?"

"What else might I want?" she asked, raising her eyebrows at him knowingly. "Surely you don't expect me to fall in love with you?"

"Careful, Kate, I like a challenge in a woman."

"Yes, but this challenge you can't handle, Jake Griffin."

"Like hell I can't," he said, leaning over to kiss her.

She sank into his arms. He was the nicest man to kiss. He took her breath away and gave her chills and made her feel like fainting all at once. But she didn't trust him. After what had happened with Harry, she doubted she'd ever trust a man again.

"Like hell I can't," he repeated softly when at last he lifted his lips and she was trembling in his arms.

"All right," she said, smiling, "so you know how to kiss. So what?"

He smiled and brushed his hand over her cheek, touched her hair, took her hand in his and explored the creamy skin. "So this," he said, kissing her hand. He smoothed his thumb over her cheek, looking into her eyes and making her heart race. "And this," he whispered, his voice low as he dipped his head and brushed his lips across the pulse that was beating frantically in her throat.

A gentle man, she realized, was much more lethal than one who tried to overpower a woman with heated kisses and passionate embraces. She was transported, gliding away as if carried by a bird into the sky, soaring and filled with heat, her body liquefied, her bones melting. She wanted him to really kiss her, but he wouldn't. It was as if he were teasing her with promises, letting her know what it could be like if only she stopped resisting.

But resist she would. She pushed him away gently and straightened her blouse. "I thought we were going to have lunch."

He sighed and sat back. "I'm sorry, it appears I got sidetracked."

"Like most men, you decided you wanted to taste dessert first."

"Surely understandable when the dessert is so delectable."

She ignored the compliment. "I'm starving. I could eat a horse."

"A woman with a healthy appetite. How encouraging."

She gave him a sideways glance and smoothed her hands over her hair. "Where shall we go? Not The Lily Pond, please. We'd likely see everyone we know."

"You want to keep our dalliance a secret?"

She thought of Harry and smiled. "Yes, as a matter of fact."

"And I want to brag about you," he said, shaking his head. "How different we are. I wonder if there's even a shred of hope for us."

"I doubt it." Kate couldn't take Jake Griffin seriously. He was too much fun to be with. She would simply enjoy him while it lasted. For today, at least, she wasn't going to worry about tomorrow.

Chapter Ten

When Jake turned into the driveway that led to Spindrift, Kate stiffened. "Actually, I'd much prefer The Lily Pond," she said.

"Come on, I want to show you what I've done with the house. There's no sense ignoring it, Kate. This house is a boulder between us. The sooner we face it, the quicker we can get past it."

"I don't care to see what you've done with it," she said sharply. "I'd just like to leave."

"I know you would, and that's precisely why we're here." He pulled up in front of the house and cut the engine. "In two weeks, I'm giving a huge party and you'll cater it. It can't be easy on you, but it'll be a lot easier if you face it now rather than later."

"Who says I have to face it at all? I'm quite comfortable with the fact that you're the new owner, Jake. Let's just drop it, shall we?"

"Not until I've shown you all around," he said, getting out of the car and going around to open her door for her. "Come along now, out of the car." He reached down and took her arm and urged her from the car.

She shook her arm from his grasp. "All right, all right," she said irritably. "I'm here now. You don't have to drag me."

"I didn't do it by myself, of course," he said. "I hired a decorator. I'm very pleased with the results." He inserted the key in the impressive front door and swung it open. "You've already seen the living and dining rooms and the sun porch. Why don't we go upstairs?"

She planted her feet firmly and refused to budge. "I don't need to go upstairs, Jake."

"I think you do."

She met his eyes, her own eyes flaring with willfulness. "I think I don't," she said stubbornly.

"You are the most disagreeable woman sometimes," he said amiably, taking her arm and escorting her toward the stairs.

She shook her arm from his grip. "If I'm so disagreeable, then take me back to Lilac Hedges."

"It's an interesting name, Lilac Hedges," he said, pausing at a window on the stair landing and nodding toward the back lawn. "There's a lilac hedge out there, leading to the carriage shed."

She stood on the landing and looked out at the lilac bushes that were now in riotous bloom. "I'm so glad you kept them," she said softly, her eyes drinking them in. "That was always my favorite spot. I used to go out there and put a blanket on the ground and read a book in front of them. The bees would buzz amidst them all day and I'd be drunk on the scent."

"Is that why you named your business Lilac Hedges?"

"Perhaps. Of course, the little cottage I bought already was surrounded by lilacs, but I think that's why I bought it. It called to me. It had grown dilapidated and needed fixing up, but I had always loved it, even when there was very little but the lilacs to recommend it."

"You love this place," he said gently.

That gentleness was almost her undoing. She felt tears well up behind her eyes, and she batted them away quickly, struggling not to give in to them. "It was my home," she said. "A little while ago, you talked about wanting a home. Well, this was mine. I grew up here and felt safe and secure and then one day it was gone. Just like that. A puff of smoke, then nothing." She touched the windowsill, running her hand along the wood, savoring the feel of the place.

She wished she could close her eyes and will the past to return, but she couldn't. It was gone. All had changed. Nothing ever stayed the same.

She took a deep breath and turned to go up the rest of the stairs. "My bedroom was here," she said when they reached the end of the hall. "Tucked away under the eaves."

Jake opened the door, then stepped back. It was the same but different. When she'd lived here, the wallpaper had been sprigged with pink rosebuds. She had had a single bed with a white canopy. There had been a pink cushion in the window seat. A maple desk had held her schoolbooks.

Now there was blue-and-white-striped wallpaper, twin beds with white-painted iron headboards, with white lace pillow shams and bed skirts and hand-pieced quilts. The white-painted woodwork was bright and clean, and the window seat was cushioned in blue-and-white stripes to match the wallpaper. It was bright and cheerful and, with some pink geraniums on the windowsill, would be every bit as homey as it had ever been.

"I used to sit in that window seat," she said dreamily, "and imagine myself married to Harry, having his children. I wanted a little red-haired boy and a blond little girl. This was going to be my little girl's room."

She touched the wallpaper and felt a painful throb in her heart. She had loved this place and now it belonged to someone else. It was no longer her home, no longer the place where she could come and leave the world behind, seek shelter from pain, close herself off from hurt.

Turning, she walked past Jake and escaped to the hall. "You've managed to keep the charm," she said. "You chose a good decorator."

He opened the door to the room that had once been her parents'. But here all was changed. He had knocked down a wall that had separated her parents' room from a guest room and made it all one space. Light flooded the room from huge, many-mullioned windows. A four-poster bed covered in blue damask dominated one wall. Two wing chairs and a love seat formed a conversation grouping near the fireplace. It was a lovely room, but it lacked something.

"Flowers," she said. "It needs flowers. I'd bring in masses of lilacs and stuff them into an antique white pitcher and put them on the bedside table."

"What's the point? If I want to see flowers, I can look outside."

"A home has to have flowers," Kate said. "Otherwise it isn't a home." Jake grunted. She smiled and went on to explain: "Flowers are the extras, like fresh linens and well-used books and comfortable chairs. A home should be a haven from the world, a place to regroup and indulge oneself. Adding flowers is one way to do that."

"The woman's touch," he said. "That's what I'm lacking." His eyes drifted to the bed. "Most definitely."

She turned abruptly, not liking the way his thoughts were obviously going. "Forget it, Mr. Griffin. I'm here on a tour, not to be a bed warmer."

Instead of coming with her toward the door, he sat on the bed and patted the place beside him. "Come here and sit next to me. Stop running away all the time."

"You're incorrigible."

"Of course. Now come on over here and stop putting up such a fuss."

"I want to see the kitchen," she said, laughing, and walked into the hall, leaving him still seated on the bed, bellowing after her.

"Come back here!" he shouted jokingly to her.

"Come join me in the kitchen."

"Oh, good grief," he grumbled, coming out from the bedroom and shutting the door behind him. He put his hands in his trouser pockets and came down the stairs after her. "You are the stubbornest woman."

"And you're the most ridiculous man. Honestly, you don't understand women at all, do you?"

"To be honest, I don't. You're foreign to me, all of you. But intriguing nonetheless."

"I told you last night," she said, leading the way to the kitchen. "Women like to be courted."

He sighed and opened the door to the kitchen. "After you."

The kitchen had been a rather dark room when they had lived here, but it had been cheerful nevertheless. Now it was light and open and airy, with white cabinets and a cooking island in the center of the room, and palladium windows over French doors on the outside wall, leading to a deck overlooking the yard.

"Oh, it's wonderful," she said, her eyes shining as she turned round and round looking at everything. "I'd spend my entire day in here," she said. "Cooking, trying out new recipes, arranging flowers for the table, snipping herbs for an omelet."

"Speaking of cooking, I'm afraid my housekeeper is out right now, but why don't I fix us something for lunch?"

"You cook?"

He shrugged. "I apply pans to heat and eat the results."

She laughed delightedly. "I'll cook. You make us drinks. Something fabulous, like strawberry daiquiris or mimosas."

"Would beer and a little white wine do?" he asked.

She shook her head at him. "You're missing out on the small things that make life wonderful. You need fresh strawberries and long-stemmed glasses for daiquiris."

"I'll have them next time."

"Who says there'll be a next time?" she said, smiling as she examined the contents of the refrigerator. "Thank God for eggs," she said. "We'll have an omelet."

"With cheese and tomatoes?"

"If you have some."

"I do, though you might have to cut the mold off the cheese."

"No problem," she said dryly. "We can stuff it back in the fridge and make penicillin."

Jake sighed. "I can't win with you, can I?"

She chose to ignore him. "Oh, for some croissants," she said, peering into the freezer. "Or sourdough bread." She looked at him over her shoulder. "You wouldn't have any sourdough starter, would you?"

"Sorry." He opened his hands as if to say his larder was empty. "I'm not very well stocked with food. My housekeeper's going shopping today, I believe."

"You know, that's something I've been thinking about," she said, finding a piece of celery and biting off some.

"My housekeeper going shopping?"

She shook her head. "I might expand my business to include delivering meals at night. With both husband and wife working now, no one wants to come home at night and cook. All they'd have to do is pick up the phone during the day and call in an order and we'd whisk it out to them at night, complete with flowers and wine."

"Sounds good to me, but it would keep you even busier than you already are."

"I'd hire help," she said, grating the cheese. "Of course, I'd need more space. My little cottage is getting tiny."

"You could always add on."

She shook her head. "I looked into it. There's not enough room. The zoning board wouldn't let me."

"Ah." He watched her as she took tomatoes out of the refrigerator. "What will you do? Buy another place and move from the cottage?"

"I haven't decided. I've thought of getting another place and having two separate businesses, one a regular catering business and the other a combined take-out-and-delivery service." She popped a piece of cheese into her mouth and sipped some beer. "Maybe we'll find a big old house with plenty of room for expansion. But that's down the road a bit. We have to pay off my first loan before we can take out another." She took a knife from a rack and handed it to him. "Cut up the tomatoes, will you? I'm going to go in search of flowers for the table."

"We don't need flowers," he said.

"Of course we do! We can't eat without flowers on the table. It's like eating out of a can."

"Heaven forbid."

"Stop being such a bear," she said, and went up on tiptoe to kiss him. "What does it take to put you in a good mood?"

"This will do it," he murmured, putting his arms around her and pulling her into his embrace. "Quite nicely, as a matter of fact."

She looked into his eyes and realized that she liked being with him, liked the way he looked and sounded and smelled. When he kissed her again, she realized she liked the way he tasted, too. Everything about Jake Griffin was appetizing.

"I have to go find flowers," she murmured.

He nuzzled his nose against her ear, inhaling her scent. "You smell like a flower," he said. "And you're prettier than any flower I've ever seen."

"You're trying to butter me up," she said, eyes dancing with amusement, "in the hopes that I'll give in and we'll end up making passionate love in that big bed of yours."

"One can always hope," he said, smiling at her.

She raised her eyebrow at him and pushed out of his arms. "Cut the tomatoes. I'll be back soon."

"I'd rather come with you."

"Then come along," she said, and swung a wicker basket off a hook.

"What's that for?" he asked, falling into step beside her.

"For gathering flowers, of course," she answered. "I just need shears."

"In that drawer."

She found the shears and they went outside. The house back here was sheltered from the breeze, the only sound the song of birds in the trees.

"Utter contentment," she said, bending to clip some zinnias and marigolds. "I love it here, always have."

"You'll have to come out again," he said. "When I have some real groceries in the house."

"I will," she said, laughing at him. "In two weeks, when I cater that party of yours." She sat back on her heels and studied the backyard. "We'll bring gas grills. But do you insist on hot dogs and hamburgers? Couldn't we do swordfish on the grill and warm potato salad and spinach salad with mandarin oranges and slivered almonds?"

"You make it sound delicious."

"It will be. And great pitchers of iced tea, sweating with condensation." She inhaled the smell of the flowers and closed her eyes. "It is so wonderful here. The sun feels warmer and the flowers smell sweeter than any other place on earth."

"I suppose you've been to every other place on earth and checked it out to compare?" he asked dryly.

"Stop being so literal," she said, opening her eyes. "You spoil things."

He looked into her eyes and brushed his hand across her cheek. "I don't mean to spoil things," he murmured. "Right now, I'd like to give you whatever you wanted, just to keep that happiness in your eyes."

"I am happy," she said, feeling a thrill go through her as she realized it was true. "This is a perfect moment. I'd like to stop time right here and make this moment last forever."

"I'll have to see what I can do," Jake said. Leaning down, he kissed her on the lips.

She could give in and let him have his way with her, because if the truth be told, it was what she wanted, too. She didn't care if Jake Griffin loved her, she just wanted to be in his arms, to experience his lovemaking. But something held her back, told her not to give herself away. *Put up a fight,* a small voice said. *Don't tumble into his arms just yet.*

"Why did you pull away?" Jake asked. "Why must you always pull away?"

She turned her head so he couldn't see the confusion in her face. "You wouldn't want a woman to fall into your arms without a fight, would you, Jake Griffin?" she asked lightly, and managed to turn and smile at him.

"Yes," he said. "If the woman was you."

She gave him a knowing look and walked toward the lilac bushes. "Oh, come on, Jake. As the old fisherman used to say, 'The longer the fight, the sweeter the fish.'"

"What's that supposed to mean?"

She began cutting off branches of fragrant lilac blossoms. "Figure it out." She dropped some branches into the basket and set out to find more. "Oh," she said, coming to a halt, "you've built a new barn."

"For my horses," he explained. "Would you like to ride later?"

She gave him an amused look. "I'm not dressed for it."

"Godiva didn't let that bother her."

"Godiva's bottom must have smarted for a week," she said, turning to go back to the kitchen. "We've enough flowers. Let's have lunch."

"You're much too practical," he said, falling into step beside her. "Why can't you be more romantic?"

She laughed out loud. "It wouldn't be romantic in the least to ride a smelly old horse and then dally in the grass, as you're implying. In fact, it would be quite uncomfortable."

"Well, there's always bed. It's prosaic and dull, but at least it's comfortable."

"Woo me a little longer, Jake, then ask." She tilted her head flirtatiously. "Who knows? You might get your wish."

"You little tease." He scooped her up in his arms and carried her into the kitchen.

She mock-screamed in delight and threw her arms around him. He came to a halt and looked into her eyes, then put her down. He took the basket of flowers from her and set them on the table. "Don't push me away this time," he ordered softly, and she didn't.

His lips were the sweetest she'd ever tasted, his arms the strongest, his body warm and masculine. He crushed her against him, kissing her long and hard, and she felt as if she were swirling and dancing in midair. She was a bird, a star, dangling in the sky. She was moonlight and sunshine all at once; she was music and thunder and snow.

She trembled as his kiss deepened and she felt his tongue enter her mouth. It was so sweet, so intimate, she moaned softly in response.

"Kate," he whispered against her throat. "I want to touch you."

Shivering, she ran her hand up his back, feeling the ripple of muscles under his taut skin. She wished his shirt was off. She wanted to touch him, too, to feel the satin smoothness of warm skin under her palm. It would be so simple, really, to let him take her upstairs. It would be delightful and delicious and could last for hours. . . .

She moaned softly and pushed away. "We've forgotten lunch."

"We don't need it," he whispered against her neck, drawing her back into his arms.

She put her arms around his neck and went up on tiptoe to kiss him lightly on the lips. "I wouldn't want you to lose your strength," she whispered, her eyes shining with laughter.

"Believe me, I'm not about to."

She laughed, a deep throaty laugh of pure sensuality. "I like my men rugged and strong," she murmured, running her hand up his chest.

He took her hand and guided it downward. "This rugged?" he asked.

She closed her eyes and swayed against him. Oh dear, things were escalating rapidly. She swallowed convulsively and rubbed her body against him. "That seems pretty darned strong," she admitted, her voice catching in her throat.

"Don't tease me, Kate," he said. "I want to make love to you. It's what you want, too, if you'd only admit it. I want to touch you and inhale your scent. I want to kiss you all over. Wouldn't you like that, Kate? Isn't that what you've wanted since last night?"

Her head was swirling, and she wasn't sure which end was up. Everything was in upheaval. Was that what she wanted? Then what about Harry? If she loved Harry so darned much, why was she feeling this way with Jake Griffin?

Jake kissed her again and all thoughts of Harry fled. She was filled with warmth and everything was beautiful—the world and Jake and her, especially her. She felt golden. She was singing inside. There was music all around them, wonderful, soaring, celestial music, and shimmering lights and even angels.

Where had she been the past four years? Lost in some dark world with no light and laughter, no music or sunshine? Just kissing Jake Griffin lighted up her life like nothing she'd ever experienced before. Why was she fighting him? Why was she fighting herself? What did she hope to accomplish by stopping the conflagration that had erupted between her and Jake?

"Ohhh," she breathed, her face shining with newly discovered joy. "Kiss me again. Keep kissing me." She laughed in delight as he whirled her around and around, covering her with kisses.

"I'll kiss you forever," he vowed. "I'll cover you with kisses. I'll—"

He was interrupted by the insistent buzzing of the front doorbell. Startled, Kate stared at Jake. She wanted to tell him to forget it, not to answer it. She wanted this magical moment to go on and on, never to stop. But the bell had rung and there was no sense ignoring it. With the tip of her finger, she lightly pushed him away. "I guess you better answer it."

"If we're real quiet, whoever it is might go away."

She laughed musically. "Uh-uh. You better answer it."

"Damn," he said, putting his arms around her. "I've lived here for three months and no one's ever come to the door before. Why now? Are the gods against me?"

Her eyes twinkled with laughter. "Stop stalling. They're not going to go away that easy."

"How do you know?"

The bell rang again, sounding even more insistent. She raised a brow. "I can tell."

Sighing, he released her. "I'll be right back."

"I'll start lunch."

"Great. Be back in a second."

She listened as he went to the front door, whistling cheerfully. She hugged herself and leaned back against the kitchen counter. What a perfect day. Not even a silly interruption could spoil it.

Then she realized that Jake's cheerful whistle had stopped abruptly. Curious, she ventured toward the door. Maybe she'd just peek down the hall and see who it was. Probably a delivery person or UPS. They were always interrupting her on her day off. She inched open the door, then froze. It was a woman, chattering gaily. Kate stood just inside the kitchen door and felt herself grow cold. It wasn't just any woman.

Angrily, she pushed open the kitchen door. "Hello, Jennifer," she said coldly. "What brings you here?"

Chapter Eleven

Jennifer's face changed from flirtatious animation to open displeasure. "What are *you* doing here?" she asked, then looked at Jake. "We had plans for this afternoon."

"Well, you did walk out on me earlier today," Jake pointed out. "I made other plans when you left me in the lurch."

She looked back at Kate, a triumphant smile transforming her face. "How does it feel to know that the man I was with made do with you, Kate? What's it like playing second fiddle?"

"I wasn't aware that I was," Kate said, spying the overnight bag on the floor by Jennifer. She gave Jake a poisonous look. "But I wouldn't dream of interfering. I'll leave right now, and you and Jennifer can continue with your...plans," she said, underlining the word with honeyed sarcasm.

"Kate," Jake said, "I swear I can explain everything."

"Don't bother," she said, untying her apron and throwing it on a chair.

"Kate, don't go," Jake said urgently, trying to stop Kate as she stalked out the front door and raced down the steps.

"Forget it, Jake Griffin," she called back over her shoulder. "I'm leaving and I don't plan on coming back. Find someone else to cater your precious party. I wouldn't be caught dead here."

"Oooohh," Jennifer cried, clapping her hands. "This is so great!"

"Shut up, Jennifer," Jake snarled, then ran after Kate. "Kate! Please, let me explain!"

"You don't have to explain," Kate said, whirling around to face him. "I already understand. Any port in the storm, right, Jake? If Jennifer finked out on you, you'll substitute with someone else, right?" She glared at him, lowering her voice to an angry undertone. "Oooohh, you're despicable. Worse than that. You're...you're..." She was so angry she wished she could slap him, but she wasn't going to give Jennifer even more to crow about—she was already beside herself with joy. "You're not worth getting upset over," she said, drawing herself up regally. Turning, she set out for the road.

"Kate, for heaven's sake, at least let me drive you back to your office."

"I wouldn't think of it," she said loftily. "I wouldn't lower myself to ride in the same car with you."

"Dammit, Kate, you're being ridiculous."

"Ridiculous!" she stormed, turning to face him. "Is it ridiculous to expect that a man means it when he kisses me? Is it ridiculous to expect a man to be trustworthy and honorable in his intentions? Oh, you make me sick. All that wonderful talk when all along you were planning on sleeping with Jennifer tonight. God, I can't believe I was such a goose that I almost believed you."

"I had no intentions of sleeping with Jennifer tonight."

"Sure, Jake, and her overnight bag is just filled with Girl Scout cookies."

"I was going to drive her to the train station, dammit."

"Jake, please. Spare me the stories."

"It's not a story, and if you're so thickheaded you won't believe me, then good riddance to you."

"Good!" Kate said. "Then we're both agreed on something at long last!"

"Lord, you are an ornery woman," Jake said, shaking his head at her. "You just won't believe me, will you?"

"That's right, I won't. And now, Mr. Griffin, if you'll excuse me, I have to run."

Turning, she did just that. She raced off, wanting to put as much space between herself and Jake Griffin as she could. She was hot and disheveled by the time she reached the road, but she wouldn't let herself stop. At least when she ran, she couldn't think of Jake Griffin's treachery. Her side hurt too much, and her shoes were killing her feet, and any dainty, ladylike scent had been whisked away by womanly perspiration in full spate.

A car flew by without even stopping to ask if she needed help. *Good,* she thought, *I don't want anyone's help anyway.*

Another car raced by, and then a third slowed down. "Hey, lady, need some help?"

It was a boorish man with a huge grin who was watching her appreciatively. "Not from you, thanks," she said, refusing to even look at him as she trotted by the side of his car.

"Okay, but I could make things a lot easier on you."

"Get lost," she snarled.

He floored the accelerator and left her in a cloud of exhaust. Choking on it, she stopped and bent over from the waist, coughing and spitting like an old truck.

Across the road, another car approached and slowed. "Kate?"

Oh, damn. It was Harry.

She straightened, then tossed her hair over her shoulder. It had come loose from its pins and was floating around her shoulders like cotton candy at a country fair.

"Kate, are you all right?" Harry asked, pulling his car off the road and getting out and crossing the street.

"I'm fine," she said, smiling heartily. "Never better. Just out taking a little constitutional."

"Well, you're very red," Harry said uncertainly. "And you're sweating like a..."

"Pig?" she supplied sweetly. "How kind of you not to say so to my face."

"Look," Harry said, taking her arm, "get in the car and I'll drive you home and we can talk about it. It's obvious you're upset."

She pulled her arm from his hand. "I don't want to talk about it, Harry. And I don't want to get in your car. Just leave me alone, please, and I'll be just fine."

Another car approached from behind and slowed down. Oh, fine, Kate thought. Now she needed Jake Griffin, too. "Kate," he said when the car had stopped beside her and Harry, "let me drive you back to your office at least."

She glared at Jake. "Where's darling Jennifer? Waiting for you in bed?"

"Bed?" Harry shouted. "What are you talking about?" He looked frantically from Kate to Jake. "Dammit, where's Jennifer? If you've hurt her I'll break every bone in your body."

"I thought you were divorcing her," Jake said mildly.

"I am, but by God that doesn't stop me from caring about her! I know all about you, Griffin. You're a damned playboy. Love 'em and leave 'em. Well, Jennifer's vulnerable right now, and it's damned rotten of you to use her for your enjoyment then just spit her out."

"What an interesting image," Kate commented to no one in particular. "Makes her sound like a peach pit."

"Kate, shut up," Harry said. "I suppose you were baiting Jennifer, too."

Kate raised her eyebrows. "Actually I was holding her hand over open flames," she said sarcastically. "But what do you care? Jennifer and Jake are a real hot item, and the sooner you face it the better off you'll be."

"And I suppose you'll offer him a warm shoulder to cry on," Jake said roughly.

"What if I do?" Kate cried. "It's none of your business, Jake Griffin."

Harry put his hands to his head and squeezed his eyes shut. "Dammit, will you two be *quiet?*" he shouted. "I can't think when you're shouting at each other like that!"

"Harry, you can't think when it's quiet as a church," Kate snapped.

Jake chuckled, and Harry's head snapped back in surprise. "What are you mad at me for?" he whined. "Dammit, I just stopped to see if I could help."

"Butt out, Grenville," Jake growled. "I'll take care of Kate."

"Like hell you will," Kate said, and took Harry's arm. "Come on, Harry, drive me back to work." She dragged him across the road to his car.

Grumbling, Harry got in and started his car. "You are the most exasperating woman, Kate."

"Is that why you never married me, Harry?" she asked, shutting out the sight of Jake reversing his car and storming off down the road toward his place.

"It probably is," he said irritably. "That and a million other reasons."

"Oh, Harry," she said, putting a hand to her head. "Please just be quiet."

Harry glanced at her. "What's the matter? You look beat."

"I am beat. I'm exhausted. Worn out. Depleted. There are a million other words for what I am, and not one of them is positive."

"What the hell has Jennifer got to do with all this?"

Kate sighed. "I was with Jake, having the most romantic afternoon of my entire life when Jennifer showed up on the doorstep. She had an overnight bag with her—"

"An overnight bag?" Harry shouted, slowing the car. "We're going back. That's all there is to it. We're going right to Griffin's place and getting her."

"Harry, don't be foolish."

"It's being foolish wanting to protect the woman you love?"

Kate stared at him. He was turning the car around and driving like a bat out of hell toward Jake's place. He looked frazzled and out of his mind with worry.

"My Lord," Kate said quietly, "you really do love her, don't you?"

Harry took his foot off the accelerator. The car began to slow down. He drove it to the side of the road and sat staring forlornly ahead. "Yes," he admitted. "I'm crazy about her. She's irritating, shallow, and most of the time she's brain-dead, but I love her. I don't want to live without her."

Staring at Harry, Kate had to face it at last. Harry Grenville didn't love her. He probably never had. He loved a woman he acknowledged to be shallow and not very bright, and he loved that woman when he could have had Kate.

It hurt for a very brief moment, then Kate rallied. There was no sense ending her life over it. It was the luck of the draw, or something like that. She wondered if she'd ever really loved Harry. Maybe it had all just been ego and hurt pride. When Harry had broken their engagement and taken up with Jennifer Holliday, Kate hadn't been devastated, she'd been furious. And wanting Harry back had nothing to do with loving him; it had more to do with showing Jennifer she could get him back.

Only she couldn't get him back, and if the truth be told, she didn't want him back. Not now, not ever.

"Harry," she said wearily, "life is a hell of a mess."

"You never used to swear, Kate," he said, staring out the windshield at nothing.

"I know. There's a lot of things I never used to do."

"I'm sorry, Kate," he said, turning his head to look at her with large, wounded eyes. "I made a mess of things, didn't I?"

"No, you probably did exactly what you should have done," she said. "It's me who's been making a mess of things."

"I don't understand."

"Forget it, you probably never would."

"What am I going to do, Kate? I love her and she's hot on Jake Griffin's trail. I swear she's after him because she wants to show you up."

"That's something I've never understood," Kate said. "What has Jennifer got against me? I never did anything to hurt her."

"She's jealous," Harry said. "For some strange reason, she thinks you've got more than she has—more looks, more money, more brains, more class."

Kate stared at Harry. "Thanks," she said wryly.

"I didn't mean it like it sounded," he said. "But it's true. She's jealous of you. She wants everything you have. She always has."

"Next thing you know, she'll be opening a catering business," Kate said sarcastically.

"I wouldn't put it past her," Harry said, nodding. "She just can't stand it when you have something she doesn't have."

"So that's why you want me to pretend I want you, is that it?" Kate said. "You think if she sees me going after you, she'll come after you, too?"

Harry nodded glumly. "Something like that. The woman is perverse. Take something away and she wants it again. The only reason she's after Jake Griffin is because she thinks you want him."

Kate shook her head. "It won't work, Harry. You two can't base a marriage on these stupid games."

"Well, we won't have a marriage unless I think of something to get her to admit she loves me."

"You mean you think she loves you but she just won't admit it?"

"I think in her own way she's as stubborn as you are, Kate. Come to think of it, I guess I think all women are stubborn. But that's neither here nor there. I think she's just being contrary. She's so used to using you as her barometer that she can't get off the merry-go-round long enough to see that having what you've got just doesn't matter."

"Harry," Kate said dryly, "you've got a lot of mixed metaphors there. Can you back it up and slow it down and try saying that again?"

"Forget it," Harry said glumly. "I guess I'm not making any sense."

Kate stared at the man who'd been her only boyfriend for over ten years. She had loved him blindly, planned to marry him and bear his children. And some residual feeling for him did still remain. She didn't like to see him hurting. Something in her stirred, compassion perhaps, or just a desire to help.

"Okay," she sighed. "I'll do it."

"You'll do what?"

"I'll pretend I want you."

"You will?" he asked, brightening.

"Yes, against my better judgment perhaps, but I see what you mean about Jennifer. She needs to find out what really matters." She glanced at Harry. "Of course, you might not like what she decides. She may actually decide she doesn't want you."

"Still, I've got to try, Kate. Anything is better than just letting the divorce happen."

"Have you tried just talking to her?"

"Kate. Be real. Have you ever tried just talking to Jennifer?"

She sighed. "Yeah. I see what you mean." She cocked her head curiously. "Just what do you see in her, if you don't mind my asking."

"I don't know, it's just—" he shrugged "—chemistry, I guess. She's infuriating and childish and she drives me crazy, but I love her."

"Proves the old adage that there's someone for everybody."

"I know you don't like her. Hell, you've got good reason not to—she's been absolutely bitchy to you all her life—but if you could know her the way I do... Sometimes she lets down her guard and she's like a kid, you know? She's full of life and zest and, I don't know, I just feel more alive when I'm around her."

That was good, Kate thought darkly, Harry had sure never shown much life on his own.

"Okay," she said, slapping him on the knee, "how do we begin?"

He was staring at a car coming toward them. "Is this Griffin?"

Kate peered out the windshield and nodded. "Yes, and Jennifer's with him."

"Kiss me," Harry said, lunging toward Kate. "And look like you mean it."

Kate kissed him. She put everything into the kiss, because while she didn't give a damn about Harry, she wanted to get back at Jake Griffin so much she was shaking. What better way than to let him see her passionately kissing Harry Grenville?

When the kiss ended, Harry looked dazed. "How come you never used to kiss me like that?" he asked, loosening his collar. "Jeez, Kate, you've been taking lessons."

"Stop talking," she said in an urgent undertone. "They've stopped the car and they're hightailing it toward us."

"Ooooh!" Harry dragged Kate into his arms and kissed her the way he wanted to kiss Jennifer. Kate ran her hand up his arm, moaning softly.

"Oh, Harry," she sighed loudly, "I want you so much. Take me here, darling. Now. It feels like I'll die if you don't make love to me this instant."

"What the hell are you two doing?"

Jennifer's strident voice broke the mood. Sitting back as if she'd been stung, Kate batted her lashes and put a hand to her heaving breasts. "Oh, Lord, where are we?" she breathed. "Harry, darling, I got completely carried away!"

"You would be," Jennifer snapped, "if the trash truck came along."

"Oh, Harry," Kate said, opening her eyes wide and pretending to be afraid, "it's your wife! She's found out about us!"

"Tone it down," Harry snarled under his breath. "You're overdoing it."

Kate smiled adoringly. "Yes, dumpling, whatever you say."

"You seem to have forgotten, Harry," Jennifer said coldly, "we're not divorced yet. I could haul you back into court and demand more money. How would you like that, *dumpling?*"

"Jennifer, if I didn't know better, I'd almost think you were jealous," Harry said complacently. He noticed Jake Griffin leaning against the hood of the car, his arms folded as he watched the unfolding scene. "And who are you to be throwing stones? You're with another man. The judge might not listen to your story if he found out you were having an affair with a known womanizer."

"Leave Jake out of this," Jennifer said.

"Then leave Kate out of it."

"Not on your life. She's been the problem all along."

Kate batted her lashes. "Why is that, Jennifer? Is there something about me you don't like?"

"Oooohh," Jennifer said, stomping her foot. "Just leave your hands off Harry."

"I don't think Harry is your concern anymore, Jennifer," Kate said, tucking a hand in Harry's arm and snuggling against him. "Are you, honey pie?" she asked, kissing his ear.

"That's right!" Harry said heartily. "I'm a free man now. If I want to date Kate again, I will. In fact, if I want to marry her, I will."

"Ohhh, Harry," Kate breathed adoringly.

"Ugh," Jennifer said. "You two are disgusting." She reached for Jake's hand and dragged him to the window. "But that's all right. I have Jake, don't I, darling?"

Jake gave Kate an angry look. "If you want me, you do," he said, putting an arm around Jennifer and pulling her close.

Kate simmered. She tossed her hair sultrily and stroked Harry's thigh. "Come on, Harry," she said in a low, throaty voice. "Come back to my place and let's...turn up the heat...."

He loosened his tie and started the engine. "Sorry, folks," he said, "but Kate and I have some business to take care of."

Jake leaned down and stared into the car, his face a mask of fury. "Kate, you're making a huge mistake."

She gave him a sultry look. "I don't think I am."

"Kate," he said, "I'm warning you. Don't do this."

She blew him a kiss, then turned to Harry and ran her hand up his thigh. "Come on, Harry," she murmured. "Let's go home and get to know each other again."

"Oh, Kate," Harry said in a shaky voice as he pulled the car onto the road, "I had no idea you could be this sexy."

She sat back, eyeing him sardonically. "I didn't used to be, Harry. I used to be a lady, remember? I followed all the rules and never had any fun. Now I know that fun is about the only thing that matters in life."

He drove with both hands on the wheel, blinking as he considered what she'd just said. "Kate, I...I don't know what to say. You've really changed. You're so...different."

"You mean if I'd been this way when we were engaged, you would have married me?"

"I would have been your slave!"

SHE HAD HER BACK to him, making coffee from freshly ground beans. It was funny, Harry thought, but he never saw Kate as the sexy woman she'd pretended to be earlier.

He came up behind her and slid his arms around her. "You know, I was thinking, maybe we could go out to dinner tonight, and then dancing. You used to love slow dancing, hmmm?" He turned her around and took her in his arms, humming as he led her around the kitchen floor. "Remember this?" he murmured against her ear. "Hmmm?" He hummed their song, "Chances Are," by Johnny Mathis.

"Oh, come on, Harry," she said. "Cut it out, will you? You've got overactive hormones or something. Save it for Jennifer. She's the one you supposedly love, though I wonder if either one of you know the meaning of the word."

"You're right," he said, releasing her and sighing. "You're always right. I'm being a cad. If I love Jennifer, I should be faithful to her."

"Were you faithful to me all those years we were engaged?" she asked.

Harry darted her a look, and his face turned red. "Kate, come on, that's water over the dam."

"You weren't, were you?" she said, just realizing it now. "You rat. You cheated on me even when we were engaged."

"Only a few times," he said. "And they didn't mean anything. They were just women."

"Who?"

"Kate, come on, don't do this."

"Who?" She folded her arms and waited.

He shrugged. "Mary Alice Kennedy. Suzie Bloch. Ann Marie Alestario." Kate tapped her foot as he scratched his head and kept going. "Linda Louise Shapiro. Muffy Connors. That's all I can remember."

"Muffy Connors! She was one of my best friends!"

He laughed halfheartedly. "Hey, it was only for a weekend. Remember that weekend we were going to Montauk but you had to fink out? Muffy was there and we just...you know..."

"Ohhh." Kate sat down abruptly, staring at the tabletop. "I was a fool," she said, shaking her head at herself. "You were sleeping with everyone behind my back and I didn't even know it."

"Hey, everyone does it, Kate. It's not all that big a deal."

"It is to me!" she said, her eyes burning. "I loved you, or at least I thought I did. I expected you to be faithful to me."

"You mean you were to me?"

"Of course I was! How can you even ask?"

Harry sighed. "I guess I was a real fool, Kate." He sat opposite her, his shoulders slumping. "I guess I never knew what I had in you. I just took you for granted." He raised miserable eyes to her. "Can you forgive me?"

"That's what's always been wrong between us, Harry," she said. "I've always had to forgive you. We were never right for each other, Harry. Do you realize that now?"

"No, if anything, I'm just beginning to realize what I lost when I broke our engagement."

"Oh, Harry," she said, shaking her head at him. "You really are a fool."

"But you did care for me once, Kate."

"And the funny thing is, I still do. But it's just caring, Harry. It's not love. It's...I don't know, it's affection or something like that. I know your worst faults and I guess they don't matter. I'd never want to be married to you, though. You'd be hell to be married to."

"I guess that's how Jennifer feels," he said mournfully. "I guess I'm not the kind of a guy a woman should marry."

"Stop feeling sorry for yourself," Kate said, standing up and getting out coffee mugs. She poured them coffee and handed him a mug. "Here. It's strong and black. Maybe it'll put a little stiffness in your backbone."

"You know, you've always irritated me when you talk like that. I feel like you're some kind of drill sergeant, or worse, my mother."

"If we were right for each other, I wouldn't have to be a drill sergeant."

"You're wrong, you know. You're still an incurable romantic. You think that if you find the right person, everything's just ducky. Well, it doesn't work that way, Kate. There are always problems, even in the best relationship. You just like to have everything under control. You spent so damn much time trying to fix me, trying to make me be the way you wanted me to be. Why couldn't you have just left me alone? I was never okay the way I was, was I? I always felt like I was defective, like I didn't quite measure up."

Stricken, Kate stared at him. "Oh, Harry, I'm so sorry I made you feel that way."

"You're right, though. We're not right for each other. But you wanted us to be and you just hung on, trying to make us right for each other. You couldn't give up."

She couldn't take her eyes off him. He was saying things she'd never thought she'd hear anyone say about her. He made her sound like her mother! She couldn't stand it, didn't want to face it. Was there anything worse on earth than to end up like your own *mother?*

"Well, if you knew we weren't right for each other," she said hotly, "why didn't you do something about it? Why'd you stay engaged to me?"

Harry shrugged. "It was easy, I guess. I'm not saying I was any prize, Kate. I'm just saying I wish you could have accepted me for what I was."

Kate felt her shoulders slump. She stared at the man she'd once thought she'd loved, and realized that she hadn't known anything about love or Harry. She'd been an even bigger fool than him. "It's kind of ironic, isn't it?" she said. "Here we are finally talking like we should have years ago."

"It feels good now, though," Harry said. "It feels like we've got some kind of closure, you know?"

She smiled. "Yeah, I know."

They sat quietly, companionably, at last accepting that there was nothing between them.

"Drive me back to work?" Kate asked after a while.

"Sure. Do you think we were here long enough to convince them we made love?"

"Sure. If they ask, tell them it was a quickie."

"We still could, you know," Harry said, raising his eyebrows, his eyes glittering.

"Harry," she said, standing up and grabbing him by the ear, "let's get out of here before I murder you."

Chapter Twelve

"You are going to cater my party."

Kate stared blankly into Jake Griffin's irate face. She had just entered her office to find him there, leaning over her like an avenging angel.

"Well, hello to you, too," she said and swept past him to her desk.

Martha looked up from putting the finishing touches on a cake. "I take it things aren't going too well with you two."

Kate glared at her, and Martha just shrugged and went back to frosting the cake.

"Now, then, Mr. Griffin," Kate said, "it appears we have a major disagreement."

"No, we're in complete agreement," he said. "The invitations are in the mail. No other caterer is available. I checked. You are going to cater my party, Miss Cunningham, or I'll personally throttle you."

"Anger is such a mobilizing emotion, don't you think?" she said sweetly, looking through the stack of mail on her desk. Bills, bills and more bills, and there was only one way to pay them. She looked up at Griffin. "Okay, I'm going to cater your party."

"Just like that?" Jake asked, stunned. "No arguments? No accusations or reasons why you won't?"

She held out the stack of bills. "Here, take a look at all the reasons why I will," she said dryly, and tossed the bills on the desk. She sat down and put her hands to her temples. "Lord, I have the most rotten headache, and you're not helping it any."

"If you hadn't stormed off like that, you might have found out you don't have any reason to have a headache."

"My headache has nothing to do with you!" she said hotly. "Just buzz off, Griffin. "You're an egomaniac, always thinking everything's about you."

"What's it about then?" he asked, "Harry Grenville? You'd have plenty of reasons for a monster of a headache if you've taken up with him again."

"Oh, no!" Martha wailed from the sidelines. "You haven't gone back with Harry, have you?"

"Martha," Kate said tightly, "this is none of your business. Kindly butt out."

"Hey, I'm sorry," Martha said, tossing her curly head and giving Kate a dirty look. "Pardon me for living."

"I'm sorry," Kate said, rubbing her temples. "I'm not myself today."

"Who are you?" Jake asked. "Dracula?"

She gave him a stormy look. "Look, buster, I said I'd cater your damned party. What else do you want? A written apology?"

"I want you to stop acting like a schoolgirl and let me explain about Jennifer."

"Fine," she said shortly. "Explain."

"She called me last night and asked if I could drive her to the train station this afternoon. She had a date with a girlfriend to go to a show in New York and then have dinner. I said I'd be glad to, and then she suggested we have lunch today while we were at it. I said okay. So when I picked her up, I asked her what was going on with her and Harry, alluding to the now-infamous water-pitcher scene at the inn. And she said he was a certified jackass. When I asked why, she said any man who wanted you had to be."

"Me?" Kate cried.

"You. And I asked why she had it in for you, and she wouldn't answer for a while. She sat there like a little kid, her lower lip stuck out, and finally she said all her life you'd haunted her. When she wanted new shoes on the first day of school, she didn't get them, but you did. When she wanted the leading part in the fifth-grade play, you got it. In seventh grade someone named Mikey asked you out instead of her. On and on it went—Kate was always first and *she* was always second or third."

Kate frowned as she listened. Is that how it had seemed to Jennifer, that Kate had always bested her? She felt the beginnings of understanding, and with that understanding came a degree of compassion. "I didn't realize how she'd felt all those years," she said quietly. "No wonder she hates me."

"She doesn't hate you, Kate. She envies you. But what's really underneath it, I think, is her own rotten feelings about herself. If she was happy with herself, she wouldn't have to always compare herself with you."

"But that's what I don't understand!" Kate said. "Jennifer is absolutely beautiful! And not only that, she's talented and smart and everything else a woman wants to be. Why should she feel so inferior to me?"

Jake shrugged. "I don't know why. I only know she does."

"Good grief, it's all so silly."

Jake let out a sigh and scraped his hand back through his hair. "Yes, it is," he said. "But then certain things can seem awfully important to a man or woman."

"What things?"

He looked into her eyes. "Kate, tell me you haven't gone back with Harry Grenville."

"I haven't gone back with Harry Grenville."

"Dammit, Kate, don't *do* that! Have you or haven't you?"

"What's it to you? I'd still cater your precious party whether or not I'm seeing Harry."

"Kate, this isn't about catering a party."

"Oh?" she asked, getting up and dipping her finger in Martha's frosting and licking it off her finger. "What's it about?"

As he watched her, his eyes darkened to a sexy smolder. "Don't tempt me, Kate."

She glanced at him and saw she might be pushing just a little too much. She shrugged. "I don't know what you mean."

He swiped some frosting and licked it off his finger slowly, sexily, his eyes pinned on hers. "No?" he asked, sucking the frosting off his finger.

She felt her stomach turn around, spin and dip and try to fly into the heavens. She had to close her eyes and shut out the sight of him. She put a hand on the tabletop to steady herself. "No," she said weakly.

He reached out and took her hand. "Come on, Kate, let's go back to my place and I'll show you."

"Ohhh," she said breathlessly, her eyes still closed, her face glowing. "I don't think we better."

"I think we should," he murmured, drawing her closer. Smiling, Martha turned and crept from the room. He drew Kate even closer, his breath whispering over her lips.

"Jake," Kate breathed, "we're in public."

"No, we're not," he murmured, brushing her hair back from her face. "Martha's had the good sense to leave us alone, and no one else is here."

She opened her eyes and looked up at him. "Please," she whispered, but she didn't know what she meant.

Jake did. He lowered his lips and kissed her slowly, lingeringly, sensually, taking her breath away, making her swirl and dance and float in midair. She put her hands on his chest and clung to him, swooning, losing contact with everything but Jake. He was all that mattered, all that existed. He was everything. She moaned softly and her arms crept around his neck. She pressed herself into his hard body, giving herself up to the sweetness of his kiss.

"Ohhh," she breathed when the kiss ended. She clung to him, afraid to let go. If she did, she'd melt into a puddle. She looked into his eyes and felt shivers dance up and down her spine. "Let's go back to your place."

"It's about time you admitted what you wanted," he murmured, smiling into her eyes.

She smiled back, curling her arms around his neck, going up on tiptoe to kiss him lingeringly. "Mmm," she said, feeling utterly delicious, "it is, isn't it? And I haven't gone back to Harry. I wouldn't if I could. Harry doesn't want me anyway, he wants Jennifer."

"What a fool," Jake murmured, brushing his cheek against hers. "No man in his right mind would prefer any other woman on earth if he could have you."

"But he can't have me."

"Can I?"

"Let's go back to your place and find out."

He kissed her again and her lips clung to his, her breasts ached for his touch, her abdomen pushed against the hardness of his stomach. Everything was sensual—the smell of his after-shave, the sound of his voice, the feel of his skin, the touch of his hands, the softness of her silken lingerie against her skin.

"But I'm still all sweaty," she murmured against his lips.

"We'll take a bath," he said. "But you're delicious when you're sweaty, all the same."

Her breath caught in her throat. She didn't know which was better—being sweaty with Jake or being in a tub with him. "*We* will?"

"Mmm," he murmured, still kissing her, "just you and me."

She felt her heart kick up its heels with joy and anticipation. "I can hardly wait."

"You don't have to," he said, moving her toward the door. "I'm parked right out back."

She stopped him and put her arms around his neck, pulling his head down for a lingering kiss. "What if I can't even wait till we get to your place?" she asked, her eyes glowing as she looked into his eyes.

"Lordy," he said joyfully, "you sure know how to turn a man on."

"Mmm," she murmured, running her hand down his chest and abdomen and pausing at the hardness at his groin. "It appears I do at that...."

Jake's breath caught in his throat, and he put his arms around her, pulling her against him, burying his head in the curve of her neck. "You're delicious," he whispered, kissing her hungrily, arching her back so her breasts were crushed against his chest. "Luscious," he murmured, dipping his tongue into her ear, his hands moving over her back greedily. "You're driving me crazy."

She was trembling and out of breath and afraid what would happen if they stayed here another moment. "Come on," she said, grabbing his hand and pulling him out the door, "let's get out of here before we get too carried away."

In his Range Rover, he took her in his arms again. "I don't see how I'm going to drive this thing," he said, talking even while his lips were devouring hers. "I want you so bad I'm in pain."

"Maybe I can ease it," she murmured, running her hand down his chest.

"I think maybe you can," he said, looking into her eyes. Fumbling with the key, he finally got it in the ignition, then sat back and took a steadying breath. "Lord," he said at last, "I haven't felt like this since I was a teenager."

She looked at him with smiling, sexy, slumberous eyes, reaching out to touch the tiny cleft in his chin. "Me neither," she whispered. "Isn't it wonderful?"

"It's better than wonderful." He took her hand and kissed her palm. "It's heaven on earth."

Her lips curved into a smile. Her eyes glowed with desire and heat and something that felt curiously like satisfaction, though they hadn't yet sated their physical desires. "You don't have much food at your place," she said, her lips parting in an even wider smile. "I feel like holing up for days with you. Maybe I better go inside and see what I have in the kitchen."

"Honey, don't even try. I just want to get you home. We can think about food later."

She shrugged slightly and nestled against him. "Okay. It's just that food can be so. . . sensual," she breathed, running her hand down his muscular arm.

"All right," he said in a strangled voice, "why don't you see what you can come up with?"

Smiling, she kissed him lingeringly, then got out of the truck. "Be back in a sec."

It felt like forever that she was away from him, but she found caviar and whipped cream, strawberries and a huge chunk of cheddar, crackers and a crusty loaf of bread, three bottles of white wine, a box of Godiva chocolates, fresh oysters, cooked shrimp and cocktail sauce. Her mouth was watering by the time she was back in the truck.

"Okay," she said, "we can stay in bed for days."

He put his arm around her and drew her against him, smiling into her eyes. "What if I want to stay in bed for weeks with you?" he asked lazily, his eyes smoldering. "Hmmm? What if I can't get enough of you ever?"

She felt her heartbeat quicken, felt her stomach do a flip-flop, felt her very blood heat up and sizzle inside her veins. "That sounds just fine to me," she whispered, kissing him softly. "Wonderful, in fact."

Against her lips he murmured, "Even better than wonderful."

She steeled herself and drew out of his arms. "Can you drive this thing?"

The corner of his mouth turned up wryly. "I'll do my best."

"Then drive, Jeeves, I'm kind of in a hurry."

A HOT TUB sounded great, and so did wine and caviar and oysters, but when you have a need so big it seemed to fill the sky, sometimes you just can't wait.

They stumbled from the all-terrain vehicle and fled into the house, up the stairs and down the hall, into his bedroom and into each other's arms. They kissed as if they'd never kissed before, hungrily, greedily, pulling at each other's clothes and gasping for breath. It seemed mere seconds till they were naked on the bed and he was inside her.

Their bodies glistened with a sheen of sweat, as, limbs entwined, they cried out softly with pleasure. Kate had never before felt as alive as she did now. As filled with heat and ecstasy. It was as if they were on a ride—a glorious ride, one that took them soaring into the sky. When at last they reached the peak, sunlight crashed around them and splintered like golden shards of glass. Then gently, softly, they lay in each other's arms and looked into each other's eyes, and there was peace at last.

SHE HAD NEVER KNOWN such exquisite pleasure. Her body hummed wonderfully. She was relaxed as she'd never been in her life, her limbs limp and filled with pleasant aching, her breathing soft and even, her body sated, pleasured, incredibly complete.

She lifted drowsy lids and watched him sleeping. She moved her head and nuzzled his shoulder with her nose. He stirred, came awake slowly, saw her and smiled a smile so dazzling it could have rivaled the sun.

"Hello, beautiful," he murmured drowsily.

"Hi."

So simple. So easy. So right.

She turned on her side and nestled against him. "What time is it?"

"I have no idea." He smiled and ran his hand down her back, pausing at the ripe curve of her buttocks. "It could be today or it could be tomorrow. Night or day. It doesn't seem to matter."

She sighed blissfully. "Yes."

"Just yes?" he asked, kissing her shoulder lazily. "Hmmm? Just yes?" he asked again, smiling, happy, sated, complete.

She smiled into his eyes. "Yes. Just yes."

"Lord, you are a beautiful woman," he murmured, trailing his fingers over her cheek, pushing back her golden hair. "Incredibly beautiful."

She turned toward his body and nestled against him, feeling his warm skin, touching him, caressing him.

"I didn't know it could be like this, Jake," she whispered. "It felt so good and so right. My body feels like it was made for you."

"And mine for you," he murmured, finding her soft and secret places and bringing her even more glorious pleasure.

"Oh, no!" She bolted upright and stared wide-eyed down at him.

"What is it?"

She pointed to him and then to herself. "Sex," she said. "I mean . . . babies."

He groaned. "I never even thought about it."

"Me neither."

"What made you think of it now?"

She flopped back down. "I don't know. It just popped into my head, like 'uh-oh, there might be a problem here.'"

He ran his hand over her belly lovingly. "It wouldn't be a problem for me," he said softly. "I'd like to have my baby growing inside you."

"You mean that?" she murmured, looking into his eyes. "You really mean it?"

He smiled at her and pulled her into his arms. "I really mean it, Kate."

She lay looking at the ceiling. "Even if I came to you a month from now and told you I was pregnant? You wouldn't be angry or scared?"

He continued rubbing her belly. "I think I'd be the happiest man in the world if you told me you were pregnant. I think I'd want to marry you in a minute."

"Marry?"

He turned on his side and went up on his elbow, looking down at her with warm eyes. "Marry. Tie the knot. Make you an honest woman. Give you my name. Marry, Kate, as in 'I do.'"

"That's kind of reassuring," she whispered, her eyes glowing. "No one's ever really wanted to marry me before."

"You just hadn't met the right man yet."

"Are you the right man?"

"I'd like to think so."

She considered all this. It was wonderful and frightening all at once. Things didn't happen this quickly, did they? She looked up at him with sleepy, sexy eyes. "I love it when you touch me."

He put his hand on her stomach again and rubbed it, then leaned over and kissed her belly gently, lovingly, letting his lips trail downward. He inhaled her scent and groaned with ecstasy.

"God, I want you," he said. "Again. And I want it to last longer this time. I want it to last forever."

She held his head and groaned when he moved his head between her thighs and found her with his tongue. She arched her back and closed her eyes and sunlight seemed to dance on her lids.

He moved his hands under her thighs and ran them under her buttocks, pulling her closer to his seeking lips and tongue.

She cried out softly and dug her fingers into his hair. She felt as if she were all liquid and fire. "Oh, Jake," she moaned, "it's still happening. It keeps happening."

He went up on his elbows and slid his body over hers. Fitting himself to her, finding her core, he entered her, sheathing himself deep inside her.

He kissed her neck and breasts, moved his hands over her shoulders and down to her breasts, found her rigid nipples and caressed them, lowered his head and licked them, sucked them into his mouth and rolled them around on his tongue. He delved into her, again and again, deeper and deeper until he was a part of her.

"I love you," he murmured, and then the heavens broke around them again and flung them into eternity.

"OYSTERS," she said, up to her chin in bubbles in the tub in his bathroom. "The most totally sensual food."

He took one from its chilled shell and fed it to her. She ate it greedily, slurping it up as the juices ran down her chin, laughing throatily. She sipped champagne. He wouldn't hear of plain white wine.

"White wine is for lunch," he had said, uncorking the champagne. "This is a celebration."

She fed him an oyster. He dipped it in cocktail sauce and ate it lazily, looking into her eyes. "You are the most beautiful woman in the world. I want to marry you right now."

"Silly," she said, wrinkling her nose at him, "it's much too soon to propose. We haven't slept the whole night together yet. What if you hog the whole bed, or I do?"

"We'll buy two king-size beds and push them together so we have plenty of room."

She settled back and rested the champagne glass on her chest, smiling at him over the top of it. "I love you, too, I think."

"You think? You mean you don't know?"

She shook her head at him, her eyes filled with warmth. "You are a crazy man, totally irresponsible."

"Marry me tomorrow."

"What about the license and the blood tests?"

He groaned. "They don't make it easy on people, do they?"

She smiled. "Paperwork and waiting. It's so people can't rush into things in the heat of passion."

"Maybe more people should. Maybe if they did, they wouldn't think and obsess and get it all wrong."

She became serious. "I don't want a divorce."

"Neither do I."

She sighed. "Maybe it's better just to be lovers."

"Never. What about our babies? They'll need love and parents and the security marriage can give them."

She couldn't help smiling. He was the most impractical man on earth. "No more foolish talk," she said. "Let's just enjoy the moment."

"I'd like to take you to Italy," he said. "Ever been there?"

"Once, years ago. It was beautiful."

"Even more beautiful when you're in love. Will you go with me?"

She smiled. "Ask me later."

"How much later?"

She considered. "A month from now, after your passion has cooled down."

"It won't," he said, touching his toes to hers. It was a mammoth tub, big enough almost to swim in.

"Wait a month anyway."

He sighed. "So practical. So bent on getting it right and not making any mistakes."

She stared at him. Was she like that? Afraid to let go and spontaneously enjoy the moments for what they were? "Have you ever asked anyone to marry you before?"

He shook his head. "Never wanted to, either."

"How can you be so sure?"

He shrugged. "It feels right with you. Doesn't it, Kate? Doesn't it feel right to you?"

She smiled. "Yes, but—" she searched his eyes "—I thought I loved Harry, too."

He tilted his head and studied her. "Did it feel this way with him? Ever?"

"No. Not at all, not even for a minute."

"Are you glad now you didn't marry him?"

"So glad I almost can't stand it," she said fervently. "I'm only beginning to see how lucky I was."

"There," he said, as if resting his case.

She smiled dreamily. "Let me enjoy this a little longer. Let me just soak it all up. It's too good to be true—" Startled, she looked at him. "See? That's what's so frightening—it's almost too good to be true."

"You've had too much pain in your life," he said gently. "It must be hard for you to believe that anything good can happen."

She looked down, sipped her champagne, then looked up at him again. "Yes. I guess I'm afraid to get my hopes up."

He smiled tenderly, and she felt so safe looking at him that she wanted to dive into his arms and hug him. Tears misted her eyes.

"Get your hopes up, Kate," he said softly. "I'm going to marry you."

"But will we be happy?" she asked in a small voice.

He nodded, so sure, so certain, as if no doubts were even possible. "Sunshine and laughter," he said. "That's what our life together will be. It happens to a very few, very lucky people. It's going to happen to us."

She sighed and shook her head, smiling at him. "Don't talk about it anymore. Let's leave it for a while."

He put his champagne glass down and moved to her side. "You comfortable?" he asked, kneading her shoulders. "Could you use a massage?"

"A massage," she groaned. "That would be heavenly."

"Then come," he said, picking her up and wrapping her in a fluffy towel. "I'll bring you back to bed. I'll give you a massage." He kissed her softly. "Then we can sleep together and see if you push me out of bed."

She put her arms around his neck and let him carry her back to bed. She was in love with him. It was as simple as that.

Chapter Thirteen

Morning. Sunlight streaming into the room. Birds singing outside. And Jake next to her.

Was there ever anything more perfect? She turned her head and he was watching her, his eyes warm, his mouth smiling. He reached out and put his hand on her stomach.

"I'm hoping there's a baby already started. Then you'll have to marry me."

Smiling, she stretched and yawned, raising her hands over her head and stretching till the nighttime aches were gone and her muscles felt like melted butter. She turned on her side and nuzzled his neck. "Mmm, you smell so good," she murmured, running her hands over his body. "And feel so good."

He sighed contentedly and held her. "Breakfast?"

"Mmm."

"What would you like?"

"Scrambled eggs and bacon and English muffins and coffee and fresh-squeezed orange juice. And the morning paper. On the terrace in the sunshine, on a silver tray."

"Done."

He picked up a phone and dialed one number. "Theresa? I have a guest. We'd like scrambled eggs and bacon and English muffins and fresh-squeezed orange juice. With the morning paper on the terrace on a silver tray. Can you do all that?" He smiled. "Good." He hung up.

"Who's Theresa?"

"My housekeeper and cook. Yesterday afternoon she was off shopping. There'll be a full larder this morning. She'll be up in half an hour with our food."

"Ohhh," Kate sighed, stretching again. "Perfect. I thought I was going to have to cook."

"Not unless you want to."

"I'd rather be waited on today." She ran her hand over his chest. "That's all we have. A half an hour?"

"I could call her and ask her to come up in an hour."

Kate looked into his eyes. He called Theresa.

IT WAS LATE AFTERNOON when Jake brought Kate back to Lilac Hedges. Martha was running around shouting directions, and the phone was ringing off the hook.

"Thank God," Martha said when she saw Kate. "I'm going crazy."

"What's wrong?" Kate asked.

"Everything. The Purdys want to change their menu. Something about one of the guests being allergic to shellfish. The Smiths need to add three more couples. The Elliots heard what the Smiths were having and want the same menu for their dinner. And Ann Hudson called—her niece's wedding is back on and she wants to have the shower next weekend."

"It never rains but pours," Kate said, smiling at Jake as she picked up the phone and dialed the Smiths. "I'll take the Smiths. Call Ann and tell her the shower's on, but only if she promises to pay for everything if her niece backs out again."

"What about my party?" Jake asked.

Kate shook her head, then said, "Hi, Mrs. Smith? Kate Cunningham. Yes, I heard. Yes. No problem. Sure. Six more people. Fine. Great. See you then." She hung up and dusted off her hands. "What about your party?"

"It sounds like everyone in town wants you to work for them," Jake said. "Will you be able to cater my party?"

"Sure," she said.

The phone rang again but Martha said she'd get it in the back. She'd no sooner picked it up than she yelled, "Kate! Ann Hudson wants to talk to you."

Kate made a face and picked up her extension. "Hi, Ann. Yes, Martha told me. Look, it's water over the dam, okay? These things happen. I understand completely.... Of course we can still do it.... Well, Martha only was saying what I told her to say. I'm sorry, but that's the stipulation. Yes. The entire thing. You will? Great, then it's all set. Yes. See you Tuesday." She hung up and plopped into her chair, sighing contentedly. "There. Everything's going like clockwork."

"Not quite," Martha said, bustling in. "Harry was here and so was your mother."

"Oh, no," Kate groaned.

"I'm afraid so. Harry was livid when he found out you left with Jake—"

"Why'd you even tell him?"

Martha shrugged. "I didn't think it mattered."

Kate sighed. "To Harry it will. What about my mother?"

"She was singing and humming and acting as if she'd just been assured by God himself that she had a first-class ticket to heaven."

"Things must be going well with Elroy," Kate said.

"Looks that way," Martha said, grinning.

"Did she say what she wanted?"

"No, she just said she needed to talk to you as soon as possible."

"What'd Harry say?"

"A bunch of unprintables. He was pretty upset. He said for you to call him the minute you got in."

Kate took Jake's hand and sat him opposite her. "I have to talk to you about Harry. I promised him I'd help him get Jennifer back."

"Why does he need your help?" Jake said, grinning. "If he were man enough, he'd be able to do that on his own."

"He's got this cockeyed theory that Jennifer only wants what I want, so he wants me to pretend I want him."

"Say again?"

Kate laughed. "He thinks if I act like I want him, Jennifer will come after him like a greyhound after a duck."

"Oh, Kate, come on, no more games, okay?"

"It's only for a few more days. He really loves her, Jake. And I promised I'd help."

"But that was before you and I got together. Jennifer will lose interest as soon as I set her straight."

"You don't know Jennifer."

"Kate, I don't like this."

"I don't like it, either, but I promised."

"Un-promise," he said. "Please, Kate. For me."

"Look, it'd only be for a couple days at most."

"I don't like it, Kate. I'd rather you washed your hands completely of the two of them. Let them battle it out if they want to and let's get on with our lives."

"Believe me, if Jennifer's still around, we won't have much of a life to get on with. She'll do everything in her power to break us up."

"As if she could," Jake said, running his hand over her cheek.

She turned her face into his palm and kissed it lingeringly. "I don't like this any more than you do, but I did promise, Jake."

He nodded. "Okay. I don't suppose they can screw things up now that we've gotten together."

"Of course they can't," she said, smiling. "Believe me, they'll be out of our hair by the end of the week."

Jake pulled her close and kissed her. "They better be. I don't want any more of your attention on Harry Grenville ever again."

"Believe me, it won't be."

Jake was about to kiss her again when the door opened and Kate's mother sailed in.

"Darling!" Laurel Cunningham trilled. "How are you?"

"I'm fine, Mother," Kate said. "How are you?"

"Just fine." Her mother stopped when she saw Jake. "Why, Mr. Griffin, how nice to see you!"

"Nice to see you again, Mrs. Cunningham."

"And are we here on a social or professional call?" Laurel asked, batting her lashes.

"Mother," Kate interrupted before Jake could answer, "I'm going to cater a party for Jake next month."

"Oh." Laurel's smile faltered, then she shrugged. "Oh, well, that's wonderful, dear." She smiled at Jake. "But you know, Mr. Griffin, my little girl can do a lot more than just cater parties."

"I'm well aware of that, Mrs. Cunningham," he said, his eyes gleaming at Kate.

"Well, just as long as you don't forget it," she said, tapping him playfully on the hand. "Katie is going to make some man a wonderful wife. She's just holding out for the right one. You have no idea how many men have wanted to marry Katie."

"Mother—"

"Now don't be so modest, Katie. You know it's true. Why just yesterday I saw that sweet Elliot Samuels in the store and he was asking about you—"

Kate sighed and put her hand to her head. Her mother went on and on and Kate looked at Jake with apologetic eyes. "I'm sorry," she mouthed to him, which stopped her mother immediately.

"What are you sorry for?" Laurel demanded.

Kate smiled. "Nothing, Mother."

"But you said you were sorry. I saw you."

"You don't miss anything, do you, Mother?"

"Not when it comes to my little girl, I don't." Laurel lifted her eyebrows and gave Kate a knowing smile. "And by the way, I just saw Harry Grenville."

"Oh?"

"Yes, and he's wearing a grin the size of the state of Texas."

"My," said Kate. "I wonder what's making him so happy?"

"Well, he's telling everyone who'll listen it's you."

"Me?"

"Kate?" Jake asked, suddenly looking like a thundercloud.

"Yes, Kate." Laurel Cunningham beamed. "It seems you two have gotten back together."

"We have?"

"That's what Harry says. He says it happened early yesterday afternoon." Laurel inched toward her daughter and spoke from the side of her mouth. "And to be honest, I'm a little put out with Harry. He's also letting it be known that you consummated your little affair at the same time."

"He's what?" Kate said, standing up abruptly as color flooded her face.

"He's *what?*" Jake said, standing up at the same time, his face filled with anger.

"Well, that's what he told Elroy," Laurel said. "And Elroy told me. Naturally, when I saw Harry, I didn't say anything about it, but it's very poor manners on his part to spread that kind of thing around. Elroy says he heard Harry at the club talking about being back with you and wondering how he ever put up with Jennifer when he could have had you."

"I'll kill him," Kate muttered.

"You won't have to," Jake said, heading for the door. "I'll do it first."

"Jake!" Kate ran after him and caught him by the hand. "Jake, what are you going to do?"

"I'm going to shut Harry Grenville's mouth for him."

"Jake, you can't."

"Just watch me." Angry sparks filled Jake's eyes. "He needs to learn a few lessons in etiquette."

"Jake," Kate said under her breath, "this must be his way of making Jennifer think he and I are back together."

"He could have picked a less public way," Jake said.

"Look, I know this is upsetting, but it'll blow over in a couple days. Jennifer just has to hear the rumors and she'll run back to Harry so fast her head will swim even more than usual."

"And meanwhile, Harry's destroying your reputation all over town."

"Jake, it's hardly going to destroy my reputation for people to think I slept with Harry. I did for over ten years and I survived."

"But you weren't going to be my wife then."

"And who says I am now?" she asked, irritation flaring. Honestly, was Jake one of those possessive men who wanted her to account for every minute she was away from him?

"Kate, I've asked you to marry me."

"But I haven't given you an answer."

"Does sleeping with Harry Grenville have anything to do with your hesitancy?" Jake asked.

"Sleeping with—" She stared at Jake, horrified. In a low voice she said, "How dare you imply that I really slept with him!"

"How do I know what you did or didn't do? You looked awfully chummy with him when he drove off with you yesterday!"

"Jake!"

"I notice you haven't denied it yet."

"If that's all the faith you have in me, I won't deny it!"

"You mean to say you're going to stand right there and not tell me you didn't sleep with Harry Grenville?" Jake asked angrily.

"That's right!" Kate snapped. "If you want to think I slept with Harry, go ahead and think it. Just don't do it on my property!" She opened the door and gestured to it. "Just get out, Jake Griffin, and don't come back until you can believe in me."

"How the hell am I supposed to believe you when you refuse to tell me what you did with Harry?"

"Why should I tell you?" she demanded. "It's none of your business!"

"It's my business if I'm going to marry you!"

"I wouldn't marry you for all the money in Swiss banks," she said in a low, angry voice. "Now get out and get out fast."

"Great," he said. "I'm going. Just don't forget you have to cater my party."

"Ohhhh," she said, her face getting redder. "Is that all you can think about? That damn *party?*"

"No, Kate," he said in a quieter voice, "but it's obvious I care a lot more about us than you do. If you ever decide to tell me the truth about you and Harry, call me."

"I wouldn't call you if you were the last man on earth," she said.

"Fine, then I guess this is goodbye." He turned and stalked out of the office.

Kate stared after him, then slammed the door. "Damn!" she shouted. "I hate men!"

"Don't be foolish," Laurel said. "You silly girl, run right out there and apologize to that man! He said something about wanting to marry you!"

"Mother, this is all your fault!"

"What did I do?" Laurel demanded. "All I did was try to help things along. It was only a little fib about Elroy."

Kate stared at her mother, horrified. "Do you mean to say Harry didn't tell Elroy we'd slept together?"

"Well, of course he didn't!" Laurel sniffed. "Harry has better manners than to say a thing like that! He told me just now about the little ruse you two hatched, so I thought I'd just make sure that nice Jake Griffin heard it."

"Mother, how *could* you?" Kate cried. "Now Jake thinks I slept with Harry!"

"But that's wonderful! Men need to be a little jealous now and then."

"Mother!" Kate looked at her as if she were looking at an ax murderer. *This* was her *mother?* She dropped her head in her hands and gave herself up to despair.

"Now what's wrong?" Laurel asked. "Honestly, Kate, you act as if it's the end of the world, and I've probably done you the biggest favor you've ever had done for you."

Kate held her hands out as if to ward off Laurel. "Do me a real favor, Mother. Leave. Right now. Don't ask any questions and don't say another word. Just get out."

"Well, I don't know what's wrong with you, Kate!"

"Please, Mother."

"All right, I'm going." Laurel lifted her chin and stopped at the door. "But you don't realize what I've done for you," she said, turning back for one last word.

"Actually," Kate said tiredly, "I do."

"No, you don't," Laurel said, then opened the door in a huff. "But I'm not going to stay around where I'm not appreciated. I'm leaving, Kate."

"Good."

Laurel slammed the door after her.

Kate slumped into her chair and stared into space. Maybe she should move to Saskatchewan. Maybe her mother would never find her there.

"Is it safe to come out?" Martha called from the back room.

"All clear," Kate said. "Mother's gone. You can take down the sandbags now."

Martha perched on the top of Kate's desk. "Did I hear Jake Griffin say what I thought I heard him say?"

Kate stared into space. "Yup."

"And you let him get away without making up?"

"Yup."

"Kate! Can't you say anything more than 'yup'?"

"Nope."

"Kate, come on, stop being foolish. If Jake Griffin's that interested in you, you can't let him get away."

"If Jake Griffin can't believe in me, I don't want him."

"Kate, you're being unreasonable."

"It's unreasonable to expect a man who says he wants to marry you to take your word for something?"

"But he doesn't really know you."

"That's the point, Martha. He doesn't know me. How can we discuss something as important as marriage when we don't even know each other's shoe size? Oh, sure, yesterday in the heat of passion everything was terrific, but now I'm not so sure. I mean, I really don't know this guy." She chuckled humorlessly. "In fact, Harry's getting to look better and better."

"Harry!"

"Hey, I know him. We dated for ten years. Yesterday we sat and talked and it was nice."

"Nice. You want nice when you can have stupendous?" Martha stared at Kate. "Are you crazy? Hey, I know you, kid. You get scared and you run back to what's safe. Maybe you're thinking life would be just ducky with Harry. Think again, pal. Harry dumped you when you needed him the most."

"You think Jake Griffin didn't just dump me?" Kate snapped, her eyes flaring with anger.

"You think you didn't help him along?"

"Hey," she said sarcastically, "maybe I should just enter the convent."

"I doubt the nuns could give you as much of a rush," Martha said, marching toward the back room. "But then maybe you don't want passion, Kate. Maybe all you want is safety."

"Passion's a hell of a thing to base a marriage on," Kate said angrily.

"You think safety's any better?" Martha asked, whirling around to face her friend. "You want to be like me, Kate? Married to the same man for fifteen years and never had one day of true happiness?"

They stared at each other, and the quiet in the room became loud.

"Kate," Martha said at last, "I wanted to get married so bad I would have dragged the nearest man to the closest altar. Tom was nice, but I'll tell you something, nice doesn't cut it anymore. And it shouldn't cut it with you. Go for the whole banana, Kate. Settling for safety and a ring on your finger just doesn't work. I know. It took me a long time to find that out, but I'm glad I did. Getting a divorce was the best thing I ever did."

"Well, pardon me for living, but do I get to make my own mistakes here or not?"

Martha sighed. "I'm sorry for interfering with you and Jake. I just wish I had a man like him in my life, and when

I see you cavalierly throwing him away, I want to shake you."

"I'm not throwing him away," Kate said. "I just don't like the way he's acting. I want a man who believes in me. Is that too much to expect?"

"I guess you two need to get to know each other better."

"But that takes time," Kate said. "And Jake Griffin doesn't want to go slow. He's rushing headlong into this thing."

"And the hotter he gets, the cooler you are," Martha said.

"Well, someone has to use their head," Kate said hotly. "He's acting like a teenager! My God, Martha, you don't ask someone to marry you on the second date!"

"He obviously did."

"Well, he was foolish. Everyone knows you need to get to know someone before you make any long-term decisions."

"Sensible Kate," Martha sighed. "I guess I just wonder if you'll wake up someday and wish you'd been a little more spontaneous instead of always doing the sensible thing."

"Is it so wrong to want a man who believes me?"

"See? There you go again, always harping on what Jake Griffin isn't doing. Why not just sit back and enjoy what he does so well?"

Kate stared at Martha, then went back to her desk. She looked out the window and saw that the sun had disappeared. The sky was suddenly gray and overcast. There would be a storm before the day was out.

Sighing, she sat down and looked at the pile of work on her desk. Menus needed to be recorded, bills needed to be sent out, other bills needed to be paid. She put her head in her hands and realized that for the past couple days she'd had an intermittent headache. In fact, she was feeling lousy.

She put it down to her fight with Jake. Anyone would feel terrible after what had just happened between them. Everything had been great one minute and the next it had all soured.

Sighing again, she told herself to forget about it. In a day or two she'd call Jake about the party she had to cater for him. Maybe then they could straighten things out. But one thing was certain. She wasn't going to apologize. If he wanted her that badly, he'd have to apologize to her.

Chapter Fourteen

Kate was lying on the couch that night with wet cotton balls on her eyes when the doorbell rang. She groaned and decided to pretend she wasn't home. Whoever it was would go away. She wasn't going to answer the door for love nor money. She had a headache the size of Chicago and wanted complete and uninterrupted peace.

"Kate?"

She groaned. It was Harry. What was he doing here?

He began pounding on the door. "Kate? Open up. I need to talk to you!"

Sighing, she took the cotton balls off her eyes and sat up. Her head felt like a watermelon about to burst, and everyone knew what a mess *that* made....

"Okay, okay," she groused, "I'm coming." She opened the door and stared dully at Harry. He was cowering on the porch under a trench coat that was soaked. It was pouring rain, and ominous flashes of lightning occasionally illuminated the night sky. "What are you doing here?" she asked tiredly.

"Kate, you look terrible."

"Thanks," she said sourly. She went back to the couch. "What do you want?"

"Kate, we've got to talk. It's true. Jake did take Jennifer to the train. She's visiting Dale Hunnicut in New York. Dale called to tell me Jennifer's blubbering all over the place about our marriage ending. She loves me, Kate! Jennifer loves me!"

"You sound like Sally Field," Kate said grouchily, kneading her temples. "Can you please stop being so damned happy?"

"But I am happy!" Harry said. "I'm happier than I've ever been in my life!"

"So go to New York and get Jennifer and be happy with her. Why are you trying to ruin my life?"

"Kate, you don't seem to understand. I can't let on that Dale Hunnicut told me. Jennifer would kill me. I still have to pretend I think Jennifer wants the divorce."

"Oh, Lord," Kate said, sinking into the couch cushions. "When is it ever going to end?" She put her head back and gingerly placed the cotton pads on her eyes.

"What are you doing, Kate?" Harry asked, staring at her. "You look like something from outer space."

"I am, Harry," she said dully. "I'm Captain Kirk from the spaceship *Enterprise.* Now please tell me why you're here so you can leave and let me be in peace."

"I'm here to plot our next move, Kate. This thing isn't over yet by a long shot."

"I knew it," Kate said. "I've stumbled into some kind of Greek comedy and the gods are angry at me."

"Kate, will you please stop babbling and listen to me? Jennifer's on her way home. Dale told me Jennifer called Jake Griffin to pick her up at the train station, but I want to pick her up. I need someone to keep Jake from getting to the train station so I can look like a hero when I rescue Jennifer."

"Don't count on me," Kate said. "I won't do it. I don't want to be any part of your schemes. Leave me alone, Harry. It's over. Any obligations to you are discharged."

"You promised me, Kate," he said accusingly. "Can't I even count on you when the going gets rough?"

She took the cotton pads off her eyes and stared at him, feeling hysteria rise inside her like an ocean tide. "Can't you count on *me?*" she echoed disbelievingly. "What about me, Harry? When could I ever count on *you?* Dammit, you broke our engagement when I needed you the most and turned tail and ran. You lousy little worm. Get out of here now! Before I do something I'll regret."

"Okay!" he snapped. "I'm going. But if Jennifer goes home with Jake Griffin tonight, I don't think I'll be the one who loses."

Kate stared at Harry. "What do you mean?"

"It seems to me you're more than a little interested in that Griffin fellow. Well, you can kiss him goodbye if Jennifer gets her hands on him."

"Oh, Harry," she said irritably, "you don't know what you're talking about. Jake Griffin doesn't care a fig about Jennifer."

"He hasn't slept with her yet," Harry said, staring at Kate triumphantly. "But he will tonight if you don't stop him."

"And sleeping with her will make him crazy about her?" Kate said. "Come on, Harry, wake up and join the rest of us on earth."

"I tell you, Kate, that woman is insatiable. She wrings a man out and tears him into little pieces, and he still comes back for more, begging, pleading for just one more night of bliss."

Kate stared at him distastefully. "You *are* sick."

"No, I'm in love, and Jake Griffin will be, too, if you don't keep him out of Jennifer's clutches. I tell you the woman is a love vampire. She sucks your blood and makes you beg for more."

Kate closed her eyes and covered her ears. "No more, Harry. I can't stand it another minute. I'll help you, but only on one condition."

"Name it."

"You never, ever come back to me for help. Is that clear? If you're on the damned *Titanic* and it's sinking, you don't call me. Agreed?"

"Fine. This will be the last time, and Kate, I promise you, if I just show up at that train station and Jake Griffin's not there, Jennifer will fall into my arms and all will be well again. I swear it."

"Sure, Harry," Kate said, feeling old beyond her years. "Can I count on that just like I can death and taxes?"

"Kate, I swear to you, I'll never bother you again, ever. Not if the whole world is collapsing and you're the only one who can save it."

"Harry, don't be rash. Just get out. I'll find a way to keep Jake away from the train station. What time's the train arriving?"

"A little after nine. That only gives us an hour and a half."

"Hey," she said, "I'm just like the Lone Ranger. I always get there in time."

"Kate, you're a real sport. I knew I could count on you."

"Harry, don't wear out your welcome. Leave before I change my mind."

"I'm going! I'm going, Kate," he sang out cheerfully. Leaning over, he deposited a huge kiss on her forehead. "Oh, Kate, I love you for this."

She nodded wearily and waved him out the door, then closed it as quietly as she could. She had a whopper of a headache, and she had a hunch it might be a lot worse by the end of the night.

"I ALWAYS GET THERE just in time," she said, mimicking herself half an hour later. "Good old Kate. Such a great sport." She sat on the couch, listening to the rain, wondering what she could do to keep Jake from showing up at the train station to pick up Jennifer. After their fight this morning, she wouldn't dream of giving Jake the satisfaction of knowing that Harry really wanted Jennifer. She also refused to tell him that nothing had happened between her and Harry. But how could she prevent him from showing up at the station so that Harry could play Captain Marvel?

She supposed the only excuse was the party she was supposed to cater for him. She grabbed an envelope from her desk and jotted down some ideas for the menu. Glancing at her watch, she saw that the train wouldn't arrive for an hour. If she'd judged correctly, Jake should still be at home. She picked up the phone and dialed his number.

"Theresa?" she said when Jake's housekeeper answered the phone, "is Mr. Griffin there? It's Kate Cunningham."

She smiled and nodded when Theresa said she'd get Jake, and all the while she wanted to throttle Harry Grenville. Why had he gotten her into this? More to the point, why had she agreed to it?

She decided to practice what she'd say: *Jake?* she said to herself, *I need to talk to you about your party.* She cleared her throat and mentally dabbed some perfume on her throat. *Jake? Are you free for a while tonight? I just need to talk to you about the party.* She squeezed her eyes shut and wished she had a plan. She needed a plan, dammit, and all she had was a lousy menu scribbled on the back of an envelope.

Hi, there, Jake! she mentally said, *You're not busy, are you? How'd you like to sit and discuss your party? No? How'd you like to screw around for a couple hours so Harry can rescue Jennifer?*

She took a deep breath and told herself not to apologize for this morning's fight. She hadn't done anything wrong; Jake had.

Oh, hello, Jake, she tried out. *I'm going to be in your neighborhood tonight and I wondered if you'd like to take me up to your bedroom and ravish me. No? Then how about I take you up there and ravish you?*

She groaned and rested her forehead against the wall. Damn Harry Grenville. Why had he gotten her into this mess? She should be lying down with her feet up and two soaked cotton balls resting on her eyes. Maybe then this rotten headache would go away.

What was taking so long? Where was Jake? In Timbuktu? She felt like an interloper. Maybe he had guests. Maybe he was in the middle of a lavish dinner. Doubt assailed her. Maybe he was with another woman....

Don't be stupid, she told herself. *He's supposed to pick up Jennifer in an hour. He won't be with another woman.*

"Well, well," Jake said when he answered, "I thought you said you never wanted to see me again."

His voice momentarily paralyzed her, but she told herself she had to do this if only to get Harry Grenville out of her life permanently.

She cleared her throat. "I need to talk to you."

"What do we possibly have to talk about?" he asked.

Great. He was playing it cool. She despised men who played it cool. "I need to talk to you about your party."

"Why?" he said. "Last thing I knew you were refusing to do it."

She smiled gamely. "You seem angry."

"I am."

"With me?"

"Who else is there?"

"Last count?" she asked sarcastically. "Over two hundred million in the U.S. alone."

"You have a real smart mouth, Kate. Too bad the rest of you isn't as smart."

"I didn't call to be insulted, Jake."

"Oh? Why did you call?"

"Couldn't I just come out and talk? You could invite me in and offer me a drink. Can't we be civilized about this thing?"

He seemed to be struggling with what to say. Finally he said, "I'm sorry, Kate, but I've got a previous engagement. I can't see you tonight."

Dammit. He was putting Jennifer Grenville ahead of her! "How troubling," she said sarcastically. "To think you don't have time to talk with the woman whom just yesterday, if my feeble memory serves me correctly, you asked to marry you."

"Are you implying that I was just using a line to get you into bed?"

Actually, it had never occurred to her. The possibility hit her now like a Mack truck. "Weren't you?" she asked hotly.

"No, I wasn't," he answered just as hotly.

"Of all the low, conniving, *rotten* things to do," she said in a low voice. "That takes the cake. I've been propositioned and I've been seduced, but I've *never* been lied to!"

"I wasn't lying to you," he said. "I can't believe I was such a fool to think we could be happy together! Lord, I'm an ass!"

"You said it, buster," she said, and slammed down the phone. Lord, she'd like to tear him limb from limb. She'd like to string him up from the nearest tree, eviscerate him, feed him to the wolves. There weren't enough bad things to do to him. She hated him!

She sat down abruptly and burst out crying. Who was she kidding? She didn't hate him, she loved him. What a fool *she* was! It was abundantly clear that Jake Griffin didn't give a hoot for her. He was just like Harry—both men left her and raced to get to Jennifer. If her ego took any more beatings at the hands of Jennifer, it would end up looking like a rag doll.

But it was senseless sitting here feeling sorry for herself. She still had Harry to think about. Her life might be in ruins, but there was no reason his had to be. She got up and began to pace, racking her brain about what she could do now. She could derail the train. She considered that idea with pleasure. At least Jennifer wouldn't bother her anymore.

Sighing, she sat down again. She didn't know what to do. There was no hope for any of them. Harry and Jennifer and she and Jake were doomed.

That thought made her so angry she sailed off the couch, grabbed her slicker and raced out the door. She'd go to the station and throw herself in front of the train if she had to, but before she got there, maybe she'd get another idea.

THE RAIN WAS coming down in torrents, bouncing off the pavement, blowing into the windshield so that the feeble attempt of the wipers to clear the rain was almost laughable.

She crawled along dark roads toward the train station fifteen miles away, peering into the bleak wind-driven rain, rubbing the fog off the windshield and cursing Harry and Jake unmercifully. She didn't need this. She needed a hot cup of tea and a steaming bath and someone to tuck her into bed.

That was when her car died. She drove through a huge puddle and suddenly the motor began to rattle and cough and hiccup, and then it died. The car rolled to a stop. The rain pounded against the roof, rattled against the windows. The wind howled. Lightning still flashed intermittently on the horizon. Thunder rumbled ominously in the distance.

Kate rested her head against the steering wheel and gave herself up to despair. "Why me?" she wailed to no one in particular. "Why now?"

No one answered. She'd bet no one even cared. It had been that kind of day.

Gathering her reserves, she fumbled in the pocket of the car and found a flashlight. She pulled the hood on her slicker over her head and got out. She raised the engine hood. She stared down at the engine by the feeble light of the flashlight. Steam rose off the engine. It looked dark and greasy. She wondered what other terrible things would befall her before the evening was through.

She slammed the hood down and peered into the darkness. No one ahead of her, no one behind. No gas stations. Not even any houses. She might as well be stranded in the Yukon. At least up there she'd probably have a dog team. She'd bet *they* wouldn't sputter and die on her.

She saw a car coming and waved at it frantically. It drove by, going a hundred miles an hour and splashing what felt like eight buckets of water over her.

She sighed and peered into the darkness. Yes, far down the road, the lights of another car appeared. She began yelling and waving and dancing up and down in the middle of the road.

"Hey! Help me! I need help!"

"You sure do, lady," a male voice growled and sped off.

She made the most unladylike gesture she could think of and turned back in time to see another car approaching.

"Hey! Stop!" She jumped up and down and waved and threw up her arms like a signal at a railway crossing. "Slow down, buster!"

The car sprayed water all over her, then sped off.

"So much for brotherly love," she groused. "Are there no friendly, neighborly folks left in this world who see a maiden in distress and want to rescue her? What about the Good Samaritan? Was that just a story in a book? An idea whose time has passed?"

She got in the car and stared glumly out at the night. Her head felt as big as a whale. She tried to start the engine. It coughed, wheezed, then died again. She put on the flashers and got out and locked the car. She'd come back in the morning to pick it up. If there ever was a morning.

She set out toward the train station. She had no idea how far away she was. The rain came down in buckets. The wind whipped her slicker back and blew rain into her face. She bent into the wind and lowered her head and squeezed her eyes almost shut, cursing her fate. Her spirits were rapidly deteriorating, along with her health. She was cold, and her wet clothes didn't help any.

At the sound of an approaching car she whirled around, sticking out her arm with her thumb pointed backward.

"Hey!" she shouted. "I need a ride!"

To her amazement, the car slowed down.

Elated, she ran to it, opened the passenger side door and threw herself in.

"Thank you!" she gasped, lowering the hood on her slicker and resting her head on the back of the plush leather seat. "Thank you so much. My car died and I've been trying to get someone to help me and all they've done is drive by and splash me. You don't know how glad I am that you stopped. You are truly a godsend."

"Kate?"

She turned her head and stared, wondering if she was hallucinating. "Jake?"

"It's me all right," Jake Griffin said grimly. "Strange how we should run into each other like this. I imagine I'm the last person on earth you wanted to see, judging by how you hung up on me."

Actually, he was the only person on earth she wanted to see, but she couldn't tell him that. Today must be her lucky day after all. He was probably on his way to pick up Jennifer. All she needed to do was keep him busy the next half hour so Harry could pick up Jennifer. Then they'd be out of her life forever. But how could she keep Jake busy? She closed her eyes and prayed for a miracle.

"Well, I see you won't even talk to me," Jake said. "Let me try again. Was that your car back there sitting on the side of the road?"

"If it was a blue BMW it was," she said shortly. Honestly, she wished he hadn't picked her up. They were taking up just where they'd left off on the phone.

"You said it died. Could you be a little more specific? Did you have a flat tire? Did the engine get flooded? Is it the carburetor, the transmission, the fuel pump?"

"How would I know?" she asked irritably. "I know enough about cars to fit on the head of a pin with room left over for *War and Peace.* But I'm so sorry if I disappoint you. In my next life, I'll sign up for Engine Mechanics 101."

"Look, I don't need your sarcasm," Jake said. "I just want a straight answer."

"You want a straight answer?" she snapped. "You got one. I was driving merrily along minding my own damn business when the car stalled. Boom. Just like that. One minute it's going, the next it's not." She folded her arms and turned her head to stare out the window. "Why don't you just stop the car and let me out? No one else stopped to help, so why should you?"

"Because under normal circumstances I'm a decent human being."

"You could have fooled me."

He slammed on the brakes, pulled the car to the side of the road and cut the engine. The rain and wind continued to batter the car.

"Let's settle this once and for all," he said. "You've had a burr under your saddle ever since this afternoon."

"I've had a burr under *my* saddle?" she echoed disbelievingly. "What about you? Getting all possessive and riled up about Harry Grenville! I told you Harry means nothing to me, but you hear the first little thing Harry supposedly said and you jump to conclusions. How can I trust you if you won't trust me?'' She stared at him with stormy eyes that barely concealed her hurt. ''And what's even worse is that you could even think I'd go directly from sleeping with Harry to sleeping with you.''

''Do you mean to say you didn't sleep with Harry?''

''What do you take me for?'' she cried. ''Some kind of hussy?'' Angrily she dashed away a tear that had escaped. ''I'm tired of men who say they care about me but fink out on me when the chips are down. First Harry and now you. All your fine romantic sentiments and lovemaking mean diddly squat, Jake Griffin, if you can't believe me when I say something and be there for me, the way I need someone to be there for me.''

By now she was crying but she didn't care. It felt as if everything in the world was going wrong, so why not get everything off her chest and be done with it?

''And do you know what *really* hurts?'' She didn't wait for his answer. She was sobbing and just kept right on going. ''Harry came over tonight to beg me to help him get Jennifer back. I have a headache the size of the Bronx, but he promised me that if I could keep you from going to pick up Jennifer at the train station he'd show up and they'd get back together. I didn't want to. I told him I was sick of all the silly games, but I finally agreed. So I called you with the excuse of talking about that silly party you want me to cater, and what did you do?'' She wrung a tissue in her hands, tearing it to pieces in her hurt and agitation. ''You tell me you have other plans! And all the time I know it's *Jennifer* you've got plans with. Jennifer! Always Jennifer! First she takes my fiancé away, then she takes you away! My ego feels like a bruised potato.''

She broke off and turned her head away, scrubbing her tears off her face and trying to stop her foolish crying. Oh, she was so silly to get worked up like this. Was Jake Griffin worked up? He probably thought she was a ninny.

''Look,'' he said, ''I'm sorry. I didn't realize you were so upset about all this.''

"That's right, you didn't!" she said, turning to look at him. "But you should have! If you really cared, you would have believed me when I said I wasn't interested in Harry anymore. But the minute you hear my mother, you jump to conclusions." She turned her head away. "Just take me home, Jake. Harry will have picked up Jennifer by now. Maybe something good will come of this farce."

"Kate, I said I was sorry—"

"I know you did," she said, her eyes filled with pain. "But it's too late, Jake. You've already shown that you don't believe me when I tell you something."

"I'm sorry that I overreacted to what your mother said, but I don't really know you well yet, Kate."

"That's the real problem," she said quietly. "I'm afraid we made a terrible mistake sleeping together so soon. We short-circuited any chance we might have had to really get to know each other."

"Maybe we slept together rather quickly, but I wouldn't call it a mistake. We just need to work a few things out in our relationship, that's all."

"Jake, after tonight, I don't want to see you again, much less have a relationship with you. Please, I just want to go home."

"I'll take you home," he said, starting the engine and heading toward Kate's house, "but I won't let you get away. Jennifer doesn't mean anything to me. It's you I care about."

"You expect me to believe that without a doubt, yet you wouldn't believe me when I said the same thing about Harry."

"Look, I'll grant I went off half-cocked, but I don't think that means we can't make a go of a relationship."

"Jake, to make a go of a relationship, you need two people who want one in the first place. You may want one, but I don't. I've had it, Jake. I'm tired of games and misunderstandings and hurt feelings. I just want to be left alone."

"Kate, I want to see you again."

"And I don't want to see you. Now if you don't mind, I have a rotten headache and I don't feel like talking."

They fell silent. Kate put her head back and closed her eyes. She'd had it with Harry; she'd had it with Jake. She hoped she never saw another man as long as she lived.

"I'll call you tomorrow," Jake said when he dropped her at her house.

"Don't bother. I won't answer." She slammed the car door and headed for her house.

"You're a stubborn woman," he yelled out the window at her. "But I'm not going to give up."

She didn't even bother to reply. She slipped her key into the lock and opened her door. There were only two things she wanted right now—a bottle of aspirin and a hot bath. Jake Griffin wasn't even a distant third.

Chapter Fifteen

Kate showed up at work the next morning none the worse for wear. Her headache was gone, and even though she felt like she was catching a cold, she figured she could fight it off long enough to get in a good day's work.

"If Jake Griffin calls," she said to Martha when she showed up, "tell him I went to Alaska."

"Uh-oh," Martha said. "Sounds like trouble."

"You could say that," Kate said shortly. "I told him last night I never wanted to see him again."

"Why?" Martha was staring at her as if she had two heads.

"Because I'm sick of men, Martha. I've had it with them. They're infantile and egotistical and I'm taking a vow of chastity for the rest of my life."

"Ha," Martha said. "Chastity's no fun, even if it is safer than sex these days."

"I thought you'd sworn off men after your fifteen years with Tom."

Martha shrugged. "I met a new guy last night. Name's Pete."

"What?" Kate whooped and flew off her chair.

"Well, after the speech I gave you yesterday, I figured I should start putting my money where my mouth is. I went to The Brass Monkey last night and there's this guy sitting at the bar, and I sit next to him and he looks at me and we danced and had a couple drinks and . . . well, one thing led to another and . . ." She grinned impishly. "It's better than sleeping alone. Not only that, he likes plump women. Can you beat that?"

The dreaded question hung in the air: Are you going to see him again? Kate was grinning, wondering if she should ask it.

Anticipating it, Martha said, "He asked me to meet him for dinner tonight when he left this morning."

"You really like him then," Kate said, studying her friend for evidence that things were really okay.

"Yeah, I do. He's a carpenter. On his days off, he builds furniture. He went to college, hated every minute of it, spent some time wandering, then settled down as a carpenter. He owns his own house and pays his bills regularly. Someday he hopes to build furniture full-time, but for now he's happy." She shrugged. "What can I say? He's not Jake Griffin, but he sure as hell knows how to kiss!"

"Believe me, you wouldn't want Jake Griffin," Kate said angrily, shoving a cookbook into the bookcase. "Stick with Pete. He sounds like the kind of guy I need to meet."

"Oh, come on, Kate, you're just angry. What I'd like to know is what you're angry about."

"Everything," Kate said, remembering last night with a thud. Her good mood evaporated. "I'm so tired of all the stupid games and deception I could scream. Last night was the last straw." She outlined last evening's events and at the end of the yarn sighed wearily. "Hopefully Harry and Jennifer patched everything up last night and will be out of my hair soon. Maybe then my life can get back to normal." She cleared her throat and realized it was becoming scratchy. Just her luck.

"There's still your mother to worry about though," Martha pointed out.

Kate sighed. "There's always Mother. If she hadn't butted in and tried to help me out, Jake and I never would have fought in the first place."

"So tell her to stay out of your life."

"I've told her a million times, Martha. Mother suffers from the same problem men do—she can't hear what's being said."

"She doesn't want to," Martha said. "She likes to be in control all the time. She thinks you can't get along unless she's constantly helping out."

"What bothers me is she does it in the name of love," Kate said, "when she doesn't know the first thing about loving me."

"Oh, I think she loves you, Kate."

"I know." Kate stared out the window, feeling frustrated and tired at the same time. "I didn't mean it that way. I meant that she tries to control my life in order to make herself feel better. She worries about me, for instance, and that makes her feel uncomfortable, so she interferes and tries to arrange things so she's comfortable again. That's what hurts so much, Martha. That's what really hurts—I long for a mother who hears me and sees *my* needs, but she's too busy trying to take care of herself."

"And now it feels like Jake's not listening to you, either, and it's driving you crazy," Martha said sympathetically.

"At last," Kate said laughingly, making a sweeping dramatic gesture. "Someone who understands!"

"You know," Martha said quietly, "in a way, we're an awful lot alike. We both keep up a front, pretending everything is fine when it's not." Martha sighed. "Maybe we're just products of our upbringing and can't escape it."

"I guess that's what I've been rebelling against," Kate said, and began to mimic her mother's instructions: "Don't swear, Kate, it isn't ladylike. Cross your feet at the ankle, Kate. Ladies don't cross their legs. Always smile and be polite, Kate, even if you don't like the other person."

She groaned and put a hand to her head. "Maybe that's why I keep getting these rotten headaches—my body's telling me to stop doing what I've been told I should do, and do what I *want* to do for a change."

"It's awfully hard to go against the old rules, though, isn't it?" Martha said wistfully. "One of my rules was to love your husband no matter what he does or how he treats you." She sighed. "So I lived in misery for years because somewhere deep inside I thought that's the way life was supposed to be."

"God, we're a couple of messes, aren't we?" Kate said. "Maybe we should just shuck the damn rules and close up shop a while and go have a three-martini lunch."

"Oh, Lord, wouldn't that be great?" Martha said, eyes shining.

"Then let's do it," Kate said, throwing down her pen.

"Where shall we go?"

"Oh, let's do it up royal. Let's go to The Lily Pond. The last time I was there I made a so-called scene that had my poor mother hanging her head in shame for a week. Who knows? If I get good and drunk enough, maybe I'll make another scene." She grinned wickedly. "And wouldn't that bust my mother's buttons?"

"You angry child, you," Martha said, grinning back.

"You bet," Kate said, hooking her arm companionably through Martha's. "Let's go, Martha. Let's live it up and not do *anything* we don't want to."

DOING ONLY what they wanted to do proved more difficult than they'd thought it would be. Entering The Lily Pond, they ran into Mrs. James Talmadge, silver-haired and impeccable in a green knit suit and white gloves.

She tapped Kate chastisingly on the wrist. "You naughty girl, you!" she said. "I hear you've been upsetting your dear mama. Now you listen to me, Kate Cunningham, your mother's been through a terrible time losing your father. You have to remember that and treat her with respect."

The old lady nodded decisively and swept out the door, not even bothering to nod to Martha.

"Lord!" Kate sighed. "In a single minute, she succeeded in making me feel rotten about myself! How did she do it?"

"Guilt," Martha said, looking after Mrs. Talmadge. "That generation thrives on dishing it out."

"You're right. But I don't have to buy into it." Her throat was beginning to hurt now, but she managed to smile at the waitress who appeared.

"Can I get you some white wine, ladies?" she asked. "A nice zinfandel, perhaps?"

Kate stared at the waitress. It was an almost automatic expectation in Connecticut that a woman would order wine, but Kate was so sick of being expected to act in certain ways she wanted to scream. "No," she said. "I'll have a manhattan, straight up."

"And I'll have a martini," Martha said, looking like a child who's just played hooky. "With three olives. Very dry."

The waitress looked as if she thought they might be a couple of incipient alcoholics, but she managed a polite smile. Polite smiles in Connecticut were de rigueur—you smiled even if it killed you. Kate wondered if it was that way everywhere, or if Connecticut had a corner on the insincerity market.

When the waitress left, Kate grinned. "I suppose the rumor will be all over town now that we're a couple of drunks."

"And harridans," Martha joined in. "Out carousing—and during the noon hour!" she said with mock affront. "I can just see those tongues wagging."

"Uh-oh," Kate said, looking over Martha's head to the doorway. "Here comes trouble."

"Who?"

"Jennifer."

"Remember your promise," Martha said. "Don't be nice to her. Don't smile if you don't want to, don't be polite, don't even be civil if you don't want to."

Kate gritted her teeth. "But it's so *hard* to do what you really want to. I mean, she's headed this way with that supercilious smile on her face and I feel like smacking her, but I can't, Martha."

"Well!" Jennifer said when she reached their table. "If it isn't sweet little Kate and her pal, Martha. And how are you today, Katie? I hear you've had a fight with Jake Griffin."

Kate stared up at her, wondering what she'd look like with a pie in her face. Sighing, she told herself being civil didn't necessarily imply liking someone. "How did you hear that, Jennifer?" she asked. "Keeping that petite little ear of yours to the ground again?"

Jennifer looked at Kate blankly. "What do you mean by that? How could I keep my ear to the ground? It would be awfully awkward."

Martha groaned and Kate almost choked. "Never mind," Kate said. "Why did you stop by? Just to ruin my day?"

"I wanted to let you know that Harry and I are back together. In fact, he's meeting me here for lunch in a few minutes."

"Well, it's about time," Kate said thankfully, then sneezed.

"You can't fool me," Jennifer said triumphantly. "I know you're miserable about it, but it can't be helped. Harry told me he's always loved me. He said he never loved you. How does that make you feel, Miss Perfection?"

Kate stared up at her and felt something release within her. She wasn't going to do it any longer. She wasn't going to play the silly games anymore. It was foolish and, even worse, destructive. And after all, wasn't that the whole point to this liquid lunch?

"You want to know how that makes me feel, Jennifer?" she asked, sitting up tall and confident. "I'll tell you. It hurts. I went out with Harry for ten years. I thought we were going to get married. And then suddenly my whole world collapsed. I wish I could get over it, but I haven't been able to. It still hurts, Jennifer. And it hurts that he loved you more than he ever loved me."

Jennifer stared at Kate, her face growing white. She looked suddenly confused, uncertain, as if she'd stumbled into a country she'd had no idea existed. Backing away, she put a hand to her mouth, then turned and fled.

"That's right, Jennifer," Kate said sarcastically. "Run away when someone speaks the truth. It's so foreign to you, you don't know how to cope with it."

"Too bad she wasn't here to hear you say that," Martha said.

Kate watched her go, then turned to Martha. "You know what?" she asked after a deep breath. "I feel better already."

"Maybe you should have done that a long time ago," Martha said. "It sure sent Jennifer packing."

"Oh, Lord, here comes Harry," Kate said, putting a hand to her head as if a headache were imminent. Her cold was coming on rapidly, making her eyes water and her throat sore. She needed to see Harry the way she needed pleurisy.

"What did you say to Jennifer to upset her so much?" Harry demanded when he reached their table. "Dammit, Kate, are you so spiteful that you couldn't let Jennifer have her day in the sun?"

Kate stared at him, feeling as if she were trapped in a déjà vu. She wondered what Harry would look like with pie in his face. Probably a lot like Jennifer would have.

"Harry," she said tiredly, "get lost."

"Oh, sure," he said snidely, "that's dear old Kate. You'd love to see me and Jennifer slink out of here, wouldn't you? Well, we're not slinking, Kate. We're staying for lunch and the hell with you."

"You're welcome, Harry," she said dryly. "I'm glad I agreed to keep Jake from going to the train last night, too. I'm so happy that you realize what I've done for you. But, please, don't bother to thank me. I know you're grateful to the tips of your tiny little toes."

"Oh," he said, realizing too late that he had Kate to thank for everything suddenly going his way. "Oh. Well, er...thanks, Kate. You were a real sport last night."

She nodded knowingly. "Just like a faithful old dog."

"Yes," Harry said, beaming, "a lot like that!"

"Go away, Harry," Kate said wearily. "Go back to Jennifer and make her feel better."

"Well, I'm going to have my hands full!" he snapped. "Honestly, Kate, I wish you'd be more thoughtful of others' feelings!" With that, he turned on his heel and dashed for the lobby, from which Jennifer's sobs were clearly audible even in the dining room.

"How did you ever put up with him all those years?" Martha asked, shaking her head as she watched him disappear.

"I don't know," Kate said, holding the tissue to her nose because she felt a sneeze coming on. "I must have been out of my mind."

"Well, you're sane now," Martha said affectionately. "You're really so much better off without Harry. You know that, don't you?"

"Yes," Kate said slowly, tracing a pattern on the tablecloth as she tried to articulate her thoughts. "I've known it for quite a while, but there's a lag time between knowing something and accepting it. I knew Harry was a jerk when he left me, but my pride was hurt. I felt like a fool for not being able to see him for what he was. My ego got bruised, and that takes awhile to recuperate from." She sneezed heartily, then groaned. It was here. She had a rotten cold.

"Sounds like you need to take some time for Kate."

"That's why I don't want to see Jake right now," Kate said. "I feel as if I've just emerged from a space capsule after circling the globe for the last four years. I'm back on earth, but I need time to decompress."

"But is not seeing Jake what you really need?" Martha asked. "After all, it wasn't Jake who was playing the stupid games. It was Jennifer and Harry and your mother. Granted, they interfered in your life and have made you miserable, but that's not Jake's fault."

"Maybe I'm just afraid to try again, Martha. I trusted Harry, and look what a fool I was. How do I know Jake Griffin can be trusted any better?"

"I guess you have to give him a chance."

"I don't feel ready to do that. I feel like I've been broken in about five different places. I'm tired, Martha. There's been so much pressure these past four years—emotional and financial and every other kind imaginable. I just need to go find a corner and curl up for a while."

"I understand how you feel, Kate, but sometimes people take time out after they've been hurt and they never get back in. Look at you. It's been four years since Harry dumped you, yet you hadn't dated anyone until Jake came along. I'm sorry, Kate, but that doesn't seem healthy. I think you have to take a chance. Sure, he let you down once, and I'll bet he'll let you down again, but isn't that what relationships are all about?"

Martha frowned thoughtfully. "In fact, I'll bet I wasn't the greatest wife to Tom all those years, but I've been putting all the blame on him. Maybe I'm really the biggest culprit because I wasn't honest with him. I let him think everything was okay when it wasn't."

"Does that mean you're going to try to patch things up with him?"

"No way!" Martha said, laughing. "What? You think I'm crazy? Uh-uh, honey, I just met a great guy named Pete who likes plump women. Tom can go to hell, which is where the fool belongs."

"Good for you!" Kate said. "It's about time you found a nice guy for yourself."

"In fact, if you wouldn't mind..." Martha looked apprehensively at Kate. "Pete told me he was taking the day off today. Maybe I could stop by his place and..."

"And what?" Kate stared up at her partner. From the look on Martha's face, Kate knew what she'd left unsaid. She smiled. "In the middle of the afternoon?"

"Don't knock it until you've tried it!" Martha said, her eyes dancing.

"Lord, listen to her! Take the rest of the day off. And tomorrow, too. I'll manage. You've been managing for me while I've taken time off lately."

"Oh, thanks, Kate!" Martha said, her eyes shining. "I'll be back at work on Monday, ready to cater up a storm, I promise."

"Have a great time."

Martha waved and dashed for the door. Kate sat looking after her wistfully. There was extra energy in Martha's step, and her face was suddenly glowing. Kate smiled to herself and said a small prayer that things would begin to work out for Martha.

As for herself, the way her luck ran, she had about as much chance at future happiness as a turtle had at winning the Kentucky Derby. Sighing, she perused the menu. As long as she was here, she might as well eat lunch.

The waitress came. "Are you ready to order, Miss Cunningham?"

"Yes," she said. "I'll have tuna salad and iced tea and—"

"Oh, Elroy!" a lilting feminine voice said from somewhere close by. Kate frowned. It sounded like her mother. She shook off the depressing thought and continued ordering. "Let's see, I'll have the tuna on whole wheat and—"

"Katie? Is that you?"

She couldn't ignore the voice any longer. Looking up, she stared at her mother and Elroy bearing down on her. Her mother's face was glowing, her eyes were shining, and she was looking at Elroy as if he were the next best thing to Paul Newman.

"Hello, Mother," Kate said. "Hello, Elroy. Nice to see you."

"Katie!" Her mother sat opposite her, her eyes shining. "You'll never guess what?"

Oh, dear. When her mother played guessing games, anything might happen. She sneezed and blew her nose. "Then why don't you tell me," she suggested.

"Elroy has asked me to marry him!"

Kate stared at her mother. Never in her wildest imaginings did she think this would have happened. Her mother and *Elroy?* She'd come up with the idea of matching them up because it was absolutely comical to even consider the two together, but here they were, looking at each other as if they wanted to jump each other's bones.

Kate broke into a huge smile. "Oh, Mother! I'm so happy for you!" She got up and hugged her mother, tears shining in her eyes, then she hugged Elroy, who was beaming even more than Laurel was.

"We're so happy, Kate," Elroy said, taking a seat. "We've decided to have a small ceremony next month. Nothing elaborate, just a few close friends."

"And I'd like you to be my maid of honor," Laurel said, tears shining in her eyes as she looked at Kate.

"Mom, I'd love to be your maid of honor."

"Oh, thank you, Kate," her mother said, taking her daughter's hand. "I know I've made you unhappy so many times with my interfering. I just want to say I'm sorry, Kate. Elroy talked to me quite awhile yesterday and he pointed out that you're a grown woman, fully capable of taking care of herself without my butting in all the time." Her mother searched Kate's eyes. "I just want you to know that if I've interfered, it was because I love you."

"I know that, Mom," Kate said gently, squeezing her mother's hand. "I understand."

"And Elroy made me call Jake Griffin and explain everything and apologize."

Kate gulped. "He what?"

"That's right," Elroy said, nodding decisively, "I told her what she'd done was inexcusable, that she had to stop trying to fix everyone else's lives and start trying to fix her own."

"That's when he asked me to marry him," Laurel said proudly.

"Well, it seems to me marriage is what you need, Laurel," Elroy said, smiling bashfully. "And a good man to love you and begin taking care of you instead of you always trying to take care of everyone but yourself."

"Oh, Kate," Laurel said, her eyes shining, "I'm so happy, darling. Elroy is the kindest man I've ever met. And we have so many similar interests and friends. We feel as if we were made for each other."

Elroy took Laurel's hand and squeezed it. "We were, Laurel," he said gently. "I believe we were."

Kate wanted to cry and laugh all at the same time. "If you don't mind my asking, what did Jake say?"

Her mother hesitated, then shook her head. "Oh, nothing, really," she said brightly. "We had a nice little chat." Laurel frowned thoughtfully. "Then he said something I didn't understand. Something about no wonder you felt the way you did about him, and I told him I thought you really liked him. And he said maybe he should find that out once and for all for himself. And I was about to say something but Elroy was frowning at me and putting a finger to his lips, so I just said yes, maybe he should and I hung up."

"And when was this?" Kate asked.

"Early this morning," Laurel said, then stared at Kate worriedly. "Oh dear. I did do the right thing, didn't I?"

"I'm glad you explained things to him," Kate said. "But I would appreciate it if from now on, you'd follow Elroy's advice and let me take care of my own problems."

"Well, of course I'll let you take care of your own problems, darling," Laurel said, smiling. "When have I ever interfered?"

Kate stared at her mother. Talking to her was a lot like finding out you'd been speaking in English when the other person only understood German. Kate shook her head, as if trying to clear it. "I'm very happy for you, Mother."

Laurel studied her daughter with concerned eyes. "But you're not happy, are you, Kate? I heard Harry got back together with Jennifer. That must be very hard for you, dear."

"No, it's not, Mom. I'm glad they're back together. Harry was never right for me. I was just too foolish to realize it before."

"Not foolish, Kate," Laurel said gently. "Young. And hopeful and in love. There's nothing ever wrong with being young and in love, Katie. I hope you can let all that go now, honey. It's all behind you. What you've got to focus on now is the future."

Kate felt tears well up in her eyes. Reaching out, she hugged Laurel, hugged her with all the love she'd always felt but had never been able to show. It was useless to fight it; her mother would never change. But Kate supposed that didn't matter. All that mattered was that, in spite of everything, she loved her mother and her mother loved her.

"Kate," Laurel said hesitantly, "I know I probably shouldn't say this, but I'm going to anyway. I really think Jake Griffin genuinely cares for you."

Kate went very still. "Oh?"

"Yes..." Laurel brushed a speck off the tablecloth, her face frowning in concentration. "Now I know you don't want me to interfere, and I've promised I won't, but I really think you should give him a chance to—"

"Mother," she said tiredly. "Please."

Elroy cleared his throat. "Now, Laurel, you know what you promised...." He gave her a meaningful look, and Laurel sighed.

"I'm sorry, Kate," she said. "It's just that—"

"Laurel..." Elroy warned.

Laurel lifted her hands, then let them fall helplessly into her lap. "I'm sorry," she said, and her voice carried genuine regret. "I guess I'm programmed."

Watching her, Kate realized how her mother felt. To Laurel, what she did wasn't interference, it was love. She'd never learned that letting go was preferable to holding on for dear life. But she was finally going to have a life of her own now, and focus attention on herself for a change. It wouldn't be easy for her mother, but Kate knew it would be worth it.

"We were all programmed, Mother," she said gently, reaching out and taking her hand. "But we need to learn new roles. We need to grow up, not just grow old."

Her mother held on to Kate's hand, squeezing it so hard that Kate winced. Then slowly, agonizingly, Laurel let go.

Chapter Sixteen

Back at Lilac Hedges Caterers, everything was too quiet. Without Martha's usual jokes and laughter, the office seemed like a mausoleum. Kate sat and stared out the window at the roses with their fat buds almost ready to burst into bloom. The lilacs had already faded. When she was a young girl, she had told herself that God gave the world roses in June to make up for the loss of the lilacs in May.

Sighing, she pulled a box of tissues toward her and began making notes about the party she would do for Jake. They still had to discuss the menu, but she wanted to do a picnic with old-fashioned homey food without resorting to the usual fare. She wanted food with heart to it, the kind of food that had made this country the bread basket of the world, food that spelled home and love and comfort and security, not money or status or class or social climbing. Litchfield County had enough of that already.

So there would be Long Island duck and steaks on the grill, an old-fashioned clambake, boiled lobsters dripping with melted butter, corn on the cob, Boston baked beans, potato salad and tossed salad and sourdough rolls and French bread. There would be iced tea and lemonade and cans of beer and soda. It would be, Kate decided, a showcase of New England home-cooked foods.

Now she just had to convince Jake that's what it would be. She made a list of ingredients she'd need, jotted down notes about the utensils and pots and pans she'd use, then typed the proposed menu neatly along with a short, businesslike note to Jake, and inserted everything in an envelope. She couldn't bear the thought of facing him in person. Thank heavens for the U.S. Post Office.

SHE WAS UP to her elbows in flour, rolling out pastry crust, when the door to the shop opened and a delivery boy came in bearing a huge arrangement of lilacs in a crystal vase.

"Flowers for Miss Kate Cunningham," he called out cheerfully.

"I'm Kate Cunningham," she rasped. Her eyes fastened on the lilacs and she felt a rush of feeling. They were magnificent—a massive arrangement of her beloved lavender lilacs in a tall cut-glass vase. But who would be sending them to her? No one knew how much she loved lilacs. Except—

She stared at the flowers and felt a faint stirring of hope. Jake knew how much she loved lilacs. She shook the thought away and smiled at the delivery boy. "They're beautiful. I hadn't realized florists made arrangements of lilacs. I thought you had to get them the old-fashioned way—go out and pick them."

"Well, ordinarily we don't. Lilacs aren't the sort of flowers most florists carry, but this man came in carrying these he'd flown all the way to Vermont to pick, and he asked us to arrange them in the most beautiful vase we had and then deliver them, so here they are, ma'am, with our compliments."

Kate looked at the envelope tucked among the blossoms. Her heart was pumping as if she'd just run a marathon. She was afraid to read the card, afraid she'd be disappointed and find out they hadn't come from Jake.

She slipped the delivery boy an ample tip, smiled at his beaming face, then reached for the card with shaking fingers. She stared down at it, excited and nervous at the same time.

"Oh, don't be silly, Kate," she chastised herself, and ripped open the envelope.

As she read the card her heart seemed to stop, then it raced on.

Kate,
I tried for hours to find the right words, and had to resort to Shakespeare. He said it much better than I ever could: "She's beautiful and therefore to be woo'd; She is woman, therefore to be won." I don't want to lose you, Kate. Let's keep trying. No one ever gets it right the first time, do they?

Love, Jake

Tears sprang into her eyes. She pressed the card to her breast and inhaled the heavenly fragrance of her beloved lilacs, and it almost made up for the fact that her head was splitting, her throat raspy and her nose cherry red. No one in her life had ever taken the time to find out what she loved, then given it to her with only one object in mind—to please her.

She sat down and gazed at the words, reading them over and over, seeing one particular sentence as if it were highlighted and outlined in gold leaf: No one ever gets it right the first time, do they?

Perhaps not, but she had wanted to. She had grown up with one idea in mind—to be Harry Grenville's wife, to bear his children, to golf with him at the country club and entertain his business clients. She'd had it all worked out, and then life had slipped her a curveball.

She felt as if she'd been buffeted about by hurricane-force winds when her father died and Harry broke their engagement. For the past four years she'd spent all her energy making sure her harbor was safe, all the boats moored tightly, hatches battened down. And then along came Jake Griffin, trying to smash every fortress she'd built against storms.

It was then she realized she was very much like her mother, trying to control events lest they overwhelm her. She sat there and tried to digest the thought, but it was particularly unappetizing to find the thing she liked least in her mother present in herself.

"Like mother, like daughter," she said out loud, and almost wanted to laugh.

Life played such good jokes on people. It humbled the exalted, and supposedly exalted the humble, but in her experience, she had yet to be exalted, perhaps because she had yet to become humble. Her pride was such a problem—her massive, uncontrollable, fervent, stinging pride. She sat at her desk and felt befuddled, incompetent and foolish.

Perhaps that, she thought wryly, was the beginning of humility.

She looked at the pile of pastry on the butcher block. Then she sneezed. She groaned and blew her nose, washed her hands and went back to the pastry. Kneading pastry or bread dough had always comforted her, but suddenly there was no comfort in the rhythmic chore.

Jake's question nagged at her: No one ever gets it right the first time, do they?

If he were here, she'd shout at him to be quiet. But he wasn't here. It was his image she fought, the memory of his eyes laughing into hers, his gentle voice, the way it had felt to wake up with him in his big bed in the morning.

She found herself smiling at the memory, laughing out loud at the way he'd asked her to marry him on only their second date. That had been absurd, preposterous, ridiculous in the extreme. But that was Jake—quick to decide, impulsive, already talking about babies when most men only wanted sex.

Stunned, she raised her eyes and stared unseeingly into the distance. Most men only wanted sex. For no reason, she remembered a snippet of a conversation with Harry that had been repeated over and over throughout the ten years they'd dated. It had always gone something like this:

Kate: "Harry, don't you want kids?"

Harry: "Of course, dear, but later."

Kate: "But we've been dating a year (two years, five years, ten years—choose one and fill in blank)."

Harry: "Honey, let's not talk about it now, hmm? Come here and cuddle up with me. That a new nightie? It's pretty, Kate . . . really pretty."

Kate struggling to get his hands off her breasts: "But, Harry, I think we should set the date for our wedding."

Harry: "Let's not talk about that right now. Let's go to bed. Tomorrow we can set a date for our wedding."

But tomorrow had never come, at least not for Harry. And Kate, ever hopeful, had let him string her along, put off by a series of ingenious excuses he manufactured with seeming ease:

"I'm just graduating from law school. Let me get my practice established first."

"Honey, I've got a really big case right now. If I win it, I'll be made a junior partner. When that happens, we'll get married."

"Kate, for crying out loud, I'm a partner in a law firm! I'm busy! We'll set a date for the wedding later, when things calm down a little."

Kate sneezed, and came back to reality. She'd just been on a short but bumpy ride. She had never before allowed herself to realize fully just what a fool she'd been about Harry Grenville. Most women would have dumped him, but not Kate. Good old Kate had stuck by her man, through thick and through thin, in good times and bad, believing him when he'd told her he'd marry her someday.

And here was Jake Griffin, almost begging her for a second chance, and she was standing around kneading dough.

"Fish or cut bait, Kate," she said to herself out loud.

She stared at the piecrust dough. If only major decisions were easy, clear-cut, simple. Why couldn't she look into the future and know what was going to happen? Why couldn't she call up Jake and gush about the lilacs so that he'd show up and sweep her into his arms and everything would be just fine? It happened that way in books; why not in real life?

She wanted to call him, but she didn't want to. She wanted to resolve all her doubts and rush to Jake and walk hand in hand into the sunset, but she couldn't quite bring herself to do it.

Sighing, she fretted. She kneaded the dough, punched it, cursed at it, turning the air purple with her words. At last, angry, frustrated and out of sorts, she made a mad dash for the phone.

Dammit, she didn't know what she'd say to him, but at least she was calling!

"Jake?" she said when he answered. "It's Kate."

His voice was so sexy it sounded like cream oozing over fresh strawberries. "This is promising," he said. "She's calling me. This is very promising indeed."

She felt a spurt of irritation. How dare he assume she'd just fall into his lap? She might have, but she wouldn't now, not when he sounded so confident.

"I called about the party you want me to cater," she said.

"Oh." There was a pause. "And here I thought you were calling about the flowers I sent you."

She felt a sting of regret at her obstinacy, but shrugged it off. "I was going to get to them later."

"When? Next year?"

"What's your rush?" she asked. "We've got business to conduct. I wrote you a note enclosing the menu I've come up with for the party, but—"

"Didn't you like them?" he interrupted.

"Didn't I like what?"

"The flowers."

She considered what to say. She decided she'd choose a schoolmarmish tone to convey the right mood—interested, but with reservations. "They're only a beginning, Jake," she said carefully. "The appetizer, so to speak."

"And here I was already thinking about marriage, but that's sort of like the main course, isn't it?"

Her heart began bumping along in her chest like a spirited filly. "It's a little early to be considering marriage, Jake," she said reprovingly.

"What would you rather consider?"

"I told you once—I want to be courted, wooed, chased after. The lilacs are a wonderful start, but that's all they are."

He sighed. "You're not going to make this easy on me, are you?"

"No." She smiled in spite of herself. "You wouldn't want me if I did."

"Sure I would, but what the heck, you want to be courted? I'll court you. How about I send over a band of roving troubadours to play guitars outside your window tonight?"

"You do and I'll brain you with one of the guitars. Martha's taking some time off and I have a party to cater tonight. On top of that, I'm catching a rotten cold. When I finish here, I'm going home and hit the sack. No interruptions, Jake, no noise, no candlelight dinners, no seductive scene, just bed—alone—and some much-needed sleep."

"Sounds boring."

She shrugged. "That's the life of a caterer."

"So who caters to you, Kate?" he asked.

His question stumped her, and her silence must have reached him.

"Kate," he said gently, "stop fighting me. Let me come over to your place tonight and take care of you. I'll draw you a hot bath and give you a massage and make you a cup of hot tea and feed you warm blueberry muffins. Wouldn't that be nice?"

Despite her resolve to hold him off, she found herself melting. Then she rallied. "No, I'd really rather just go home and hit the bed alone. Call me when you get my note about the party. We can talk about it then."

She hung up, then tore at her hair. "You fool! You imbecile! He would have given you a massage and drawn you a hot bath!"

"Who would have, dear?"

Startled, Kate whirled around to find her mother standing in the doorway. "Mother! You scared the life out of me!"

"Well, small wonder," Laurel said, closing the door and advancing toward her daughter. "You were talking to yourself, dear. It's serious when you start talking to yourself. I know, I've been doing it a couple years now."

Kate stared at her mother. If she didn't know better, she'd think she was developing a sense of humor. "What do you want, Mother? I'm harassed up to my eyeballs. I've got a party to do tonight and I've got a rotten cold."

"I thought you were looking a little peaked at lunch. That's why I stopped by." Laurel tilted her head consideringly. "Who were you talking to when I came in?"

"Myself."

"No, silly, I meant on the phone."

"Oh." Kate shrugged, trying to sound offhanded. She didn't want her mother getting on the scent of this thing with Jake; she'd be worse than a bloodhound after quail. "Jake Griffin," she said reluctantly.

Laurel's eyes widened. "*He's* the one who would have given you a massage and drawn you a hot bath? Why did you refuse? You don't just throw away these kinds of opportunities, you know. Didn't I teach you *anything?*"

Kate rolled her eyes. Here it was—the full frontal attack she'd come to know and not love. She sneezed, then blew her nose. "Mother, it's not a big deal. Honestly. We've only been out a couple times."

"So what? It was on our third date that Elroy asked me to marry him."

"Well, that's one more than Jake Griffin needed," Kate said breezily.

"You mean he's asked you to marry him and you've refused?" Laurel blinked, as if looking at a rare specimen of flora.

"Yes," Kate said, "I refused. Take it or leave it, Mother, I'm still your incorrigible daughter."

"And I'm still your interfering mother," Laurel said. "Call him right back. Tell him you'll see him tonight. When the bull enters your yard, darling, take him right by the horns."

"What do I do when the bull's my mother?" Kate asked sharply, her hands on her hips.

Laurel blinked. "What do you mean?"

"Mother, you just got finished telling me you'd stop interfering in my life, and here you are, just like taxes on April fifteenth. I can't stand it anymore! I'm livid! Leave. Me. Alone." Kate blinked. It felt good to yell, so she added, even louder, "Forever!"

"All right," Laurel said, lifting her chin haughtily, "I'll not talk to you again about it. You can just make a mess of your life if you want. I'm wiping my hands of you. You can just—" Laurel was shaking she was so angry "—you can just stew in your own juices, to use one of those horrible cooking references you like so much."

She turned and stomped out of the shop, slamming the door after her. Kate put a hand to her head. Good lord, was there never to be any peace?

AT NINE-THIRTY, Kate pulled into her driveway. She was beat. Her cold had blossomed into what felt like walking pneumonia. She sat dispiritedly in the car and stared at the sidewalk that led to the front door. It was much too great a distance to navigate. Maybe she should just sit here in the car and let her eyelids close the way they wanted to. She could sleep for hours, even if her head landed on the car's horn and it honked all night.

Then she spied a light on in the house. Dammit, if she didn't stop leaving lights on, her electric bill was going to be as big as Con Edison itself. Groaning, she opened the car door and eased her weary body out of the car. Feeling like a damp rag, she shuffled toward the front door. When she put her foot on the first porch step, three strolling guitar players stepped out of the darkness and began to serenade her.

"*Vaya con dios,* my darling," they sang in hokey Hispanic-sounding voices. "*Vaya con dios,* my dear."

They wore ridiculous black velvet suits with skintight pants and absurd little vests that were covered with sequins and scarlet braided trim. On their heads were mammoth sombreros. They looked as if they'd just stepped out of a Cisco Kid television episode. Unfortunately they sounded that way, too.

Kate leaned against the porch railing and wiped her brow. Jake's hand was so evident in all this, his fingerprints would probably be all over her house.

"Okay, guys," she said wearily, "fun's over. Run along home now. The maiden is distressed."

The men smiled and kept on playing, making a professional segue into what sounded like a Mexican hat-dance tune. All it needed was castanets and she'd be in Acapulco. Kate cast a furtive eye toward her nearest neighbor's house. She saw a shade pulled aside and could just imagine old Mr. Renfrew's shaggy gray eyebrows rising over startled beady eyes. Any minute he'd be over here threatening to call the police.

She was about to shoo the singers away when the front door opened and Jake appeared.

"You're home," he said.

"And you're not," she said flatly, puffy red eyes blazing at him. "Who are these buttonholes? Is this your idea of a joke?"

"You're angry," he said, taking her hand and signaling the men to leave. "And here I thought you had such a great sense of humor."

"Not when I'm sick," she said, quivering with rage.

"Run along now, boys," Jake said, waving the men away. "Come on, darling, let Jake take care of you."

She let him lead her into the house because that's where she wanted to go anyway and she didn't have any more strength to fight. Everything drained out of her the way water runs out of a bathtub.

"Okay," she said, exhausted beyond belief, "you've had your little joke. You can leave now."

"Not just yet," Jake said gently, and came up behind her and placed his hands on her shoulders near her neck. He began kneading her tight muscles. "That's it," he crooned. "Relax."

She went limp. Jake caught her just in time and carried her upstairs. She managed to open her eyes to see that her bed was turned down, made up with fresh, snowy-white sheets. There were at least a couple dozen pink roses in a vase on the bedside table, and the lights were turned down low. A quiet, calming symphony played on the sound system. There was a silver tray by the bed and two china teacups set out beside a silver sugar bowl and cream pitcher.

"What's this?" she asked when he set her down on the bed.

"Hot tea," he said, easing her blouse off her shoulders. "But let's get you into the tub first. I'll pour you tea when you're feeling better."

"I get it," she said. "I died and went to heaven."

"No," he said, grinning, "you got sick and came home to me."

She heaved herself up on her feet and reached up and put her arms around his neck. "You dear man," she whispered, clinging to him. "You dear, wonderful man." Tears glittered in her eyes. "Thanks for not listening to me. Thanks for being here, for all this, everything...."

"Hush," he whispered, and picked her up and carried her into the bathroom. The tub was filled with bubble bath. Even through her clogged nose she caught the scent of roses.

Incoherently she turned to him, pressing her head into his neck. "Thank you," she whispered. "With this cold, I felt like warmed-over mush all afternoon. The dinner party went crummy. It was a total disaster. I couldn't smell anything and oversalted the food. I've probably lost a client. All I wanted to do was come home and drop."

"This too will pass," he said gently, easing her out of her clothes. He helped her into the bath. When she sank into the hot water, she let out a moan of pure pleasure. She began to make little whimpering sounds, like a puppy chewing on its first bone.

"I've changed my mind," Jake said when she was relaxed and lolling in the tub, sipping a cup of hot tea and sniffling into a series of tissues.

"You've changed your mind about what?" Kate asked morosely, then groaned when she sneezed so violently she sloshed water all over the bathroom.

He took the cup and placed it on the sink. "About the party you're going to cater for me."

She fixed him with eyes that would have been murderous if they weren't so red. "After all this time, you're not going to give it?"

"Oh, no, I'm still going to give it, but I don't want a picnic anymore."

She sighed philosophically. "Okay, what do you want now?"

"Something more formal—still outside, with a big blue-and-white-striped tent for the guests in case it rains, but instead of being early in the afternoon, it'll be a little later, with white linen tablecloths, elegant china and sterling silver, the best crystal, roses in silver bowls—the whole nine yards."

"It sounds more like a wedding than an open house."

He took her hands. "Marry me and it could be our reception."

"Forget it, Jake," she said sourly. "Now is not the time to propose marriage. I feel about as matrimonial, if that's a word, as a waterlogged porpoise."

He leaned over and kissed her on the forehead. "If it's any comfort, you're lovely with a red, stuffed-up nose and a voice as low as a foghorn."

She pushed him away. "Careful, you'll catch this thing and it feels deadly."

"I'm charmed," he said, grinning. "Men in love always are."

She stared at him. "What?"

"You heard me."

"I'm not sure I did. My ears are blocked."

"I said," he shouted, "men in love don't catch colds! They're charmed!"

She didn't know what to say. What did you say to a man who insisted on asking you to marry him on only the second date? And who crept into your house when you were sick and went to all kinds of trouble to make himself indispensable?

"Just get me out of here," she said, pushing any response out of her mind. She couldn't deal with proposals of marriage right now; she had more pressing things to deal with—like incipient pneumonia.

Jake lifted her from the tub, toweled her dry, put a fresh, snowy-white nightie over her head and carried her back to the bedroom.

"A cup of hot tea, madam?" he said, smiling down at her as she lay propped up on the pillows.

Her eyelids lowered, then fluttered open. "No thanks," she whispered. "I'm so sleepy." She yawned heartily, then her eyes flew open. "Jake!" She sat bolt upright.

"What's wrong?"

"How'd you get in my house?"

"Oh, your mother gave me her key."

"My mother!" She didn't know what to do. She was crazed, driven beyond her limits, shaking and frustrated and helpless all at once. She felt like the Wrath of Khan—she could have eaten up the bed, destroyed all the furniture in the entire house, gone on a rampage that would have made a tornado look like a gentle breeze.

Instead she flopped back down on the bed. There was no escaping Laurel Cunningham. Like an oil slick on the ocean, she was everywhere. Heartsick, Kate stared at the ceiling. Her world was a prison. She had no freedom of choice, she couldn't make her own decisions, couldn't map out her own course. Her mother was always ahead of her, steering her like a ship.

She looked up at Jake. "You better leave now, Jake. You might catch this thing and it's a doozy."

He began unbuttoning his shirt. Astonished, she stared up at him. "What are you doing?"

"I'm going to stay with you tonight," he said, smiling.

"Oh no, you're not!" she shouted, sitting up and pointing toward the door. "Get out! Now!"

"Kate, be reasonable. You're sick."

"And I can take care of myself," she said with a shaking voice. "Now, leave, before I throw you out myself."

"Kate—" Jake stared at her, frowning. "What's the matter? You've gone berserk on me."

"It's my mother!" she said, lifting her hands helplessly. "The minute you mentioned her, you were doomed, Jake. She's driving me crazy. She interferes, manipulates, controls, she makes plans for me and tells me how she wants things done, she steps in right when I'm trying to do something. It's horrible, Jake. She's like a force from hell!"

"So when you rebel against me," Jake said gently, "it's not really me you're rebelling against, it's your mother."

She lifted sorrowful eyes, nodding dully. "I suppose so. I don't know. All I know is, I've got to make my own decisions. I've got to call the shots, Jake, not have someone call them for me."

"But, Kate, what your mother wants doesn't have anything to do with us," Jake said reasonably.

"Of course it does!" Kate cried. "She came running into the Letterers' kitchen the other night telling me she'd found the perfect man for me. Do you know who it was?"

Jake shook his head.

"You!" she shouted, then dropped her head in her hands. "Don't you see? My mother picked you out for me! Do you know how that makes me *feel?* Like I want to kick you halfway to Chicago!"

"Kate," he said, sitting on the edge of the bed and taking her hand in his. "I don't have a damn thing to do with your mother. I wanted you the first time I saw you. Just like that—I saw you and loved you. Thud. Boom. Crash. I didn't know who you were, didn't know your name, didn't know a thing about you. All I knew was I wanted you. Forever. I know it's illogical. Hell, maybe it's even crazy, but it's the truth. Kate, your mother didn't choose me for you, I chose you for myself!"

"But I haven't chosen you!" Kate shouted, then took a shaky breath. She felt calmer suddenly, more in control. She stared into Jake's eyes, determined. "Please leave, Jake. Until I know what I want for myself, I don't want you around."

"Aw, Kate, I just want to be with you. You're sick. Let me stay and take care of you. I just want to hold you."

"Jake!" she said exasperatedly. "I have a cold!"

"So?" He shrugged. "These things happen." He patted the pillows. "Come on, sweetheart, lie down."

She refused to budge. "Harry never stayed with me when I was sick," she said stubbornly.

"Harry was an ass."

She considered that. "You're right," she said.

"So I can stay?"

She folded her arms. "Not tonight. Please, Jake, humor me on this."

He shook his head as if exasperated at her, but he stood up. "Okay, I'll leave."

"And leave my mother's key with me, please," she said coolly. "I don't want her to have it, and I don't want you to, either."

Quietly Jake took the key out of his pocket and placed it on the bedside table. He met her stormy gaze, then lifted his shoulders in a shrug. "You'll know where I am when you want to call," he said, walking toward the door.

"*If* I want to call," she corrected him obstinately.

At the door, he turned to look back at her. "You are a very stubborn woman, Kate."

She nodded. "Yes, I am. You might think about that awhile, Jake. This is how I am. Could you live with that?"

He looked at her thoughtfully, then turned and opened the door. "I guess we both need to think about a few things."

"I guess we do."

He shut the door and she felt her heart fall. But she couldn't go after him. She wouldn't relent. This was too important. She lay down and drew the freshly laundered sheets up to her chin and felt tears begin to trickle down her face. She was stubborn and perhaps even foolish, and she wished sometimes she wasn't, but this was who she was. Like it or not, she'd had to do what she'd just done.

Sighing, she turned on her side. Her throat was raw. Her sinuses were full, her nose clogged. Great. It was another wonderful day in the full and glorious life of Kate Cunningham, part owner of Lilac Hedges Caterers and mistress of her own fate.

Chapter Seventeen

Kate threw herself into her work. Her anger was a powerful source of energy. She whizzed when others dragged, sailed when others lagged. She was a rocket, a power surge, the next best thing to a nuclear reactor.

"Kate," Martha said a week later, "why don't you slow down? I can't keep up with you."

"Comes from too much lovemaking," Kate said tartly, eyeing Martha pointedly. "You can't burn the candle at both ends, my dear, without feeling the result. Not when you're our age."

"You're jealous!" Martha grinned. "Why don't you just give in, Kate, and tell Jake Griffin you'll marry him?"

"If I decide I want to marry him, I will," Kate said shortly. "Until then, leave me alone."

"It's these damn flowers!" Martha moaned. The shop was full of them—roses, mums, petunias and daisies. Every day Jake sent Kate a bigger bouquet. Every day Kate refused to talk to him when he called. They were at a standoff—Jake was determined to wear her down, and Kate was equally determined to resist.

"So refuse to accept the next batch," Kate said offhandedly. "I could care less about the damn things."

Martha put her hands on her hips. "You're impossible, Kate."

Kate smiled. "I know, and I love it."

"You're going to lose him if you're not careful," Martha warned.

Kate shrugged. "That's my business, isn't it?"

Martha gave up. Nothing worked. Kate was obdurate; she would go to her grave this way, she proclaimed, as long as she got to call the shots.

"ALL RIGHT," Laurel Cunningham said one day a week later, "this has got to stop!"

Kate looked up from her desk, peering over the new horn-rimmed glasses she was wearing. Her headaches, it turned out, had been the result of needing glasses. Now, even when her mother was at her bossiest, Kate's head stayed cool.

"What has, Mother?" she said. "If I listened to you the way you listen to me, nothing would change."

"You are ruining your life out of spite for me," Laurel said angrily, "and I won't have it!"

Kate threw down her pen. "Tough."

"Ohhhh, you drive me mad!" Laurel said, clenching her hands. "You willful, headstrong, *stubborn* girl!"

Kate picked up her pen and went back to writing out a menu. "So when's the wedding, Mother? You haven't even told me, and I thought I was supposed to be the maid of honor."

"Put that damn pen down and I will tell you," her mother said coldly.

There was something new in Laurel's tone, some undercurrent of anger that had never been there before. Kate swiveled around slowly, a sly smile on her face. "I'm getting to you, aren't I? You know how? By using your tactics. I never listen to you anymore. Doesn't it just drive you mad? Doesn't it make you want to kill me?"

Laurel stared at her daughter, two patches of red in her otherwise perfectly made-up cheeks. "Has it really been like this for you?"

Kate nodded. "All my life."

Laurel sighed. "It must have been pure hell." She sighed and picked an imaginary piece of lint off her suit. "The past couple of weeks have been for me, that's for sure."

Kate's eyes softened. "You should be happy, Mother. You're getting married."

"But I want you to get married, too," she said in a small, almost childish voice. "Dammit, Kate, I can't stand to be happy when you're not."

"Mother!" Kate said wonderingly. "You swore!"

"Yes, I did. I'm doing a lot of strange things lately." She choked on a laugh. "I even found myself laughing at myself the other day. Can you believe it?" She dabbed at a tear that crept from her eye. "Me? With a sense of humor? It's what you've wished for all your life, and here it is and you won't even talk to me so you can enjoy it."

Kate reached out and drew her mother into her arms. "I love you, Mom."

"Oh, Katie," Laurel said, squeezing her eyes shut, "and I love you. So very much, darling. I'm sorry. I must have been a terrible mother."

Kate shook her head. "Never," she said softly, hugging her mother. "You're a wonderful mother."

"How can you say that? I drive you crazy—you tell everyone I do, even Jake."

"I love you. You are my own wonderful mother, faults and all."

Laurel drew back, searching her daughter's face. "I don't think I understand. You really mean it? You're not just humoring me?"

Kate shrugged. "I mean it. I wouldn't humor you if I could."

"Oh, Kate, please stop fighting with Jake. He loves you, Katie. He's crazy about you."

"Let us work that out, Mom."

Laurel took a deep breath. "Well, maybe you can when you see him on Saturday."

"At his picnic, you mean?"

"No, at my wedding," Laurel said matter-of-factly.

Confused, Kate stared at her mother. "But Saturday is Jake's party. How can I cater that and be your maid of honor, too?"

"Well, it should be relatively simple," Laurel said, looking uncomfortable despite her words. "You see, dear, Elroy and I are getting married at Spindrift."

"Spindrift?" She stared at her mother, unable to assemble this new piece of knowledge.

"In the beginning, Jake was hoping it could be a double ceremony," Laurel said, "but I guess your refusal to even speak to him except about business has put the kibosh on that idea! So, we'll have a simple ceremony and that will be that."

"But...why?" Kate stared, frown lines creasing her forehead. "Mother, it's Jake's place now. It's not yours anymore, or your family's or even mine. It's Jake's."

"The day I saw you at the restaurant with Elroy, when I told you we were getting married, when I'd spoken to Jake on the phone that morning?" Kate nodded and Laurel went on. "I told him then that Elroy and I were getting married, and he was pleasant and asked where the ceremony would be. I was just chattering on and on, not making sense as usual, I suppose, and I said the Tracy women always got married at Spindrift. It just sort of came out, and then of course I was terribly embarrassed. But Jake was such a dear, so understanding and kind. He said he'd found out recently that Spindrift was my family home and he said, in that lovely gentle way he has, why didn't I continue the tradition? And then he said, 'And if your daughter will have me, maybe we can make it a double ceremony.'"

Everything suddenly became clear. Kate sat back and digested this news and saw everything that had happened in the past two weeks in a new light. No wonder she was driving them mad! She was spoiling everything—except she hadn't known.

"It would have been much simpler if Jake and you had just told me," she said. "Can you see that now?"

Laurel nodded miserably. "Yes, I know. We were both so taken with the idea that we never even gave it a thought that you might not be."

"I like to be in on the major decisions in my life," Kate said wryly. "It's a quirk I have."

"Jake realized it before I did, what we'd done. He understands now how important making your own decisions is. That's why he continues to send you these ridiculous flowers. He said he'd send the damn things till he wore you down and you called him on something other than business."

Kate sighed. "He could have just called me himself."

"I'm afraid you haven't been very receptive, Katie. But maybe you can change that before Saturday."

Kate laughed and sat back. "Don't push it, Mom."

Laurel kissed her, then stood up. "Okay, I won't. I'll see you at the wedding."

"There's no rehearsal Friday night, no dinner?" Kate asked.

"No. I've been married before, and Elroy says he doesn't need to rehearse, he's been getting ready for this all his life." Laurel laughed. "He is *such* a nice man! And to think he's been right there under my nose all those years."

"Well, I'm glad I had the idea of getting you two together," Kate said, laughing.

"*You* had the idea?"

"Why, yes," Kate said casually. "I guess you didn't realize that. Martha put a bug in your ear the same day she put one in Elroy's."

Astounded, Laurel sat back down abruptly. She stared at Kate, then slowly she began to laugh. "Well, I'll be damned! You paid me back, didn't you? You little devil!"

Kate's smile grew until she was laughing with her mother. Martha heard them in the back room and stuck her head around the door. "What's going on? Are you two actually *laughing?*"

"Would you believe it?" Kate said, wiping tears from her eyes. "Mom just found out whose idea it was to fix her up with Elroy."

A slow grin grew on Martha's face. "I'm glad you can laugh about it, Mrs. Cunningham."

Astonished, Laurel stared at Martha. "So am I, dear. So am I. . . ."

"Maybe this is as good a time as any for my announcement," Martha said.

"Your announcement?" Kate echoed.

Martha held out her hand. "I'm engaged."

Kate shot out of her chair and raced to her partner. Laurel hugged Martha and congratulated her.

"Let me see!" Kate shrieked, laughing and hugging Martha and gaping at her ring all at the same time. "It's beautiful! I'm so happy for you! It's so soon!"

"What can I say? There've been a rash of hasty engagements going around, so we figured we might as well jump on the bandwagon." Martha grinned. "Also, I thought maybe you needed some encouragement, Katie. I'm sick of seeing all these damn flowers cluttering up the shop. Maybe if you see your mother and me getting married, you'll find out it's not so bad as you think it'll be."

Kate hugged her friend and partner. "I'm happy for you, Martha," she said softly. "My very best wishes to you and Pete. He's a sweetheart."

"And you and Jake?" Martha asked.

Kate stepped back. "Let's just leave that subject, shall we?"

Martha met Laurel's eyes over Kate's head. "You're still holding out, eh?"

"Still holding out," Kate said brightly. "Sorry if that bothers everyone."

"I just feel bad for Jake," Martha said. "He's the one who's bearing the brunt of all this."

"What do you mean?"

"You don't think this is hard on him? He doesn't have any idea where he stands with you, Kate."

"Sure he does," Kate said airily. "He's in the doghouse and he knows it."

"And you're just going to leave him there?"

"For a while," Kate said, then turned away. "Don't worry, Martha. Things will turn out okay."

"I wish I could be so sure," Martha said darkly.

"You and me both," Laurel chimed in.

At her desk, Kate sat and picked up her pen. Outwardly she might appear serene and confident, but inside she was as uncertain as her partner and mother. What was she doing? Why was she holding out?

Sighing, Kate pushed the questions from her mind. She'd deal with Jake when the time was right. Just now, she had work to do.

KATE WAS ABOUT to lock up the shop late that afternoon when she found Jennifer Grenville standing in the doorway.

"Jennifer," she said, surprised. "Is something wrong?"

"There always has been between us," Jennifer said. "Hasn't there?"

Kate shrugged. "It's always seemed that way."

Jennifer sighed and closed the door behind her. "I hoped I'd find you alone."

"Why?" Kate asked wryly. "Did you bring a gun? Are you going to do away with me altogether now?"

Jennifer didn't bother to reply. She stared at Kate, then walked slowly toward her. "I came because I wanted to say something."

"Say it," Kate said shortly, "then kindly leave."

"I guess I deserve that."

"I know you do."

Jennifer took a deep breath. "I've hated you all my life, Kate Cunningham—until the other day."

"What happened then?" Kate quipped. "Did hate turn to outright loathing?"

"You've always been so quick," Jennifer said. "So witty and sharp. I'll never forget the first time I saw you. My mother had just dropped me off at kindergarten on the very first day. I was scared, but she told me to stop being a baby. She pointed to you and said, 'Look at that pretty little girl! She's not crying. Why can't you be more like her, Jennifer?'"

Kate stared at Jennifer, feeling a lump grow in her throat.

"All my life," Jennifer whispered, tears in her eyes, "I've wanted to be like you. I've hated you, Kate. I've been so jealous of everything you do, of what you are. You were always smarter than me and prettier and more popular. No matter how hard I tried, I could never measure up to you. Never. Until the other day."

Kate swallowed thickly. "What happened?" She knew, or thought she did, but she knew Jennifer needed to tell her.

"You weren't quick and you weren't funny anymore. You were hurt. And you let me see it. It stunned me. I felt as if I'd been slapped across the face. You weren't this perfect person, always doing everything right and happy all the time. You were unhappy, too, maybe even unhappier than me."

Kate nodded. "And even a little jealous—of you."

Jennifer lowered her gaze. "All of a sudden, you didn't seem to matter as much. You lost your power over me, Kate."

"I never wanted it even if I had it," Kate said.

"I realize that now. I wanted to say I was sorry." Jennifer shrugged. "For everything. All the years. All the stuff..."

"Thank you," Kate said softly. "That means a lot."

Jennifer lifted her gaze and met Kate's eyes evenly. "I love him, Kate. He's not the stuff heroes are made of, but I love him."

Kate smiled. "He loves you, too."

For the first time, Jennifer smiled. She was radiantly beautiful. "I know. It's incredible. I feel as if I've awakened from a bad dream. You wouldn't understand that, I'm sure, but that's how it feels."

"Oh, I think I know how you feel," Kate said. "I've been discovering a lot of things for myself lately, too."

"Ha," Jennifer said knowingly. "You've never done anything wrong. You just don't make mistakes." Then she grinned. "Except for Harry."

"Yeah," Kate said softly, smiling. "Except for Harry..."

Chapter Eighteen

When God created Connecticut, he got everything right but the weather. Mark Twain had made a joke about it, saying, "If you don't like Connecticut's weather, wait a minute."

To say the weather was fickle was putting it mildly. Yet the entire week leading up to the day of the wedding—Jake's "party"—had been perfect: mild, sunny days, crisp nights, blue skies dotted with white clouds, mountain laurel and rhododendron massed with blossoms, roses growing riotously in gardens across the state. The weathermen were delirious, as if they themselves could take credit for the incredible week.

Saturday, though, was a disaster. The day dawned hot and muggy, with high humidity and the ominous threat of late-afternoon thunderstorms.

"Thank goodness Jake ordered a tent," Kate said as she supervised the final decorations on the wedding cake. There would be only one hundred guests—all old friends of the family and a few relatives.

Kate wiped perspiration from her forehead and ordered more ice. "This damn cake will melt if it sits out in this weather very long," she muttered to Martha.

"So we'll keep it in the refrigerated truck till the last possible moment."

Kate nodded and sighed. "I can't believe my mother is actually getting married and I'm not only catering it, I'm her maid of honor."

"Is your dress ready?" Martha asked, looking up from the shrimp toast triangles.

"It's home waiting for me. Which reminds me," Kate said, glancing hurriedly at her watch, "can you take care of everything while I change?"

"Piece of cake," Martha said, grinning.

Kate smiled. "This is fun, isn't it? You know, I remember when Dad died and I found out he'd just declared bankruptcy. Out of all my friends, you were the only one who was really there for me. Then good old Harry dropped me and I thought I'd been hit by a ten-ton truck."

"And I suggested we start this business," Martha finished for her.

"Thank God you did," Kate said fervently. "I don't know what I'd do without it sometimes. Or you." She smiled mistily. "I'm so happy for you and Pete," she murmured. "He's really terrific."

"So's Jake Griffin, if you'd give him a chance," Martha said breezily.

Kate didn't respond. She stared at the bride and groom on the top of the wedding cake. She could have been getting married today, too. Hadn't Jake said that this party could be their reception if only she'd marry him?

She smoothed a hand over her stomach. She couldn't put it off any longer. The time had finally come to talk to Jake.

SPINDRIFT had never looked lovelier. The grounds were manicured, the shrubs clipped, the gravel in the driveway combed like the hair of a child about to receive First Communion.

In the kitchen, young waitresses raced around in white uniforms and pink aprons, flowers festooning their hair as they giggled and flirted with the boys who would serve the drinks and tend bar. The food arrived in huge aluminum pans, carried in from the vans and deposited on tables, countertops, in the stove and on it.

"Have the tables all been set?" Kate called over the din and clang of stainless steel, crystal, aluminum and brass.

"Everything's done," Martha assured her, taking her by the arm and marching her into the hall. "Now just stay out of the kitchen. Let me take care of things today. Just enjoy yourself. You slaved over the food enough already."

"It looks beautiful, doesn't it?" Kate breathed, peering out the back window at the blue-and-white-striped tent. White triangular banners flew from its top, making the backyard look like a Hollywood set for Camelot. The musicians were tuning up, their coats doffed, their shirtsleeves rolled up, ties drooping in the heat. The preacher was standing with his hands clasped loosely behind his back, gazing at the roses, occasionally leaning over to sniff a particularly appealing blossom.

Upstairs, Laurel was aflutter. Her hair and makeup were flawless. She would wear a blue princess-style dress with cap sleeves and a low, rounded neckline. She had borrowed Kate's pearls.

Elroy stood smiling in the living room, surrounded by male cohorts and well-wishers, beaming and comfortable and more at ease than he'd ever been in his life.

"You're not nervous?" Kate had asked when she kissed his cheek.

"Kate, this is the happiest day of my life. I feel terrific!"

Smiling, she had kissed his cheek again. "I'm so happy, Elroy. You're going to be wonderful for Mother."

"Just as she is for me," he said, then took Kate's hand. "Are you all right?"

She nodded, feeling momentarily speechless. A lump was lodged in her throat. It felt like a boulder.

"Have you seen Jake yet?" Elroy asked.

"No." She shook her head and glanced around nervously. "Have you?"

"Oh, yes, he's around somewhere." Elroy patted her hand. "You'll be fine, Kate."

Startled, Kate looked at him. "Well, of course I will!"

Elroy cleared his throat. "Speak of the devil."

Turning, Kate came face-to-face with Jake.

HE STOOD in the doorway, his broad shoulders seeming to touch both sides of the doorjamb at once. He wore a white dinner jacket and black trousers. His dark hair was still wet from his shower. He looked fit and lean and trim, and his eyes were glued on hers.

She went to him without even thinking, holding out her hand and rushing, stumbling almost, in her desire to get to him, to put her hand in his and feel his skin.

"Are you all right?" he asked when she reached him. He took her outstretched hand and held it, squeezed it reassuringly.

"I'm fine." She felt nervous and breathless, not at all sure of herself. "Why? Don't I seem fine?"

"You look beautiful," he said, holding her away from him and looking her up and down. "Simply beautiful."

She wore a simple pale pink dress, with rounded neck and puffy sleeves that ended at her elbows. Without her pearls, she felt naked. Even in her heels, she had to look up at Jake. She squeezed his hand. "Could we talk?"

"Of course."

She loved that about him—his immediate response to her, being there, accepting her as she was. She let him lead her into the library. He closed the door, and the commotion and noise in the rest of the house automatically fell away, leaving them alone together, as if on an island in some remote, calm sea.

She knotted her hands together and walked slowly toward the windows that overlooked the back lawn. "It looks lovely."

"Is that what you wanted to talk about?"

She turned and looked at Jake, her eyes wide and filled with apprehension. "There's no easy way to say this."

"Then perhaps you'd just better say it," he said gently.

She took a small breath. "I'm sorry I've been so difficult lately, but I had to wait to see what happened."

"What happened?" Jake looked confused. "What do you mean?"

"I had to see if I got pregnant."

A series of expressions crossed his face. She had no trouble identifying them in turn—concern, understanding, relief, fear. He lifted his hands. "Well? Are you?"

She looked at him with large, serious eyes. "What if I were?"

He let out a breath and advanced to her, taking her hands and clasping them. "Kate, I don't care if you are or aren't. I love you. I want to marry you." Then he shook his head and made a growling noise. "No, that's not what I meant! I *do* care whether you are or aren't! That is, I'd love it if you were, but I don't mind if you're not." He searched her eyes, looking worried. "Look, I don't know what the hell I'm saying. I just can't stand what's been going on the past few weeks—me sending flowers and calling you and getting no response except to talk about this damned party."

"You don't care about the party?" she asked innocently.

"I—oh Lord..." He let out a frustrated groan and pulled her into his arms. She went up on tiptoe and kissed him with all the pent-up frustration and worry she'd been holding in for weeks.

"Kissing doesn't solve problems, Mr. Griffin," she whispered when the kiss at last ended.

"Like hell it doesn't," he murmured, brushing his forehead against hers.

She closed her eyes, inhaling his scent, feeling the imprint of his hard body all down the length of hers, swimming in the sensations that shook her sensitive body. "I wanted to be sure how I felt about you," she said at last, her voice shaky, as uncertain as her words.

"And?"

"I love you," she whispered, tilting her head up to look into his eyes. Her own eyes grew warm, filled with love. "I love you, Jake. I just didn't want you walking into my life like some ape-man out of some prehistoric jungle, sweeping me up into your arms and taking me off to live happily ever after. My life is my own, Jake. I need to make my own decisions."

"And have you?"

She nodded, her eyes serious again. "Yes."

Her voice was no more than a whisper. He sighed and held her tightly, rocking her back and forth. "And?"

"When I marry you," she said, smiling into his eyes, "I want to have my own wedding, not share it with my mother. I want you all to myself, and my own day in the sun, under a blue-and-white-striped tent."

Whooping with joy, he swept her into his arms. "Yes! She's going to marry me!"

She laughed joyfully, throwing her head back, hugging him, her eyes dancing, her face radiant. "You foolish man! Put me down, this instant! This is no time to announce an engagement, not when the organist's already warming up for my mother's wedding."

"Well, how long shall we wait? Five minutes? Ten? Half an hour?"

"Just long enough to let Mother and Elroy have their time in the sun. Later, we can tell them that next year around this time, we'll all be celebrating wedding anniversaries, and a birthday, too."

"You don't mean today's your birthday?" he said. "Happy birthday, Kate."

"It won't be my birthday we're celebrating," she said softly.

"No?" Jake said, frowning. "Then whose?"

"The baby's," she said, her eyes soft and filled with love.

"The—" He sat down abruptly. "Oh my God."

She stared at him, aghast. "Is that a problem?"

"You mean you are pregnant?" he asked, his voice rising with hope.

"If you can believe at-home pregnancy tests, I am. I'm going to see my doctor on Monday. I guess he'll make it official."

"But earlier you said..."

"I said I wanted to be sure how I felt about you," she said, sitting down next to him and taking his hand. "And I wanted to be sure you really wanted to marry me, that you wouldn't do it just because I was pregnant."

"But you . . . did you ever consider not keeping it?"

She shook her head. "No, that wasn't ever an issue. I knew I'd keep it even if we didn't get married. Right from the start, the problem has been my mother's telling me she'd found the perfect man for me. When she said that, you almost didn't have a chance. I fought it tooth and nail, like I fight everything she suggests. If my mother says right, I say left. It's a knee-jerk thing with me. Automatic reflex. I needed time to separate the issues, to find out what *I* wanted, to decide for myself."

"And when I swept you up in my desire to get married right away, it felt like I wasn't letting you decide, either."

She nodded. "It's a problem, Jake. I need to be in charge of my own life. I've had my own business for four years. I'm autonomous. It's scary, thinking about all the sharing and compromise that marriage entails."

"And yet you decided to do it. You decided to say yes."

She nodded, her eyes serious. "Sometimes your heart tells you what to do," she said softly. "Sometimes you're scared, but you can't let that stop you. Martha told me once I wanted safety more than passion. I realized she could be right, if I didn't take the chance with you."

"It would have been easier then, if you hadn't gotten pregnant."

"Infinitely." She put a hand on her stomach. "But that's what's so strange. Now that I am, I want to be. I like the idea of being a mom." Tears misted her eyes. "A few months ago, I couldn't have said that, but in the past few weeks, I've gotten to know my mother a lot better. For some reason, that makes it easier to want to have kids of my own."

He stroked her hair back from her face. "It will be a completely democratic marriage," he said softly. "I won't force my opinions down your throat if you won't force yours down mine. We'll have to agree to discuss things and respect each other. Despite the fact that I don't even know when your birthday is, I think we've got a shot at this thing."

"And something to work for," she said, placing her hand on her stomach.

"Yes. Something to work for."

Hand in hand, they went to join the wedding party.

HARLEQUIN PRESENTS®

Zsa Zsa Gabor and Jack Ryan

Jack Ryan and Zsa Zsa first met as neighbors. She lived three doors away from him in a one-bedroom home. Ryan's house on five acres had eighteen bathrooms, seven kitchens and one hundred and fifty telephones, along with trapdoors, secret passageways and a tree house. Zsa Zsa confided that "he wanted to get married in that tree house of his, but I thought my mother would be shocked." They had a two-month courtship, during which they "never went out," according to Zsa Zsa, and were then married at Caesar's Palace by Judge Charles Thompson.

Ryan, a Yale graduate and inventor, made his fortune by creating the Barbie doll and Chatty Cathy for the Mattel Company. This marriage, Zsa Zsa's sixth, was her first to a younger man. She listed her birth date on the marriage license as 1948, but she was really born in Budapest in 1918.